Taking the Cake

NATALIA WILLIAMS

For anyone who has never felt good enough.

Contents

Fullpage Image	VII
Note to the Reader	VIII
1. Sabrina	1
2. Sabrina	21
3. Gray	25
4. Sabrina	34
5. Sabrina	45
6. Gray	61
7. Sabrina	69
8. Sabrina	85
9. Gray	94
10. Sabrina	99
11. Sabrina	110
12. Gray	120
13. Sabrina	130
14. Gray	151

15.	Sabrina	160
16.	Gray	165
17.	Sabrina	180
18.	Gray	203
19.	Sabrina	208
20.	Gray	225
21.	Sabrina	241
22.	Gray	251
23.	Sabrina	260
24.	Sabrina	272
25.	Gray	278
26.	Sabrina	291
27.	Sabrina	298
Epilogue - Sabrina		305
Acknowledgements		313
About the Author		315

Taking the Cake

NATALIA WILLIAMS

NOTE TO THE READER

Hello reader!

Thank you for picking up this book. Before you begin, please note that this book features themes such as:

parental abandonment (off-page), parental separation and cheating (past), death of a grandparent (off-page), brief mentions of body image and diet culture, alcohol consumption, adult language, and on-page consensual sex.

Thank you, and take care,
Natalia

ONE

SABRINA

MY HANDS SHAKE AS I tear open the sugar packets and pour them into my steaming mug of coffee. I'm sitting outside under the awning of the café at our usual table - heavy white chairs surrounding a round white table - while I wait for Liz.

The sky is almost blindingly blue, cloudless, the sun a bright spotlight. We're heading into the hotter months now. The kind of oppressive Florida heat that makes it hard to breathe, makes getting dressed a chore because no matter what you'll end up sweaty and sticky, hair frizzing uncontrollably. It's still early enough that the heat of the day hasn't really taken hold yet, so I practice schooling my features until she arrives.

I'd seen it this morning, my terrible habit of scrolling through social media as I awake and start the day. I'd stumbled upon it as one does any terrible news: unsuspecting, a punch to the gut. A punch to my heart.

And now I sit here, mindlessly stirring creamers into my coffee, the spoon *clink-clinking* occasionally on the bottom of the mug. Just then Liz arrives, stumbling into her chair across from me, all chaotic energy and hot pink hair.

"Sorry, sorry!" She throws her bag down, adjusting in the chair. "Jeff and I stayed up late last night binge-watching some new show about witches and murders and maybe fairies? I don't know, I couldn't keep up. I think I passed out on the couch at some point, and I woke up this morning with a killer headache and neck pain. I'm too old for this shit."

"You're thirty-two, Liz," I tell her, still stirring in the creamers one by one.

"You try sleeping on a lumpy couch! That thing is on its last leg. What a nightmare." She turns to our server who has come back over and holds up her mug while the steaming coffee is poured in. "Thank you!" she happily calls out, taking a big whiff, closing her eyes to relish it for a moment. Her choppy bob sways with her movements, framing her face. The pink of her hair makes her deeply tanned skin glow in the sunlight. "Mm, that smells so good."

We order our usuals - banana pancakes for me, granola and yogurt bowl for Liz – and then she looks over at me and pauses.

"What's wrong?"

"What? What do you mean?" *Shit.*

"You're being quiet."

"It's early," I say, almost defensively.

"Your wings are off."

"What?"

She points to her own eye, making a swoop to get the point across that my makeup is sub-par this morning.

"What are you talking about?" I reach for a mirror in my bag.

She stares at me for a beat. I didn't want to have to do this now, not when I just found out myself, but I know I can't keep anything from her.

I stop rummaging and sigh, something sad and forlorn probably, while I gather up the nerve to tell her. "Ben got engaged," I say, taking a sip of my coffee. It burns on the way down. Maybe it can sear my vocal cords and then I can avoid talking about this anymore today.

She balks at me, mug frozen mid-air. "Uh. Shit. *Shit.* Are you okay?"

I roll my eyes at this. "Yes!" I lower my voice. "Yes, I'm fine". Another sip of coffee, another burn.

The truth is I don't know how to feel about it. Ben and Monica have only been together for nine months. Nine months of a social media spectacle that I tried my best to avoid, but still managed to catch: vacations, family parties, casual weekends, Sunday brunches with all their friends. I figured this day would come at some point. Probably.

Granted, he was never the marriage type before. Especially not after nine months, let alone years.

But what do I know? People change. People figure out the things they want and sometimes they're very different ideals from when they were eighteen and wanted to just have fun. Or when they were twenty-four and loved you, but they would never be the commitment type. And now they're thirty-three and committing just fine.

Maybe it wasn't them; it was you.

"You alright over there?" Liz motions to my face with a spoon. Our food had arrived, placed in front of me before I even noticed.

"Sorry." I jolt back to the present. "Maybe I am just having a minute."

"Well. Who knew he could commit, huh?" There's acid in her tone and I love her for it.

Certainly not me.

I try to school my features again. A quick lift of my eyebrows and tilt of the head in agreement. Another sip of coffee, but this time much warmer. Can she fill my cup again? Can she make it scalding again?

"So, how is Ben Sadler these days anyway?" Liz asks around a mouthful of yogurt.

"Oh, you know. Engaged. He's doing great, obviously."

"How did you find out? Don't tell me he sent you an invitation."

"He would never. I saw it on Instagram this morning. A quick way to ruin your day if you're looking for ideas."

"First of all, he absolutely would fucking invite you because that's the unique kind of asshole he is – "

"Liz."

"And second, you need a social media ban. You get into all kinds of trouble with it."

"You're not wrong," I groan. "But he's happy. I'm just happy he's happy, you know?" I hope my voice doesn't give me away. I hope she can't hear the years of longing lodged in my throat.

Waiting, hoping, desperately wishing to be good enough, perfect enough for him.

The pancakes feel like lead in my mouth as I chew and swallow.

Liz Garrison and I have known each other since middle school and she's known me through my relationship with Ben – well, all iterations of them. Clearly, she isn't a fan. She never really was, only dealing with him because of me and playing nice when she had to. She plays nice well, but Liz also has no qualms about stomping on his balls with her boot. It's nice to have her on my side.

I poke my pancakes a little more before deciding that I don't have much of an appetite today. "We've got a lot to do this week. Can we go and get started?" I tell her.

She takes one last sip of her coffee, nodding quietly in agreement. She's bummed for me, maybe upset for me. She might even be plotting her revenge in silence. I've gone through most of those feelings since this morning. Right now, the sadness is lingering the most – the thought of him forever committed to somebody else. Somebody that I so surely thought would be me. It's a hard blow to take.

We pay the check and gather our things, walking together to the small huddle of buildings across the street. In that humble plaza is my pride and joy, my sweat, my never-ending hard work: Sabrina's Sweets.

My banana yellow Crocs and Liz's boots hit the pavement, the only noise between us as we head to the crosswalk. It's early enough, but the day is in full swing now. Clouds have come out to dot the bright blue sky. Cars zoom down the roads, pedestrians head to breakfast or the beach. We are a couple of miles from it nestled near the high rises and fancy corporate buildings in our downtown city of New River – a mix of business and pleasure with everybody you see walking down the street.

In a span of about seven years, I've managed to become a preferred wedding cake vendor to many luxury oceanfront resorts. There have been write ups in local newspapers and magazines; a small feature on a local television station; plenty of social media mentions. It is both exciting and exhausting to look at the success of the business, the one I built myself from the ground up with my own two hands in my tiny one-bedroom apartment. I feel a sense of accomplishment - this is my dream job, truly - but I always worry, is it enough?

And with so much time being taken up by my work, it leaves even less room for romantic pursuits of any kind. The days are long and sugar-filled; the nights are lonely. Maybe I should have found my Ben replacement years ago, but I wonder if the best I can hope for these days are occasional dates with occasional men, some stale conversation, something casual.

Even though I dream of companionship, too.

Liz and I walk to the shop, the silence from me its own unwelcome guest. Luckily, Liz keeps it at bay by telling me more about whatever show she was binge-watching with Jeff last night and making me smile.

"So, this witch can see into the future, right? But she also commits occasional murders. I think the fairies are bad so maybe she's like a vigilante? I don't know what the fuck I was watching, honestly. I even told Jeff, 'What kind of bullshit are we watching? Just put on *Cold Case*' but he wants to give everything a chance," Liz rolls her eyes.

She's a lucky one; she's got Jeff.

"That's one of Jeff's more redeeming qualities," I tell her.

"I know." She smiles.

I pull the shop keys out of my bag, reaching for the door. I lucked out when I found this spot about four years ago. Located at the corner end of the plaza, the bakeshop is small, but the perfect size for us.

The shop has floor to ceiling windows in the front so people can walk by and peek at us working. As I pull open the door, I step in behind Liz and click the lights on, walking past the large wood table I use for my cake tastings.

Liz takes a big whiff next to me. "So good," she sighs.

The scent of butter and sugar and vanilla has probably been embedded into the walls by now. It lingers and wafts in the air, draping us in the scent every time we walk in.

"It is, isn't it?" I smile over my shoulder to her as I walk past the stainless-steel tables in the middle of the room, the large mixers that line the wall. We head toward the small hallway that leads to my office – a place I rarely find myself in – walking past tall metal shelves with cake pans and tools, walking past the bright floral wallpaper I joyously draped over the walls after I signed the lease. My heart was bursting with excitement, ready to give these four walls character and color, ready to fill it with cake and so much love.

Liz throws her bag down on the desk while I look over emails and contracts, writing a to-do list for the day.

When I decided to branch out of my apartment, I knew I would need some help. Liz was working at the Gap looking for a way out.

"I thought people were trying to fall into the Gap," I'd said to her.

"You're hilarious. But, no, nobody wants to fall into the Gap. It's not 1998 anymore."

She had a point. She also loved to bake. Liz and I met in middle school, but really became close in high school where we both signed up for the culinary class to reap the benefits of midday chocolate chip cookies and croissants. When I was running the business out of my apartment, I knew I could always call her up in a pinch to help. It was a no-brainer when I moved into this space that I would bring her with me.

We make our way back to the front, to-do lists in hand, and the front door jingles as it opens. James Hall walks in, tall and lanky, dark hair brushed back from his face.

Four years ago, when I started landing more hotel contracts and preferred vendor spots, I brought in our mutual friend James who was working in various hospitality jobs: part-time at a local bread bakery overnight, bartending on the weekends at the fancy bar downtown. He was looking to leave the overnight shifts, and while he still only works part time for me, he completes us.

This is it - my little shop of sugar and dreams. We're a trio of baking misfits in this unconventional, whimsical, and creative bakeshop. A place I'd always dreamed of. It's my favorite place to be.

"What's up nerds?!" he calls out, grabbing his apron as he greets us.

***

"So, Marc wanted to watch that new show *The Witching Hour* last night," James says, as he pours chocolate cake batter into prepared pans and gets them ready to go into the oven. James and Marc met a year after I moved into this space, and they were serious almost from the beginning. I've been surrounded by whirlwinds of romance – Liz meeting Jeff right after college and still going strong, James and Marc's love blossoming into a beautiful relationship that I adore to watch grow.

Ben getting engaged to his sweetheart Monica. *After nine months.*

"You too?!" I hear Liz say as I come back to the conversation.

"Jeff put it on last night, too. Isn't it the worst?"

James laughs. "It really was terrible."

"Well now I feel like I'm missing out. Do I need to start watching this show?" I dunk a cake scrap into a leftover vat of buttercream and shovel it into my mouth.

"It's so ridiculous, Bri. Right up your alley." James winks. I do have a love for ridiculous TV.

James places the chocolate cakes into the oven and I check the time. We're ahead of schedule.

"Alright, I think it's time for a break. My brain needs fuel. Anybody want anything? I'll head over to Amelia's," I tell them.

"The usual," Liz responds, not looking up from the stovetop where she's making a batch of caramel.

"Same," James calls out, weighing out the ingredients for the lemon cake batter.

We're slowly getting out of our busy season - a grueling, nonstop seven months where I'm always impressed at how we manage to make it out (almost) unscathed. The weekends are filled to the brim with cake and dessert orders. I never try to overbook or do more than I can handle, but that still means about ten to twelve cakes in a week, plus any desserts.

Some weddings are small – family affairs with less than thirty guests held in backyards or a small corner of the beach. Other weddings are spectacles – three hundred guests, a tower of a cake, desserts to match, and one hell of a reception. I love it all, but I have to balance it all, too.

My striped apron gets hung on a hook by the door while I tuck some cash into my pocket and head outside. Our shop sits right at the end of the plaza that's filled with other local businesses. We're almost like a small town: supporting each other, commiserating, probably in each other's business more than we should be. I walk by Beach Waves Hair Salon run by Tina; she waves, scissors in her hand. Next is Christine's office. She's a realtor, recently divorced. She moved in here about six months ago, but she does very well for herself, selling beachfront condos and oceanfront property to whoever can afford it. I cannot, but a girl can dream.

There are a couple of clothing boutiques, a record store opening soon, and a larger store selling home wares and odds and ends. The plaza is busy today, familiar faces coming and going and those on vacation just taking a stroll.

One of the locals comes up to me now to chat about a cake I made for a wedding he attended last weekend. He talks animatedly, and I welcome it, smiling with him. I love these conversations that I can have with neighbors, a perk of my job that allows me to fill my social cup.

Once our conversation ends, Chantal from the property management office finds me mid-stride and stops to chat about a charity event the plaza will be hosting in a couple of months, asking if I could donate any small items for it.

Because these businesses are all local to New River, we have a lot of regular clienteles. Well, specifically, Amelia's does.

Amelia runs her namesake coffee shop from the other end of the plaza, and she brings the people in. Not only is her coffee fantastic, but she's created an ambiance, an experience, if you hear her tell it. I can already see mostly familiar faces inside as I approach.

It's then that I spot him, sticking out like a sore thumb, looking right at me.

He's a new face around here. Not that that's out of the ordinary, but I would have certainly remembered a face like that. *Or at the very least forearms like those.*

He's sitting on a bench directly across from the entrance to Amelia's, arms bent, hands clasped between his knees. His head hangs a little low, and he seems deep in thought, a line forming between his brows as he tries to work something out in his mind.

At first, I look away, taken aback by his stare, but then I look back over and catch his eyes again. I'm ogling; it's embarrassing, really, but I can't help it because *wow, he is handsome*. He is all broad shoulders and long arms in a perfectly fit white T-shirt. His hair is deep blond, messed up like he's been running his fingers through it all afternoon. Wavy, mussed, it reminds me of the beach. He reminds me of the beach. Sticking out like a sore thumb and yet he looks like he belongs here.

And if that ogling wasn't embarrassing enough, my focus on his face causes me to stumble on the sidewalk, tripping over my own two feet in their Crocs. A small smile plays on his lips, a bite on the inside of his cheek like he's trying to keep from laughing.

I get a hold of myself and continue to walk. *One foot in front of the other, you idiot. There you go.*

I give a small smile in return and quickly sneak through the door into Amelia's for coffee.

Ben Sadler was the big relationship for me. And when it ended, really, truly ended, it broke me. I've spent some past years dating - or at least trying to. The dating pool is a petri dish, but all of that aside, I've been the difficult one. Most dates haven't made it past third dates. Either my work-life balance is too non-existent for them, or I play the comparison game. A dangerous slippery slope that leaves me thinking, *you aren't Ben and I wish you were.*

I haven't gone out on a date in well over a year, just throwing myself and my energy into work instead. But now here I am succumbing to the loneliness and the sadness that is being a single girl in New River working way too hard while Ben Sadler puts a big fucking rock on Monica's finger. *After nine months.*

Dammit. I need a coffee.

Amelia's Coffee is busy as usual when I step inside. A study group is huddled in the corner and girlfriends are chatting by the window. In a similar set up to Sabrina's Sweets, the windows in Amelia's are also floor to ceiling in the front. Amelia decorates them with twinkling lights and changes décor to fit the seasons. Right now, it's like a greenhouse – bountiful plants in ceramic pots on shelves, small ones on the tables, even a couple of big Monstera plants by the door. She brought two of them over to the bakeshop last week and placed them right at the front entrance. All the tables are gorgeous dark wood, handmade by her husband. Cozy armchairs are scattered throughout the space. The corner on the right boasts a bookshelf encouraging guests to take or leave a book. Amelia even had James write the menu on a large chalkboard wall right above the register in fancy script.

Aside from the bakeshop, I love Amelia's coffee shop more than anything. This is her labor of love, too. Every piece was picked out and designed by her with her perfect vision in mind. She works hard, she's passionate, and I'm so lucky to call her a friend.

"Hey Bri!" she calls out when she sees me come up to the counter.

"Hey Amelia." I smile in return. She's busy with a customer so I wait my turn, walking over to peer into the glass cases she has lined up to the side filled with different baked goods.

Shortly after I moved in, she reached out to me to supply the coffee shop with some simple baked goods – scones, tea cakes, muffins. I jumped at the chance to expand my business and we became good friends through it. I continue to do it now, a small break from always baking and decorating cakes, delivering a box of goods to her every other day.

"The usual today?" she asks when it's my turn in line.

"Yeah. Liz, James, and I are working." She nods and gets to work on our coffees. Susana, another barista, helps with the order.

"I've always wished I could be familiar enough in a place to have a usual." The deep voice startles me. Coming from behind, it's unfamiliar and yet so soothing. I feel it settle over my skin like honey.

I turn and it's the handsome guy from the bench. My eyes widen slightly in surprise. Man, he is tall. I'm taller than average, but I think I come right up to his shoulder.

"So, what does your usual consist of?" he asks. It takes me a second to realize that he's talking to me. That he's smiling at *me*. I take a moment to look at him, really look at him, and his eyes meet mine – blue like the ocean at the beginning of summer. Bright, clear, dazzling. They shine and I immediately think how I would want nothing more than to dive into them, swim in them – these magical blue eyes. He lifts his brow, waiting for a response.

"Oh. Uh." I clear my throat. "The iced Nutella Delight," I tell him, vaguely pointing to the menu above the register.

He looks up and spots it.

"'Espresso, hazelnut syrup, milk of choice, a swirl of Nutella, whipped cream optional'," he reads the description. "Do you opt for the whipped cream?"

Just as he asks that, Amelia sets my coffee down, a mound of whipped cream well above the rim of the cup. She passes me a straw and I place it in my coffee, taking a sip, smiling around it.

"That would be a yes," he determines, the corner of his mouth pulling up ever so slightly.

"That would be a yes."

"The locals know best," I hear Amelia say, a smile in her voice.

He turns to her. "Hi." A dazzling smile. "Amelia, is it?"

Oh boy, he is *charming*. She stands there staring for a beat, but I see her eyes shift to me briefly, a question in them.

"I would love a large, iced Nutella Delight, please," he tells Amelia. "*With* whipped cream." He winks in my direction.

I look back at Amelia, eyes wide. Are my panties on fire? Is the heater on? Who the hell is this guy? I continue to watch his charming interaction, as he pays for his coffee and leaves a tip in the jar.

Amelia's comment about locals piques my interest. This guy seems like nothing but trouble, and yet I'm curious about him. More curious than I have been about anybody in a long time and I'm not sure why.

"So, where are you from?" I will the words to come out of my mouth.

"Here," he says. He must see the look of surprise on my face, so he elaborates. "Well, sort of. I lived here when I was younger, but then moved away to college. I moved back about three weeks ago."

"Ah, so you're like a pseudo-local."

He laughs. "Is that what they call it?"

"That's what I call it." I take another sip of my iced coffee. His eyes dart to my mouth for a second then back up. Those same eyes then quickly move down my body – a quick flash of it and then it's gone - and I control the urge to squirm at the attention.

Shit, is he checking me out?

"Nice shoes." He nods to my banana Crocs.

"Thanks. Nice face." My eyes widen. *Did I seriously just say that? Jesus Christ.*

He tilts his head back and laughs, a joyous sound that reverberates through my bones and I feel all the way down to my toes. "Thanks," he says, the tops of his cheeks turning the lightest shade of pink.

I smile into my coffee cup. There's something about this guy that just makes me spew out whatever is on my mind. I like it. Maybe I should keep up this kind of momentum if I ever do date again.

The rest of the orders are ready now – Liz's caramel cold brew and James' classic Americano - and I gather them carefully in my hands.

I look up to catch him watching me, his mouth twisted into a smirk-almost-smile.

"More usuals," I tell him. "Her caramel cold brew is also wonderful."

"I'll make a note of it," he grins.

I nod once, turning to leave. I need fresh air; I think his cologne is messing with my brain.

"Leaving so soon?" he calls out.

"I need to get back. Enjoy your coffee, though."

"But I didn't even get your name."

I keep walking towards the door, a laugh threatening to escape my lips. This guy is something else. I'm sure he flirts with girls in coffee shops all day long.

"That's Sabrina," I hear Amelia say. "Everybody around here knows Sabrina."

Small town, and all that.

I turn and push the door open with my back, carefully balancing the coffee in my hands while I wink back at him. What the hell, I'll never see this guy again. Though I try not to think about what a shame that is, because he is a sight for sore eyes that's for sure.

He smiles again, the smallest crinkle in his nose as it lights up his eyes, and it knocks me out. I manage to power walk back to the shop so I don't have to answer for my weak knees and my furiously beating heart.

Shit, maybe I just need to get laid.

"Okay guys let's call it a night. Tomorrow we've got an eleven A.M. cake tasting, and we need to put finishing touches on several cakes. The Hartman wedding is on Saturday at the Beachcomber. Delivery is at three P.M. The Rhodes wedding is happening on Sunday afternoon. Hopefully we can square everything away without a hitch."

I'm dictating notes from my old clipboard, the corner end frayed from years of use. Once we've had a brief rundown for the upcoming weekend, Liz and I start cleaning up the tables, scrubbing as we go. James washes the mixing bowls and runs other remaining utensils through the dishwasher. Floors are scrubbed and mopped. Thirty minutes later, I lock up and we all head to our cars.

"I still can't believe that asshole is engaged," James says.

I shrug. Liz makes a dramatic gagging noise. Earlier in the day, I had told James about Ben's engagement news. "He's *what?!*" James had said.

"What kind of trouble are you guys getting into tonight?" he asks now.

"Jeff and I are probably going to watch more of that *Witching Hour* show," Liz answers.

"You said it was awful," I tell her.

"I know, but it's so bad, it's good. I can't stop now, I'm in too deep! What about you Bri?"

"I've got a hot date."

They both look at me expectantly.

"With a pint of ice cream and my bed," I tell them.

They both groan.

"Bri, I love you, but you need a life," James says.

"I have a life. A wonderful one, in fact, which includes the both of you."

"You need more excitement in it than a pint of ice cream."

"Have you even *had* Jeni's Whiskey and Pecans?"

"More excitement, Bri," he repeats as we reach his car. He gives Liz and I quick kisses on our cheeks before getting behind the wheel and driving away.

Liz turns to me, "You know what he means. You know what we both mean."

"I'm happy where I'm at Liz," I sigh, trying to make those words sound believable to my ears. I know she sees right through my bullshit, but it's much harder to have to admit things. To say out loud to somebody else, *I'm not happy. I'm lonely and I didn't realize just how lonely until now.*

"Yes, I'm sure you are. You are running a successful business and you have us, and we have you, but it's not about all work and no play. There is more out there. You deserve more than you're allowing yourself. That's all."

"Is this about Ben?"

"No. Maybe. I don't know." I know what she's trying to tell me. I should date again. I should find somebody to spend time with outside of Liz and James who have their own significant others. I'm the single odd friend out; I know this. I just don't know how much of me really wants to put energy back into that again. How much of me wants to throw myself back into the carnivorous dating world that may just chew me up and spit me back out.

I nod briefly at her. "Night, Liz. See you tomorrow?"

"Yes," she sighs. "Night, Bri."

I watch as she gets into her car and drives away just like James did, both of them going home to their respective houses with their respective partners. And only after she pulls away do I allow the thought to creep in, the one I try to keep buried so very deep down: *what if I just never get over him?*

Two

Sabrina

I'VE HAD A SWEET tooth for as long as I can remember. When I was little, my dad would wake me up every Saturday morning and take us for a drive. The first stop was always to our favorite doughnut shop. His favorite was jelly-filled.

"And what do you think Sabrina?" he'd always say. "What will it be today?"

It was always a strawberry frosted with sprinkles.

We would take half a dozen to go and then take the long way home, driving along the beach. The windows would be rolled down, the salty wind would whip through my hair, and dad would sing along to whatever was on the radio. Every now and then he would laugh, and his eyes would crinkle at the corners, salt and pepper hair moving gently in the breeze. When we'd get back home, my mom would have a pot of tea ready and a cup of orange juice in a teacup poured for me. Every Saturday was filled with sugar and sprinkles and love.

Well, for a while anyway.

Weekends are magical when you're a kid, but as you get older the curtain gets pulled back some more. And maybe you realize your parents weren't as happy as they seemed. Maybe life is more hectic than you imagine. Maybe the things you thought you knew, you realize were lies.

I throw my keys on the table when I get home, kicking off my Crocs and shuffling to the freezer. My phone buzzes with some notification and I resist the urge to pull up my social media accounts again. Some years ago, I found my father on social media. An uncomfortable discovery that only served to fuel my anger and heartache. And anyway, Liz is right. I do get into too much trouble with it.

I grab a spoon from my drawer and uncap the pint of ice cream as I head to my couch. My legs don't ache like they used to. They've grown accustomed to the long hours, the constant standing, but I still feel a certain wave of relief when I finally crash onto my couch and put my feet up. I dig the spoon into the creamy concoction, savoring the bite of whiskey, the velvety mouthfeel of cream.

I started baking when I was around thirteen, a life raft that kept me afloat in the roughest of waters. A cake was always a perfect gift for birthdays, family gatherings, or holidays. So, I baked and baked until my heart was content. And then I gave it away because I loved seeing the happiness in others' faces. Because if I couldn't have a happily ever after, at least somebody else could.

I'm getting too sappy now. The pint of Whiskey and Pecans sits half-eaten on my lap as I tried to keep busy to avoid any sort of social media. I grab the remote and think about starting *The Witching Hour.*

I remember about a year after I started Sabrina's Sweets, still working from my apartment, when I got a small write up in the local paper. The excitement was so *real*. There I was getting a taste of the success I had hoped for, and people could read about me, this business.

But would the important people see it? I wondered if my father would grab the paper, browse, and stumble upon an article about his daughter doing something successful. Would he see me worthy then? Would he read it and think *I should have stayed?*

Would Ben ever read it?

Once the shop was opened, the same writer came to interview me again. She had followed my career from the start and wanted to do a larger piece on the opening of the shop. Front page of the Food & Lifestyle section and still, radio silence from those I hoped would see it. Well, except for my mother. She frames them and plasters the articles all over the walls in her house. I love her for it.

The success is necessary. I need to be strong; I need to stand on my own. I need to be seen as worthy.

Because if I'm not what I do, then who am I?

When I stumbled upon the engagement news, it was attached to an album of pictures. Monica with tears in her eyes, staring at the ring on her perfectly manicured finger, then at him. Ben elated and looking at her like she was the only thing he saw. There was a visceral reaction to it almost - seeing those pictures plastered all over social media. The realization of how truly lonely I am. How he dipped her slightly when he kissed her, and he did that with me so many times before. How he gazed at her and held her, his strong arm wrapped tightly around her waist, his fingers gripping her side. And how, like a phantom limb, I can still feel the weight of his around me.

I still feel tethered to him, invisible strings pulled taut.

I sigh deeply and start the first episode of *The Witching Hour*.

"Wow. This really is terrible."

I continue onto episode two, letting the noise lull me until I'm fast asleep on the couch.

THREE

GRAY

"Hey, Pop. I'm back," I call out into the house, closing the front door behind me.

I went out for a run early in the morning to try to clear my head. My mother had called me last night, and I just needed to get some air.

We don't talk much these days – or rather, I try to avoid her calls whenever possible. Just like I did last night. She's in Richmond now with Dave, her boyfriend. She's been there about two years so that's two years too long for her to stay anywhere. I'm sure she'll be packing up and hitting the road soon enough.

I see Pop on the back porch, so I grab a bottle of water from the fridge and head outside to join him. He's reading an old James Patterson book, glasses perched on his nose, thin hair slicked back. I slump into the chair next to him, twisting the cap to open the bottle.

"How was it?" he asks, not looking up.

"Hot." I gulp water, still a little out of breath.

It's quiet this time of day, just the birds chirping in the trees, the occasional sound of a car driving down the street. His house sits on the water, a small manmade lake running through the neighborhood, houses on either side. I love how peaceful it is, how calming. I've always loved it here.

"Did you take your pills this morning?"

"Yes," he drawls.

"Good. I'm going to hop in the shower," I tell him, getting up to go inside.

I'm back in New River now, living at Pop's house, in my old teenage bedroom. I ruffle through my bags for some clean clothes. I'm still living out of suitcases and duffel bags, a haphazard pile set in the corner of the room. My old desk sits against the wall in the same place it was in high school, my laptop perched on top of it where I do all my web design. I've switched out my teenage twin bed for a roomier queen, but almost everything else remains the same, a nostalgic step back in time. Band posters, an old street sign I found after a hurricane, staples still clung to the wall after I tore down whatever was up. At least it doesn't smell like it did when I was sixteen, so there's that.

Growing up, I moved around a lot, my mother chasing the next best thing. She split with my father before I was even born and he was not interested in any relationship with me, so it was always just us. She loved the open road, change. She craved new beginnings and had no problem packing us up and moving me around. I was seven years old and starting a new school again, eight years old and struggling to find a sense of belonging, nine years old and barely able to make friends. We came to visit Pop, her father, whenever we could, but when I was twelve, I was overwhelmed and tired. Twelve years old and drifting away, out at sea in need of an anchor.

I told him I wanted to stay here with him. I wanted to have a home for once. My mother overheard, sadness and hurt marking her features, but she steeled her spine, had a long conversation with Pop, and agreed. She was gone days later, and we stood at the front door watching her drive off. He wrapped his arm around mine, and held me close. It was the first time I felt anchored in a very, very long time.

The water is hot once I jump into the shower, the steam fogging up the mirror, the feeling welcome on my skin.

That's not to say that things were easy. Not at first and not for a while. But I got there slowly. I started to breathe a little bit easier. The loneliness started to wane as I settled in and made friends. The anger started to clear like a fog with Pop's patience, with his persistence.

Being back in New River feels like giving back. Like honoring all the years Pop took care of me. Those volatile years when I was an angry teen just looking for somebody to love me, give me stability, a sense of belonging. But it's been harder to get settled this time around, my belongings scattered around this old room. The itch is still under my skin, prickles of it, a restlessness I can't seem to wrangle.

I lather up, letting the hot water run down my back and wash me clean.

***

"You workin' outside today?" Pop asks me, looking up from his book. He's moved inside, sitting in his favorite rocker, a weathered plaid with frayed cushions that looks very well-loved.

"Yeah." I nod. "Just going to work on a couple of things." I gather my bag and shuffle some papers around on the dining room table. "Need anything while I'm out?"

"Don't think so. Nancy's coming by in a little bit."

Nancy is Pop's neighbor across the street. She's also a home nurse so she likes to come over and spend time with him under the guise of hanging out, but she's really keeping an eye on him, too. They've been neighbors for about twenty years, but Pop has had this house longer. This house is the one he bought with Gran when they were looking for something quiet that could also be a welcoming home for their daughter and new grandson.

"Good to see you getting out," he says, immersed in his book, rocking back and forth in a slow rhythm. I catch myself smiling.

I've been making it a point to work outside more. I tell Pop I want the fresh air, that I want to people watch. But really, there's only one person I've been curious to watch and it's her - who comes in at different times, always in those same comically bright yellow Crocs, a big bun of brown hair right on top of her head. She consistently looks focused, on a mission, in for coffee and out to continue with her day. Even then, she always stops and chats with Amelia, kind and patient, asking how she is doing and waiting for the answer.

I've run into her three times now. I feel so drawn to her, a rare feeling I find myself chasing. She's beautiful, sure, but there's also an energy about her – one that radiates kindness, warmth, comfort.

The second time I saw her, I was sitting at a small corner table, huddled over my laptop working on a client's request. My iced Nutella delight was in my hand, whipped cream dangerously close to the rim, and I was licking it off the top to avoid any catastrophe with my work. She walked in mid-lick, amusement coloring her features. When she spotted me, I saw the reaction instantly – the surprise in her eyes, the flush in her cheeks. A small smile graced her face, the barest nod of acknowledgement in my direction. She probably wasn't expecting to see me again. I honestly wasn't expecting to see her again either. I figured that first time was a one-off, a fluke, but here she was again. Maybe a small part of me came back to Amelia's because I wished I could see her again.

"I take it you're a fan?" she'd said, a laugh escaping her lips.

I put my cup down, trying not to laugh. I could have leaned into that comment, played the same cards I did when I first ran into her. A wink, some charm, a smile. But that's not really me. She probably thinks I'm just some asshole hanging out at coffee shops trying to pick up girls.

"Chatting up any other locals today?" she'd teased.

I don't know why I struck up a conversation with her that very first day, just that I wanted to. And I hadn't wanted to do something like that in a long time.

I saw her coming down the sidewalk, people stopping to talk to her, and she had stopped to give them all her attention. Her face was kind, her smile welcoming. I can't explain it, but I wanted to know her, too. I wanted that welcoming smile direct-ed at me.

I got up off the bench and followed her inside, ramping up the charm. I wanted to seem effortless and cool, but the more I stood with her the less I wanted to put on an act. The less I wanted it to seem like a throwaway encounter.

The third time I saw her, she'd placed her orders and then made her way back around to me, taking a peek at my laptop and the Solitaire game I had pulled up on the screen. She grabbed the chair across from mine and sat down, chin resting on her hand.

"Working hard or hardly working?"

"A little bit of both. You seem to be in that same boat, taking quite a bit of coffee breaks," I'd teased. "Unless," I'd considered, "you're the office coffee girl and your job is to get everybody else coffee."

She'd laughed at that, a loud and joyous sound that startled some of the guests, but she didn't even care. "You got me," she'd said, hazel eyes twinkling, full lips curved into an amused grin. She got up to grab her orders – those same three drinks - and then walked right out the door, calling, *"Have a good day!"* on her way out.

I had started to pack up my things when Amelia called me over.

"Hey Casanova. Weekends are busiest for her, so I'm just going to save you the trouble of a visit tomorrow." I played dumb for a minute, telling Amelia this was a great work spot, but she wasn't buying it. We both knew why I was there so often.

"No offense to your coffee," I'd told her sheepishly.

"Oh please, I know you love my coffee, but she is pretty great, too," she'd supplied, a knowing smile on her face. Amelia studied me, drying her hands on a dish towel, and I'd fidgeted under her stare. She'd leaned in close over the counter then, lowering her voice slightly, and said it: "End of the plaza, just around the corner."

"On second thought, maybe get me one of those fancy coffees you were raving about yesterday," Pop says as I drift back to the present.

"You got it, old man." I give him a quick squeeze on the shoulder and head out.

My phone rings on the way to the car and I grab it quickly, looking down to see who's calling. I hesitate, the guilt creeping in, but I answer.

"Hey mom."

"He's alive!"

"Yeah, sorry," I sigh. "I've been meaning to call. I've just been a little busy."

"Well. Busy is good." Her voice is raspy, familiar. I close my eyes at the sound of it.

"How are you doing?" I manage to ask, pulling it out of me.

"Doing alright. The bar is crazy this time of year, you know how it is."

Every move meant a new job, but my mother found hospital- ity the easiest to keep up with – serving, bartending, even hotel jobs. There's a loaded silence on the line, like she's been calling for a reason. *Where is she moving to now?*

"So, listen. I've been trying to get a hold of you cause Dave and I were thinking...maybe you'd want to come spend some time up here this summer? We...uh, we wanted to get together, talk about some things. It's been so long. We could have a good time together just us three."

I...was not expecting that.

I haven't spent any substantial time with my mother or Dave in years. They seem happy and stable, and I want nothing but the best for her, but that doesn't mean it's been easy for me to let go of the unstable years she gave me. The cramped studio apartments we would try to make a home, the one-bedroom apartments where we crashed with her old friends. It may not be fair to hold her to that standard, I know that, or to blame her for everything in my childhood. She was a single parent working through grief and loss doing her best. But it's still a hard time to think back upon, memories that leave me feeling unsteady and anxious.

"Um. I'm not sure about that, Mom."

"It was just an idea." She sounds defeated and I'm surprised to find that I don't like being the cause of it.

"I don't know if I could just leave Pop," I tell her. Yes, I'm here because I want to be, but I'm also here because nobody else is.

"How is he?" she asks then, a little concern in her voice if I've ever heard it.

"He's doing good. The doctor has him on high blood pressure medication, a bit of a controlled diet. He's okay."

"That's good to hear."

There's a silence that follows on the line and I don't know where else to take this conversation.

"I have to get to work, Mom. But I'll let you know about this summer, okay?" I can think about it. This much I can offer.

"Sure, sure. Just think it over." I can almost hear the nod on the other side.

"Talk soon."

"Love you, Gray."

"You too," I tell her, even though it's been hard for me to say back.

Four

Sabrina

The Hartman wedding is being held in the Grand Ballroom of the gorgeous oceanfront Beachcomber Hotel. The Grand Ballroom being the one that holds one hundred and fifty guests and boasts stunning views of the ocean seen from floor to ceiling windows lining the far wall. Fourteen floors up you feel like you're on top of the world, floating on water. The Beachcomber itself is part of a stretch of luxury hotels on the beach that the locals call Luxe Mile.

Liz and I unload the cake boxes from the delivery van and load them onto our cake cart. We make our way through the vendor entrance, into the service elevator, and then into the ballroom where the wedding is being held. Once we locate the cake table, we get to work.

The room is exquisitely decorated – an absolute dream of white and green florals and sparkling gold candles. Classic gold Chiavari chairs line the tables covered in luxurious navy satin tablecloths. Each place setting has a printed menu for the evening along with gold rimmed champagne glasses.

A sigh slips out. I love weddings.

Liz starts to unbox the cake tiers – three in total – and I start to assemble. Sometimes, depending on the cake design, it's easier to deliver cakes unassembled and then assemble and add the finishing touches at each location. I grab my spatulas and extra buttercream then stack the cakes one by one. Rebecca, the bride, wanted to match the aesthetic and colors of the reception– brushes of gold and a deep navy blue with bountiful white flowers placed around the tiers. I grab the floral tape and Liz and I wrap each stem while we chat. Some things I've done so many times that they've become second nature.

"I watched that witch show last night," I tell her, my hands wrapping around stems and then placing the blooms artfully around the cake tiers.

"You did? So bad right?" she asks.

"So bad that it's good."

"Ha! See?!" she says, and I laugh at her response. "My mom's making pastelón tomorrow night, by the way. James and Marc are coming over, too."

Liz's Puerto Rican mother is an excellent cook, and every so often she turns it into a party. She loves to make trays of pastelón and invite family, friends, neighbors. Her house becomes a revolving door of guests, and we spend the night laughing, talking, blasting music until the very early morning hours. You'll usually find Marc and I passed out the couch around midnight while Liz, James, and her cousins dance the night away.

"Perfect. I've been craving it," I tell her, referring to both the pastelón and the need for social interaction.

"Marcos will be there," she jokes in a sing-song voice, and I snort. "I think he's bringing his new girlfriend." Liz's cousin Marcos is, above all else, a smooth-talking, desperate romantic.

"Oh! Good for him."

Once the cake is assembled, we step back, take some pictures, and then look everything over.

"We did good Elizabeth," I tell her, hands on my hips.

"We did good Sabrina."

Liz and I high-five, clean up and make our way back downstairs to the van and then back to the bakeshop.

***

It's close to five o'clock by the time we make it back. I spent the morning handling a cake tasting and consultation while James finished up the Rhodes wedding cake – a delicate two-tier lemon cake with a lemon syrup, layer of blueberry jam, a blueberry buttercream, and a good slather of vanilla bean buttercream coating the outside – for a small backyard wedding delivery tomorrow. Liz spent a good chunk of time on the phone with potential new clients and hotels, finalizing some paperwork for me. Liz and I delivered the Hartman cake and James left for the day shortly after we got back.

The crowds are out today, walking past our front windows and peeking in. They love to catch us working – baking cakes; wrestling with big batches of luscious buttercream; spinning a cake wheel while the spatula moves left and right, a mesmerizing twist of the wrist as a cake gets frosted and decorated. It was a little strange in the beginning, feeling like you're in a fishbowl and everybody is staring at you, but I've grown to secretly love it.

I'm sitting at the end of a stainless-steel table, my legs dangling, while I look at plans for next week when I spot somebody tall walking by out of the corner of my eye.

"Holy shit, who is that?" I hear Liz ask.

The person in question walks slowly, does a double-take, and comes to a stop. I look up with mild interest and then my eyes slowly grow wide.

It's that handsome devil from the coffee shop. He stands at the window smiling that perfect smile with one hand in his pocket and the other wrapped around what looks like a caramel cold brew. He's wearing a faded black T-shirt that looks like it was made for him, forearms flexing as he grips that coffee.

"Is he...smiling at *you*?" I hear Liz's voice laced with wonder and amusement.

"I have no idea. I don't even know who that is," I lie.

"Oh my God, do you *know* him?!"

Okay, so I'm a terrible liar.

I let out a long-suffering sigh. "I've been running into him at Amelia's all week. We make small talk and then go our separate ways."

"He's been hanging out at Amelia's all week waiting to see you?" She stands staring, waving.

"That's not what I said."

"He's been hanging out at Amelia's waiting to talk to you?"

I roll my eyes.

"And is that a caramel cold brew?" she looks at it longingly. Or maybe she's looking at him longingly. I can't tell.

"Looks like it," I say and head towards the door, a magnetic force dragging me over to him. Once I open the door and step outside, I get enveloped in warm summer air and the salty scent of the neighboring ocean. There he stands in the middle of it, hair on his head like the swell of the ocean, scruff along his jawline, and there my heart goes again: *wow, you belong here.*

"Hi stranger." He grins like he's genuinely happy to see me.

"Hi yourself." I smile back; it's contagious. "So, I see you've found me."

He winces a little, maybe something like guilt crossed over his features. "If I'm being honest," he leans in a little conspiratorially, "Amelia told me where you worked."

"I'm not surprised," I chuckle. I can't decide if I should thank her for that. "And I see you got a caramel cold brew this time," I nudge my chin in the direction of his coffee.

"This," he says, lifting the cup, "is delicious. Another excellent recommendation. The locals really do know best around here, I guess," he jokes and a small laugh bubbles out of me.

"I'm Gray," he says, voice deep and rich, locking eyes with mine. Those bright blue eyes I want to swim in every day of my life. "I realized I've never introduced myself."

"Hi Gray," I say, smiling. "I'm Sabrina. But I think you already knew that."

His smile gets wider before he clears his throat. Does he ever stop smiling? Can he never stop smiling?

"Hi Sabrina." He says my name in the most delicious way, like a prayer and a wish and smooth bourbon and all I can envision is how I want to lick it out of his mouth. *Get a fucking grip, Bri.* "So. You bake." He gestures to the bakeshop with his coffee.

"I bake."

Gray must notice the bakeshop sign, the one in delicate calligraphy marked Sabrina's Sweets.

"'Sabrina's Sweets'," he reads. "This is your place? That's very cool. And you make wedding cakes?" The sign also advertises *Custom Wedding Cakes. Appointment Only.*

"And other things. But yes, mostly wedding cakes."

"Giving everybody their happily ever after."

I still and he regards me like he's discovered a secret, like he can't wait to find out more.

"Something like that," I narrow my eyes at him. "So, what brings you down here?"

"I was doing some work, wanted a caffeine break," he answers, tugging at the strap to his laptop bag. "Didn't wander this far down the plaza last time so I figured I would. And I found you." He says the last part a little quietly, the words dancing on my skin while my cheeks start to burn hot. *What is this effect he keeps having on me?*

"Do you live nearby?" I find myself asking.

"About twenty minutes or so." He takes a sip of his coffee. "I live with my grandfather. Part of the reason I moved back. I lived here with him when I was in high school, but Pop's getting older, you know? So, I decided to come back and look after him."

His eyes look a little lost as he tells me this, a little dazed, so I keep my response simple and honest. "It sounds like he's lucky to have you."

"I'm the lucky one, really." He's back just as quickly, a very small smile on his lips. "Well, this plaza has been updated a bit since I've been here." Gray looks around, probably noticing the large buildings that have been built up around us and the new businesses that have emerged in these spaces.

"Yeah." I lean against the windows, following to where his eyes are fixed on a high-rise. Just beyond it, dark clouds are looming, bringing the late afternoon summer rain. "I moved in here four years ago and it's been great, but New River has definitely transformed from when I was in high school, so I can imagine what a shock it must be for you to see it. It probably doesn't even look the same anymore."

Gray continues to nod, looking around. "I wonder what has stayed the same."

"Stayed the same?"

"Yeah, like all my old local haunts. I wonder what's left of any of it. What about Harry's Hoagies? Is that still a thing?"

"Bite your tongue. Harry's Hoagies is an institution," I tell him, getting a laugh out of him.

"What about The Grand Prix Arcade? They had that wooden roller coaster."

"Definitely not. They tore the whole thing down about six or seven years ago. That roller coaster was a lawsuit waiting to happen."

Maybe the first time I met him was a toe dip into a pool, unsure of the temperature, but now it's like swimming freely. Our conversations move easily, comfortably - a push and pull, a give and take.

He laughs quietly, that crinkle in his nose so endearing. "Well, Sabrina, I guess I'll let you get back to work." He shakes his almost empty coffee cup, eyeing the skies.

"Yeah, try to beat the rain out of here."

"Well, at least I can count on that to never change," he chuckles.

"Nice seeing you again, Gray." I smile.

"Likewise," he says, those parentheses framing his face. He lifts his hand in a small wave goodbye and I hurry back into the bakeshop only to come face to face with a shocked Liz, jaw hanging down to the floor. And Liz is rarely shocked about anything.

"What was that?" she asks.

"What do you mean?"

"Sabrina, have you met somebody?"

"What does that even mean?"

"Have you been banging him in secret for the past week?!"

A ball of laughter rolls out of me, perhaps a combination of Liz's hilarious assumption and the giddiness I feel having just talked to Gray.

"Liz, you are ridiculous. We've seen each other at Amelia's, we happened to see each other again near Amelia's, we chatted about coffee and Harry's. The end. He might as well be Tina from next door."

"Harry's?"

"Yeah. He used to live here a long time ago and asked if it was still a thing. He also asked about the Grand Prix Arcade, which made me laugh," I chuckle silently to myself.

"The Grand Prix Arcade?!" Liz is practically at full volume.

"Yes. Why are you yelling?" I walk around the bakeshop organizing things as I go while Liz follows behind, stating her case.

"Look, I know you don't want to hear this, but you need to get back out there again."

"You're right. I don't want to hear it."

"What's his name?"

I stop walking and look at her. "Gray."

"*Ugh*! So hot! Well, Gray seems nice."

"We don't really know Gray."

"So, we should get to know Gray! Sabrina Moss, listen to me." She places her palms flat on the stainless table in front of her, across from me. "Find him again at Amelia's and get his phone number."

"Elizabeth, are you nuts?"

"Yes."

"Liz!"

"His *fucking phone number* Sabrina! Are you blind? He is gorgeous and he smiled at you like you were the goddamn sun! The man wants to bang you."

I chew the bottom corner of my lip. Is she right? She might have a point. "Okay. Maybe he is kind of...sort of...very hot."

Liz's hands fly up into the air, the well-known sign for *thank you universe!*

"But I don't know that he necessarily wants to bang me…"

"With a capital B, Sabrina." Her eyes widen slightly like an idea has just popped into her head. "You think he likes pastelón?"

"Liz," I start, an exasperated tone taking over. "I'm not looking to date right now. Why are you and James pushing this so hard?"

Her answer is a groan, part annoyed, part exhausted. "Okay, fine. You're right. Maybe we're being a little pushy, but I think getting out more could be good for you."

When my father left, my mother broke down for a long time. There were days and nights where I found her in the kitchen silently crying over a cold cup of tea, but she eventually started going out again. She discovered new hobbies and friends, new activities that she would drag me to any chance she got. She even began to date again - a very slow, very calculated step into it.

I look at Liz, not fighting anything she is saying this time. Is my life mimicking my mother's? Do I need a calculated step into whatever this is?

"Besides, nobody said date this guy. Just have some fun. Let me live vicariously through you!" Liz says.

"Is Jeff not fun enough for you?"

"Oh, he is plenty fun," she answers, a mischievous gleam in her eye.

"Okay. Moving on."

She giggles. "All I'm saying is…maybe start saying yes more? Be like that Jim Carrey movie."

"I did like that movie."

"Exactly! That's it."

I mull this over, consider her words, chew my bottom lip some more. I want to give in so she'll leave me alone, but there's a smaller part of me that is close to acknowledging that I probably should get out more.

"I can try to say yes more," I tell her. "But, for the record, this guy isn't asking anything for me to say yes to."

"Not yet," she smiles.

I look out past the windows, where Gray was just standing, the lingering feeling of something swirling inside me. It's been a very long time since I've felt interested in anybody – or anything – else. It's flustering, kicking me off balance. It's also exciting. An excitement I feel like I've been wanting for too long.

Not yet, Liz said. *Not yet.*

FIVE

SABRINA

"ALRIGHT, LET ME WALK you through the flavors."

It's Friday again and we've got a busy weekend ahead of us. I've been elbow deep in paperwork and planning all week, setting up orders from our purveyors and finishing cakes. I have occasionally peeked out the window, just casually looking around. I've also been the one to go on all our coffee runs but there has been no sign of Gray. Not that I've been looking, of course not.

But it's like we went from daily interaction to...nothing. Maybe he found another coffee shop? Maybe he found somebody else to talk to.

Who cares? See?! Liz's pep talk got my hopes up.

This afternoon I'm handling three cake tastings in the shop.

"Here on this platter, you will find all of the cake flavors we offer," I say, pointing to a large wooden serving board covered with mini cupcakes. We bake all our cakes as mini cupcakes for cake tastings then offer fillings and frostings separately. The cake tasting becomes a choose-your-own-adventure of sorts in which couples can mix and match flavors to get the desired cake they want for their special day.

"Here you will find our fillings. And then over here you will find our frosting options." Three separate platters sit in the middle of the table where I host the tastings. I set out stools for clients to sit, offer bottles of water, and let them get to work while we chat and I ask questions.

Evelyn, the bride, eyes the platters. Her hands sit demurely on her lap - perfectly manicured nails atop a perfectly tailored cream pencil skirt. Most of my days are spent slathered in buttercream and avoiding any sort of nail polish that can chip into the food. A gross visual, but an honest one. Some days I wish I could be an Evelyn: put together, graceful and elegant, with a wardrobe that consists solely of fashionable pieces. Instead, I live within a mountain of leggings and T-shirts, frightened to even own anything cream colored. She's more appealing than I could probably ever be.

"The approach I recommend is to take a mini cupcake, add a filling, add a frosting, and then take a healthy bite. See how you like the flavors. Do you love them? Do they work? Would you prefer something else? Mix and match until you find something that appeals to the both of you. If you can't agree or nothing is enticing you, then let me know. I'm very flexible and open to other flavor suggestions. This is your day, and this is your cake. Please, begin."

The groom, Greg, starts to slather frostings and fillings on cakes, taking bites here and there, stuffing them into his mouth like he might have skipped breakfast and lunch for this. It's happened before.

Evelyn, on the other hand, is taking the much more polished approach. She grabs a cupcake as carefully as one can and very slowly spreads frosting on it. Vanilla bean on vanilla bean, it should be noted, because if there is one thing I can tell you about cake it's that people's favorite flavors tend to match their personalities.

She chews slowly, thoughtfully, then looks over at Greg, eyes wide.

"Gregory! You have cake crumbs all over your mouth!" she whispers across the table.

He sheepishly wipes them away with a napkin from a stack I keep on the table. I decide to jump in as delicately as I can.

"Oh, it's okay! He's just enjoying the cake. I love to see people enjoying my cakes. What do you think about the flavor, Greg?"

He smiles, mouth full of more cupcake, and nods.

"Evelyn, what do you think?" Her mini cupcake sits on her plate, half-eaten.

"Very good," she nods once. "I do love vanilla." She browses the other flavors I have set out on the table, nose turned up at them, then looks back at the half-eaten one on her plate. "Can't eat too much, you know? I have a dress to fit into!" she says this almost hysterically.

I just bob my head up and down like I agree, like I have any clue about holding back on cake to zip into a wedding dress.

"So...would you like to try other flavors...or...?" I hedge.

From the corner of my eye, I see Greg chewing on a chocolate cupcake slathered in salted caramel.

"The chocolate with salted caramel is delicious. Want a bite?" Greg extends a cupcake her way.

"Don't love chocolate," she says.

"The coconut is also killer," he says. "Try it with the key lime curd."

"Don't love coconut."

He looks at the offerings now, considering which flavor she might like. "Spiced orange? Probably like that pumpkin spice thing you love so much."

I snort, and they both look over at me.

She hesitates. "I'm sorry, Sabrina. I just...I like vanilla."

"You don't need to apologize to me," I tell her reassuringly. "Vanilla is an incredibly popular choice and for good reason. It's a great blank canvas – simple, but still elegant. And a crowd pleaser."

"Evie, honey, I will eat a vanilla cake all day if that's what you really want." Greg has swallowed the cupcake now, holding her delicate, manicured hand in his gruff palm. "If you don't like any of the other flavors we can absolutely go with vanilla. Whatever makes you happy. And what will make me happy is not what kind of cake we have at our wedding, but the fact that you're going to be my wife and I get to be your husband." He kisses her knuckles, giving her a small smile.

Damn, Greg.

She seems to release the breath she's been holding.

By the end of the tasting, they've decided on – not surprisingly - a vanilla bean cake with vanilla bean buttercream. We talk briefly about designs, Evelyn pulling out what looks to be a binder dedicated to wedding planning. She flips to the cake tab and shows me picture after picture of what she had in mind.

"Okay, I can definitely work with these ideas." I nod, calmly looking at the pictures one by one, listening to what she likes about each one. Greg looks at me apologetically as I take notes, adding them to my own file for the couple.

I smile back, mouth *It's okay*. I love it when people know what they want, or when couples come in with visions and folders. Just like I love when they have no idea and we can walk that path together to the end result.

Once they've left, I throw myself onto the stool, head resting on the table while Liz and James chat behind me.

"Damn, Greg had me almost tearing up back here," James says, spinning a cake wheel, working frosting with a thin spatula.

Liz responds, "Right? He was so romantic," stuffing a cake scrap into her mouth.

"I hate vanilla," I tell them both, my voice muffled by my arms that I'm resting on.

"We know," they say in unison.

"I'm going to take it off the menu."

"You can't do that," Liz whines.

"I know," I sigh. "It's just so boring." Now I'm whining. It's been a long day and it's only mid-afternoon. I busy myself setting up for the next scheduled cake tastings while Liz and James quietly fill and frost cakes behind me. One of our weddings this weekend also asked for chocolate truffles and strawberry-lemon tarts.

The day goes by in a whirlwind, barely giving us time to catch our breath. It's late, the sunset coloring the sky orange and deep purple, when there's a knock at our door. I look up to find Jeff holding up bags of what look like take out.

"Jeffrey, you angel!" I call out as I let him in.

"I figured you guys were busy today and probably hadn't eaten." He leans in to give me a quick kiss on the cheek. "I couldn't decide on cheeseburgers or tacos, so I got both." He holds the bags up with pride.

I gasp. "Liz, you lucky bitch!"

"Tell me something I don't know," she says, coming up to kiss him in greeting, one that's slightly inappropriate and has me looking away while I take the bags from Jeff's hands and James clears off one of the tables for us to eat at. We pull things from the bags – sliders, fries, containers of chicken tinga and al pastor tacos – and set them out. I grab drinks from the fridge.

"Have you guys been to that taco stand down the road? It's great," Jeff says, coming over to the table.

"Yes! Marc and I went last week," James chimes in.

"This is very thoughtful of you, Jeff. Thanks for this," I tell him.

Once we're all seated, we start to dig in. Some fries here, a taco there. Liz picking from Jeff's plate, James picking things from mine.

"So, how's the business going these days, Bri?" Jeff asks, mouthful of slider.

"Oh, you know. Sweet."

"That was terrible," Liz says, taking a bite of an al pastor taco. I shoot her my middle finger.

"It's fine. We're heading out of busy season so we'll be able to breathe a little bit coming up. Can't complain, though. This past season was probably our best yet. I've got a great team and I'm surrounded by baked goods," I shrug.

"We love you, too," James winks at me.

"Have you thought anymore about the expansion?" Jeff asks.

Last time we were all together, I brought up the idea of opening the shop up to the public. The response was surprisingly, overwhelmingly positive.

"Birthday cakes. Cupcakes. Cookies?" James offers suggestions. "I say let's do it."

I nod, telling Jeff, "I've still been thinking about it, but it would require so much more of my time. More planning, more adjusting. I need to really sit down and look at the logistics."

"We're here for you no matter what you want to do, Bri, but I think it could be fun to really open this place up to the public," Liz says.

"Could you make pies? I love pie," Jeff adds.

"I'll think about it." I take another big bite, stuffing my mouth full, when Jeff points to the window.

"Somebody is staring."

"Yeah, we get that a lot," I say, waving it off.

"No, I think he's trying to get your attention."

I look up at Jeff and before I even look out the window, I know exactly who I'm going to see.

There stands Gray in all his sexy glory wearing a dark blue T-shirt that hugs his shoulders, joggers hanging dangerously low on his hips, and my favorite smile. It's unfair how good he looks. My heart is doing somersaults in my chest, I'm worried everybody at the table can hear. I don't know that I've ever been so elated to see somebody.

He's amused as he looks over at me, my mouth full of al pastor, cheeks puffed out. My face is probably giving him literal heart eyes. Am I blushing too? I'm a mess. I stand and head over to the door, making sure to swallow this damn taco before I open it. *But now I need a drink.*

"Sorry, am I interrupting something?" he asks.

"Just dinner." I lean against the door frame, throat dry. *I really need a drink.*

"And what's for dinner?"

"Jeff brought us cheeseburgers and tacos."

"Who's Jeff?" His brow furrows.

"Jeff is the perfect man sitting over there that brought us cheeseburgers and tacos." I point my thumb in the direction of the table.

"Is that the bar for perfect?"

"Bringing us food? It's definitely on the list."

From behind me I hear Liz yell, "We have extra! Come join us!"

Then I hear the shuffle of feet. James has gotten up and is coming over to the door. "Honestly Bri, where are your manners? Please come sit with us, Sabrina's new friend!" He grabs Gray by the wrist and leads him in while Gray just grins at me. James might as well be an eager grandmother trying to marry me off.

"I would love to," he says. "My name is Gray by the way," he tells the table.

"Oh, we know," Liz says.

"You know?"

"We know." She points to the food in the center of the table. "Help yourself."

"Are you sure? I didn't mean to impose on your dinner tonight."

"Yes, it's fine. We have plenty," I tell him, wanting him to stay and sit and enjoy dinner with us. Wanting him near again. The feeling is a strange one I don't want to pick apart, but I'm finding it important for him to be here with us. "This is James, by the way. And Liz. And Jeff, who is with Liz." I feel the need to elaborate on that last part just in case he wondered about Jeff.

Liz catches it, and she smirks. "Yeah, he's all mine. Sorry."

Gray says hello to everyone then sits down in the chair next to mine. He slowly grabs a slider, almost reluctantly, and takes a bite, while looking around the bakeshop.

"Would you like something to drink, too?" I ask, walking over to the small fridge, reaching to guzzle a bottle of water. "I've got water or some iced matcha drink that James brought."

"Antioxidants, bitch!" James yells out.

"Water would be great. Thank you," Gray chuckles. "This is a cool place you've got here."

I feel myself start to shrink. This place, while on display for the public through those windows, is very much a personal space. My personal space. This is a big chunk of my heart and soul laid out bare around these four walls.

I place a water bottle in front of him and sit down, my remaining al pastor waiting for me.

"Isn't it great? Isn't she great?" Liz says, smile plastered on her face.

I kick her boot under the table.

"She is," he laughs, looking over at me.

"*And* she's single," she mutters under her breath, a stage whisper if I've ever heard one.

"Elizabeth," I say in warning. Jeff shoves a French fry into her mouth.

Gray just takes it all in stride, laughing softly while my face burns like the surface of the sun.

"So, what do you do Gray?" James asks.

"I'm a freelance web designer."

"That's cool. How did that come about?" Liz asks, getting to the questions before I do.

"Oh. Well, I was working with a design firm up north, but when I moved back here, I decided to go my own way. I work from home most of the time, but I found Amelia's last week and it's been a great place to work and people watch."

"Amelia's is pretty great," James nods in agreement.

"Haven't seen you there this week," I add in.

"Noticed, did you?" he smirks, and the table erupts into heckles. He turns to me, gives me his attention as he speaks quietly. "Had some things to tend to with my grandfather. Doctor's appointments, things like that," he shrugs, looking down. "So, I worked mostly from home this week."

My mouth sounds out a small oh of acknowledgment, like we're close friends sharing inside stories about things nobody else at this table would know about.

"And that's how you and Bri met?" Liz throws another question at him.

He takes another bite, nodding in response to her question. Once he's swallowed, he answers with a simple, "Yeah. We struck up a conversation one day and then I saw her almost every day after that."

He says it like it was the most natural occurrence in the world, like we started a conversation one day like we were old friends and then just didn't stop.

It's almost alarming how accurate that description is.

"Hmm," is all Liz says, looking over at me, a smile pulling at her mouth.

"This is delicious by the way. Thank you for this," he says genuinely.

"You like pastelón, Gray?" Liz asks then.

"I...don't know what that is." He shifts his eyes to mine in question like, *Should I know?* I just shake my head.

"All in due time," she murmurs quietly.

"Are you enjoying life down here?" James asks. "Bri mentioned you used to live here and just moved back."

"Oh yeah? What else has she said?" he laughs as I give James a death glare and scarf down another taco. "Yeah, I lived here as a teen. Went to West Bay High School here," he continues.

The table explodes into a chorus of *"oooohs."*

"Careful. You're sitting at a table full of New River High graduates," Liz teases.

Gray's answering laugh is hearty and warm and delightful. "Should I see myself out?"

"Nah. You can stick with me," Jeff chimes in. "I didn't associate with these nerds until college." He goes back to eating his cheeseburger.

"And just look at how much richer your life is for it, babe!" Liz says, wrapping her arms around him.

"And let's be honest, who gives a shit about high school rivalries and politics anymore anyway?" James adds.

We lift our drinks in toast to that.

"But where did you go to college? That's the real question," Jeff says.

"Nobody cares about that either, babe," Liz adds.

"You're just saying that because your college sucked."

"It would be quite unfortunate if you choked on your burger."

James and I snort at that.

"Well, I got a full ride to the state university. Really the best one of them all," Gray says smugly, with a hint of a laugh in his eyes.

I can't help but cackle at that, this sparring between friends old and new. This welcome playfulness that I've missed, that had been tucked away for only my closest friends. And the laughter continues while the rest of them join in, booing him in jest.

We finish up the food in the middle of the table. Gray sits comfortably in his chair like he's settling in, fitting into our space perfectly. He seems to be genuinely enjoying his time with us here and I'm happy to see it.

"But to answer your question, I am enjoying my time back here. I haven't had a chance to explore much yet though. Except for the local coffee...and the local wedding cake baker," Gray adds, as he chances a look at me. It's a shy look, a quiet one on the surface, but bubbling just underneath.

His words make me dizzy, but I stand anyway, grabbing empty bags and containers to bring over to the trash can. "Just going to clean this up," I murmur while I excuse myself and whatever the hell is happening at this table.

"Oh, let me help," Gray offers as he immediately follows. Of course, he does.

James is smirking. Liz's smile is about to take over her whole face. Jeff gives a wink and a lift of the eyebrows while still shoving some fries into his mouth.

"Thanks," I grumble.

He starts walking slowly, taking everything in. He walks past the ovens, the shelves along the wall. He leans over the cakes cooling on the racks and takes a big whiff. His hands are in his pockets as he slowly peruses. The slower he walks, the more excruciating it becomes. I'm an onion, layers being peeled back painfully slow.

He looks at the framed pictures I have on my wall, the front-page feature in a local magazine. Liz had long purple hair at the time in two buns on top of her head; James looked timeless and cool in his favorite black pants and apron, dark hair brushed back from his face; and I stood in the middle with my favorite striped apron and my hair down in a tumble of waves, long arms crossed in front of me, wide smile plastered to my face.

I remember when the issue came out and we went to grab it, reading and laughing at how unconventional, how *fun* it all was. How this misfit kitchen of ours made the front page and managed to be the most successful wedding cake vendor that year. How we were voted best wedding cake bakery in the county, and I'd turned to them and squealed, *"They actually like us?!"* He hums quietly as he takes a closer look.

He walks past the comic strips I have taped on the fridge doors, laughing softly as he reads them. And that's when I notice it.

"You know, speaking of coffee, you don't have one in your hand today."

He turns to look at me. "You're right. I didn't go to Amelia's first."

"So...you came here first?" "I did." He stops to open the freezer door and take a peek.

"What are you doing? Do you also do this when you visit peoples' houses?"

"Maybe."

"You're weird."

He turns to look at me directly. "Want to go to lunch?" he asks.

"What?" Behind me, I think I heard James gasp.

"Do you want to go to lunch? With me?"

"She would love to!" Liz screams from the other side of the room.

I close my eyes at that, roll my lips inward to keep my face as neutral as I can.

He tries not to laugh. "Well, we had that conversation about Harry's Hoagies and it got me thinking it would be a nice trip down memory lane. Also made me crave their Italian sub. I thought maybe you could join me if you'd like."

He says this so calmly, so rationally, as if he's not leaving me completely dazed. He was a stranger - a stranger now slowly becoming a local friendly face - and he's just asked me to lunch. Is this how people get murdered?

I need to stop watching so much Cold Case.

I think back to what Liz told me last week – try to be more open to things, try to say yes more. And here Gray is, asking a question for me to say yes to.

My palms feel clammy, I feel flushed. Not sure if this is a heart attack or just nerves. It takes me a minute to stutter my way through an "Alright. When?"

I'm rewarded with that nose-scrunching smile, the one that meets his gorgeous eyes and makes my heart skip. "Whenever you can," he says.

"Um. Does Monday work for you?" Weekends are trickier for me to schedule around, but weekdays are harder for the rest of the world.

"I can make Monday work. How about 11:30?"

"I can meet you there," I add quickly. I can take my own car, keep my distance. This is a platonic lunch with a stranger. It is *not* a date. I look over my shoulder as discreetly as I can where I find Liz shooting lasers at my face mouthing the words *PHONE NUMBER!*

"Should we...exchange numbers?" I ask, trying to sound completely nonchalant and absolutely failing.

His mouth lifts at one corner, the beginnings of a smirk or a laugh, I'm not sure which. "Good idea," he says, and we pull out our phones.

Once numbers are exchanged, he starts walking toward the exit, passing the table where everybody is quietly chatting. "Thank you for inviting me in and for the food. It was great to meet you all." Then he turns to me, as I'm following to walk him out, meets my eyes and says in a low, delicious rumble, "I'll see you on Monday, Sabrina."

The door jingles as it closes, and I think I might faint.

"Oh. My. God," I hear Liz say behind me, laughing with delight.

I turn around, face in flames, my hands pressed to my cheeks, and realize that plastered to my face is the biggest smile I've had in a very long time.

Six

Gray

THE SUN IS STARTING to peek through the blinds, bits and pieces of light funneling through. A world waking up. I found myself alone last night with no plans and Pop urging me to go out and hang with all the young people, whatever that meant. Nancy had come over to play dominoes and so I begrudgingly left. I drove around aimlessly but there was only one place I found myself wanting to be.

When I got to the plaza, I didn't even bother going to Amelia's for coffee. I didn't need that security blanket, didn't want it. I just wanted to see her, but what I didn't expect was a big group of people. She was in the middle, a communal table and a mountain of food between them. Hands reached over as they shared everything, enjoyed a dinner together. There was laughter and conversation. I almost left, not wanting to squeeze myself into this part of her life that was not meant for me, but something pushed me to knock anyway. To my surprise, they invited me in, and I felt welcome. Their questions were basic, get-to-know-you questions, but the delivery was like we'd been old friends. Like they wanted to hear the answer.

I haven't felt that...well, in a very long time.

Being on the inside, both literally and figuratively, was another peek into her that I desperately wanted to grab and hold onto, white knuckled. How they joked and jabbed, how they were so comfortable together, how they cared for one another. Her bakeshop displayed, so subtly, all these pieces of her, coming together to add to the puzzle.

And even during it, Sabrina made – *makes* - me feel like I'm just as important as anybody else. It's a little bit unnerving.

I hadn't planned on asking her to lunch when I walked in, but as the night progressed and I found myself wanting to get more puzzle pieces, the words just rushed out. I wanted a chance to see her outside of her work environment, a chance to see her outside of the space where there's always Amelia's Coffee and the comfort of her work. How is she outside of these walls? Could we be as comfortable outside of this?

And why am I so interested in that?

I roll out of bed, hair on end. It's still so early, the sun just starting to rise, but I feel compelled to unpack. To finally get the shit out of boxes and bags and really dig my heels into this place. I go to the corner and grab my suitcase and duffel bags, dumping all my clothing and nonsense onto the bed, sorting as I go: laundry, dresser, closet. I unbox my books, move around some furniture and finally work to get myself settled in like I've been meaning to.

Pop must hear the noise because I see him in my doorframe minutes later, glasses perched atop his head, hands in his pockets.

"What the heck are you doing this early in the morning?"

"Just wanted to organize," I shrug.

"You decided to organize at six in the morning on a Sunday?"

"There are stranger times."

"Maybe so." He looks around, probably assessing the mess, the tornado that's hit this room. "You want breakfast?"

"Breakfast sounds good. You cookin'?"

He barks out a laugh. "Absolutely not. Let's go to the Broken Egg."

He jerks his head in the direction of the door. The Broken Egg is a diner nearby, one that Pop and I frequented a lot when I lived here. It was a weekend treat, a chance to get out of the house and talk. I look back at the mess in the room. It can wait.

"Let's go." I smile, wrapping my arm around his shoulders as we walk to the car.

"So, how are you doin'?" Pop asks, mixing the berries into his oatmeal.

I look up from my own plate – an omelet and hash browns – and try to decipher his tone. I think he's worried.

"I'm doing okay." I take a bite and chew.

"You gettin' out?"

"Yeah, I've been doing work at that coffee shop. It's been nice."

He nods. "Got any fun plans tonight?"

"Tonight?"

"Yeah. Don't the young kids hang out on Sunday nights somewhere?"

"The young kids? Pop, what is going on?"

"I'm just making conversation."

"Are you worried about me again?"

"I'm always worried about you, Gray."

"And I told you I'm doing okay." My tone is probably harsher than I intended.

He breathes in deep, levels a look at me. "I am very happy to have you back, you know that. But I didn't need you to give up your life in order to do it." I start to protest, but he puts his hand up and continues. "Now, maybe this move wasn't even about me. I can understand that, too. But whatever the case you're here now and I want to make sure you're alright."

After college, I found everybody pairing up, getting into serious relationships. And I found myself drifting again, just floating by but not really looking for that anchor. Until I was. A loneliness and a homesickness that snuck up on me slowly and then swallowed me whole. I wanted nothing more than to come back here, to the place I last felt anchored, to the only place I've considered home.

"You sure you want to give up your life there, Gray?" he'd asked me. But I was so sure, so ready. I had been itching for it, unknowingly, for months.

"My life isn't here, Pop," I'd told him then.

I take a sip of coffee and wince slightly - my taste buds now ruined by Amelia's - and look back at him. "I missed you. I missed it here. I wanted to come back home. Maybe –" I pause, think about the words that are about to come out. "Maybe put some roots down somewhere for once. Not just pretend to, I guess."

"Roots?" He arches one eyebrow.

I shrug a little, take another bite of omelet.

He studies me for a minute. "Talk to your mother recently?"

"Not since last week."

He nods again. "I'm glad that I could be a home for you, Gray. I know things weren't always easy, but I hope that I gave you comfort and safety when you needed it."

I look at him then, unsure of what to say.

"But I also wouldn't be upset if you wanted to get your own place. You don't need to be living with your grandfather."

I balk at him. "Are you kicking me out?"

"No of course not," he practically rolls his eyes. "I'm just trying to make sure you don't feel stuck is all."

"I'm not stuck, Pop. We talked about this before I even moved down. I want to be here with you, and I want to look after you." I fidget as I scoop up my potatoes, shoveling them into my mouth. "You're the one stuck with me."

He sighs then, mouth twitching at the corners, and sips his coffee. "Well then, I hope I can push you to get out of the house more at least."

"You think that's what I need?" I say lightly.

"You've always longed for connection, Gray. We both know that. So yes, I think you need to get out of the house and hang out with your friends."

I expel a deep breath. Why do I feel like I'm being reprimanded like a teenager again?

"Is anybody still here?" he asks.

"Not really." I knew moving back here that a lot of my school friends would be gone. A few have lingered but they're busy with work, with significant others, with life – the caveat nobody tells you about once you hit your thirties.

"So, let's get you to meet new people, then," he says like it's the easiest thing in the world.

Though, meeting Sabrina was much easier than I would have imagined.

"You don't need to spend all your time with me, Gray. I'm fine."

I level a look at him, one that suggests *you know you're not.*

"Besides, I know Nancy likes to check on me no matter how much you guys try to deny it."

I laugh quietly at that. "I'll try to get out more, Pop, but not at the expense of you or your health."

"Fine. It's a start."

And I realize then that maybe what I want - what I've wanted first and foremost - is to be Sabrina's friend. More than anything else. I want that energy, that attention directed at me. Maybe that's what I was doing when the words rolled out of me, my heart knowing what to do before I could even make sense of it. We'd talked about Harry's so I thought lunch could be an easy sell. Granted, she looked like I asked her if she wanted to go eat some dirt.

I take the last bite of my omelet, chewing as I think. This could be a nice lunch between us. But maybe this could be...the start of something more. A plan starts to work in my brain, a little muddy, but taking shape.

"Wheels are turning," Pop smirks at me.

"Maybe," I smile. "Reach for connection, Gray." Words he used to tell me to push me out into the world. "Love deeply. Remember?" More words he would tell me. Ones that would remind me that I didn't have to shut the world out just because I felt it shut me out, just because my mother did. That I should push for the good, push for the love anyway. Feel the feelings, jump in the pool.

What is life if you're not risking things, Gray? What is life if you're not living? His words bouncing around the walls in my room as he sat on the edge of my bed, bouncing around in my head late at night on the nights I couldn't sleep. Echoing in the silence before, during, and after Moriah.

And now.

"Speaking of being social, how are the Old Fishermen doing these days?" I smirk around a forkful of potatoes.

He barks out a laugh. "Those grumpy assholes. I love 'em."

Pop lives a quiet life now, mostly at home with his James Patterson books and sudoku. Gran passed away before I moved in with him, and I always wondered if part of the reason he said yes to me was to have somebody else in the house with him again. He's got a good, true friend in Nancy and a monthly fishing club meet up with his old work buddies. They call themselves the Old Fishermen; they go out to the lake to fish, yes, but mostly just to grumble about life. It's good for him. I can see the joy in his eyes when he talks about them and it brings me peace to know he's got friends, he's got people that care for him. And yes, maybe that's exactly what he wants for me.

When we get back home, I retreat to my room again and finish unpacking so I can finally give myself a chance to settle in. A chance to maybe lay down roots.

SEVEN

SABRINA

I HAVE NO IDEA what I'm doing, but I'm doing it. *Famous last words.*

At this point I'm acting like I've never been out to lunch in my life. I've been out to lunch! I've been out to lunch with friends. Plenty of times! *This is all totally normal!*

I'm stressing out again.

It's Monday and I'm tiptoeing around my clothes strewn all over my floor to get to my closet to try on yet another outfit that I will probably hate. I've been at this for about thirty minutes - trying to pick clothes that scream *"casual!"* and *"it's just lunch!"* and *"this is not a date!"*

It's not a date, right?!

I'm tossing clothes into piles, cursing myself for never shopping for proper clothing, for always sticking to way too many leggings and never bothering to buy something nice for this sort of nonsense.

I take a deep breath and call Liz.

"Tell me to calm down," I say when she answers.

"Calm down."

"Tell me none of this matters."

"Eh…" "It doesn't matter! Tell me!"

"It matters enough that you're calling me, freaking out."

"I don't have anything to wear."

"Sure, you do. Wear a pair of shorts and a that T-shirt you own with the sheep wearing pearls."

I groan in response.

"Bri, it's just lunch. It's lunch with a really hot guy, but still. It's just lunch. At Harry's! It's just sandwiches and conversation. And judging by how effortless your conversations have been, I think you're going to be okay," she tells me reassuringly. "But also, it's eight hundred degrees outside so dress accordingly," she adds.

I stay silent on the other line, taking in her words, trying to remember how to breathe.

"He saw you in your banana Crocs and still wanted to talk to you. That's commitment."

"You're hilarious."

"I know," she says. "The only person you have to be is you. That's it."

She's right. I know that. In the years after Ben, I found myself having to figure out Sabrina again, having to find Sabrina again. And it wasn't easy when I realized I didn't even know who she was anymore. But she was in there, buried deep beneath a whole mess of shit. I found her, and I've been letting her grow and thrive ever since.

I'm trying to be more open and honest. I'm trying to say yes to things – clearly with Liz's push. Like this lunch. Like conversations with a stranger in a coffee shop. And I've been better for it. This Sabrina is my favorite Sabrina because she's trying and she's learning to give it her all.

I *want* to see Gray again. It's an odd feeling, one I haven't felt in so long. I like seeing him. I like talking to him.

"Thanks, Liz. Love you." I end the call and throw on the most comfortable shorts I own. I pair it with a loose graphic tank and take a look in the mirror, studying my reflection. A mess of brown waves that I've thrown up into a high ponytail, grown out bangs falling around my eyes, winged eyeliner on point. The curves of my body are on display in these shorts – curves I've hidden behind shirts and aprons. This time I stand up a little straighter, my eyes following my hips down. I throw on sandals to replace my banana Crocs. "It's just sandwiches and conversation," I tell myself. "All I have to be is me."

And if it sucks, I can call Liz and feign an emergency.

I grab my purse and head to my car.

The sun is beating down, clouds barely covering the bright blue sky. Liz wasn't kidding – the heat has arrived, and it is almost unbearable. I roll the windows down as I drive, my eyes focused on the world flying by, this city I have lived in my whole life. Palm trees line the streets as I zoom past, tall trunks reaching to the sky, a burst of green palm fronds exploding at the top. I love it here; I love the charm. Locals and tourists alike crowd sidewalks and stores, a sea of people coming and going, emitting the nostalgic smell of sunscreen: coconuts and salty ocean. Seasonal rentals are starting to fill up and I can't help but smile. The sunrises in New River feed my soul and the waves on the beach wash me clean.

This city is buzzing with something electric, a tangible energy I want to harness, and I feel it in my veins.

I drive past the 24-hour Walmart, the one where Ben and I spent hours past midnight roaming the aisles, talking and laughing one summer. The Dairy Belle where he'd kissed me with vanilla soft serve lips. I speed past the newly constructed apartment buildings that used to be the Grand Prix Arcade, where Liz and I rode that death trap of a rollercoaster till we puked. So much has changed, but the memories remain.

By the time I pull into a parking spot, I see Gray is already there waiting for me outside. He smiles as I get out of my car, coming over to greet me.

"Hi," he says. How does he make that word sound so perfect? One syllable, two letters, and I'm a puddle at his feet.

"Hi," I say back. This is great. We sound fifteen.

He's wearing shorts today, too – blue ones - and a faded T–shirt that looks to be of a famous old local band called The Triangles.

I laugh a little at that, my own memories conjured up by it, telling him, "Nice shirt."

He looks down, running his palms along the front to smooth it out and smirks. "Thanks. Nice face."

The little laugh has now turned into a cackle, a loud one, right here in the middle of the parking lot. My head tilts back as I release the booming sound right into the sky and I almost want to rein it in. I remember the first time Ben said something really funny and I laughed, that obnoxious cackle, and he winced. His face scrunched up and he looked around like he was embarrassed, mumbled, *"Ssshhh. Bri. Quiet."*

Gray doesn't tell me to be quiet now. Instead, he laughs with me, those blue gems lighting up like twinkling lights as he watches me.

"I found it mixed in with a bunch of old clothes. I thought it would fit today's theme," he grins, proud of himself.

"It's a great shirt. I loved The Triangles." My laugh still lingers.

"Me too! Saw them at The Downtowner my senior year. Great show."

I nod, smiling at his excitement.

"Should we...?" He signals to the entrance, and holds the door open for me as we walk in.

It's the Monday lunch rush and we walk into a symphony of loud voices, chairs scraping against tile floors, and the register's *cha-ching!*

I've been coming to Harry's Hoagies since high school, but it's been around much longer than that. The main gimmick is they make the subs directly in front of you, the glass partition separating you and a smorgasbord of toppings. You tell them what you want, they slice the meat to order, and then toss it into the air to the person waiting on the other end with an open hoagie roll. Lunch with a show.

"They still throw the meat around!" he says, joy and excitement on his face. It's so cute. Gray looks around in wonder. This place hasn't changed since I've been in high school so I'm sure it's a step back in time for him. "Everything is still the same. It's wild."

"Isn't it?"

"It's crazy how much I love it." He smiles at that.

"I get that. It's familiar and comforting. And delicious."

The very first time I came here I was in high school and a group of us stopped by after school. Walking into the shop, I spotted him immediately – sitting in a corner, being loud with his friends. Ben looked perfect in his trendy T-shirt and messy hair. Before I realized I was staring, he casually looked over and spotted me. I lifted my hand in a small wave; he nodded in acknowledgment. And that was it. He was with his clique, and I was with mine. That day I ordered a small turkey hoagie on wheat. I ate it slowly, daintily at a corner table making sure to look as cute as possible in case his eyes were ever on me. It wasn't until I got up to refill my diet soda that I realized he wasn't even there anymore. He had already left and didn't even say goodbye.

I'm not usually thrown off by thoughts of Ben, the memories that creep in during the day when I'm doing something that conjures up a feeling, or the ones that seep in at night when my mind is racing a mile a minute and I can't get it to slow down.

But what I do realize is this: the thoughts of Ben that have emerged when I'm with Gray are different, not like the ugly comparisons my mind would drift to whenever I was out on a date or even just talking to somebody else.

I'm brought back to the present when I see the older man taking orders wave us over.

"We're up," I tell Gray.

"You first." He motions for me to go ahead.

"Hi, how are you?" I say to the man. "Can I have a large Italian hoagie please?"

The man jots the order down and another employee, who looks to be a young college kid, slices the meats on the slicer.

Gray steps up and recites his. "Hi. Can I have a large Italian as well?"

Now I know the only acceptable order at Harry's is a large hoagie, one overflowing with meats and vegetables, large enough to last until the next day. If there are any leftovers.

"The only acceptable order at Harry's," I hear Gray say next to me, echoing my thoughts and surprising me.

We watch as the meats are sliced – salty ham, spicy capicola, fatty mortadella – and arranged on a sheet of wax paper. Then the kid grabs them and in a quick flick of the wrist tosses it over to somebody else standing, waiting with an open hoagie roll.

Our sandwiches are loaded up with toppings – a layer of provolone, mounds of shredded, crisp lettuce, jeweled tomato slices, a drizzle of oil and vinegar. I get an extra sprinkle of pepper, Gray gets a flourish of sweet peppers and we look on as they cut them in half, and wrap them in a ridiculously large piece of butcher paper. We move down the line, heading to the register next. He pulls out his wallet and quickly pays for our sandwiches then hands me a cup for a fountain drink.

"Oh, you didn't have to pay for my sandwich!" I manage to sputter out too late.

"My treat. Thank you for joining me," he says. "You can get the next one," he adds with a wink.

Once we fill our cups and find an open table, we finally sit down, and I have a minute to breathe. I watch him unwrap his comically large piece of butcher paper and take a healthy bite. His eyes flutter closed, and he groans; I almost spit out my Birch beer.

"This is even better than I remember," he says.

I take a large bite of mine, relishing the perfect taste. The meats, the cheese, the soft roll. I love the bite of the vinegar mingling with the juiciness of the tomato slice.

"So good," I say, mumbling around a mouth full of Italian sub. *Classy, Sabrina.*

He looks at me with amusement, still chewing, eyes dancing in delight.

I wipe my mouth with a napkin, offering some semblance of manners.

We eat in companionable silence for a moment, and I think how so very *nice* this is. How nice it is to get out of the house, out of the bakeshop. How nice it is to enjoy lunch with somebody different. He's funny and fun, with childlike wonder, enjoying everything.

It's been so long since I've felt like this, I almost forgot what it was like. He looks over at me and gives me the tiniest smile. A quick lift of his lips. Something starts in my belly, working its way outward. Bubbles. Fizzy, bubbly, light. The effervescence of poured champagne, rising to the surface in a glass.

"So, what else do I need to know about you Gray? You do freelance, you live with your grandfather, you got a fancy scholarship to college."

"You've been paying attention," he grins and my face heats, the blush to end all blushes overtaking my face.

"Hardly," I mutter, and he laughs, reading me like a damn book. "So, you couldn't stay away from New River, huh?"

"Didn't want to," he says. "I'm happy to be back. It's always been home."

"Is your grandfather the only family you have here?" I ask delicately, unsure of his family dynamics.

He shakes his head. "My mom and dad split up before I was born. He didn't really want anything to do with us so I moved around a lot as a kid. My mom was...always looking for something else, something better. So, I went to a lot of different schools and lived in different cities. I decided I didn't want that anymore so I asked Pop if I could stay with him."

I feel like I've asked the wrong questions, pried too much into his life. "I'm so sorry, Gray."

I'm not sure what my face looks like, but he must see something in it, because he assures me, "It's okay. Once I moved in with him, I felt much more...settled."

"Where is your mom now?" I ask.

"She's got a boyfriend now and they moved back to Virginia a couple of years ago. They've been all over the place. They love to travel, and I love that for them, but that was a hard thing to deal with when I was a kid just looking for stability, you know?"

"Of course." I see a little sadness in his eyes, but it's gone just as fast.

He takes another bite, chews, then swallows. "This lunch turned into a bummer. Sorry about that," he laughs softly.

"No. Don't apologize," I say, shaking my head. "Where else have you lived?"

He tilts his head, thinks about it. "Virginia, for starters. A stint in Maryland. Up and down the state. One year in Georgia."

"Wow." I must seem like an absolute recluse to him, stuck in this place and never opting to leave it.

"What about you? What's your story?"

"Don't really have one."

"I don't believe that for a second."

I shrug. "I've lived here my whole life. Your opposite." I give him a small smile.

"The grass isn't always greener."

I consider that. "I went to school here, went to college here. Started baking in high school. I loved it so much that I decided to pursue it. I started my business about seven years ago in my apartment, then moved into the shop, and now here I am."

"That's impressive. You must be very proud of yourself."

Those words echo in my brain before I can manage to respond. *You must be very proud of yourself.* And I am - so proud. I've fought for myself every step of the way into that shop and the position I'm in. *But then why is external validation so important to you, Sabrina?* His voice brings me out of my thoughts.

"What got you into baking?"

Heartache. Anger. Disappointment. Sadness. Pick a reason. "I've always had a sweet tooth," I say instead. "Once I started to learn the basics of baking, there was no stopping me. I started with birthday cakes first and got into wedding cakes much later."

"It must be a fun job."

"It definitely has its perks." I smile. "I love what I do. So much. I love to bake and create, but I also love the customer service aspect of it. Like designing a couple's ideal cake for their day, sitting with them to brainstorm about flavors and decorations. I love when I get it right. Cake makes everybody happy," I laugh sheepishly. "I could talk about this all day." *But I should know my limits here.*

And yet, his answering smile, his attentiveness as I speak does something to me. The champagne bubbles are slowly turning into soda can bubbles. A soda can left in the trunk of a fast-moving car. "What's the craziest cake you've made?"

I let out a breath, think about his question. "We've had some unique wedding themes. Zombies, pirates, more mermaid themes than I care to count."

His eyebrows lift, laughing as I list them off.

"Not my cup of tea, but we had a lot of fun with them. And it made people happy."

"Any cake disasters?" He takes another bite of sandwich.

"Oh, plenty," I huff out a laugh. "Burned cakes, underbaked cakes. Melted buttercream in the summer heat. One disastrous cake delivery that ended with a cake tier on the floor and me in tears."

"Oh no!" He laughs with me.

"Had a bride tell me after the wedding that she thought the cake was terrible and she was going to let everybody in the city know about it," I wince, remembering that memory.

"Wow, a bride Yelper."

I lift my eyebrows in agreement, taking another bite of my sandwich.

"Do you have any family here?"

"It's just my mom and me. It's been just us for a while now."

He looks at me briefly before setting his eyes on his sandwich, nodding slowly. "Yeah, I can understand that. My mom was a single parent for a long time and then she met Dave. But it's really just been me and Pop most of my life."

There's a tug in my chest when he says that. A common denominator where I look at him and think *yes, you know how it feels to be left behind, too.*

"Do you enjoy what you do?" I ask.

"I do, yeah. I love the creative aspect of it, too, like you. A different kind of creative. I love the technical side of it. I like being on my own, but it has its own stress factors. I'm trying to pick up more clients, get some more work."

"I might know some people," I suggest, inserting myself into this man's job like we're old friends.

I think back to Liz's words on the phone, how we've been so comfortable together that lunch would probably be a breeze. And it has been. An easygoing, comfortable time that I have not felt with somebody new in a very long time.

"Oh, thank you." He nods, probably just trying to be agreeable.

"Not to shove myself into your work or anything." I laugh now, a little embarrassed.

"No, not at all. I appreciate it."

"Thank you for inviting me here, by the way. This was a great idea," I tell him, deflecting.

"You're very welcome. I'm full of great ideas, just you wait."

He sits back in the chair, a look on his face that I can't quite decipher.

I narrow my eyes at him. What's coming?

"So, I have a proposition for you."

My eyes widen for a second. *A proposition? Like – sex? Is he about to ask me for sex? Is he buttering me up with a sub for sex?! I mean, A for effort. I love a good Harry's Hoagie.*

"Oh God, that sounded bad. No, no. Just...an idea."

"Okay...what kind of idea?"

He takes another bite, chewing thoughtfully before he answers. "I was wondering if you would want to show me around."

I stare for a beat. "Show you around what?"

"Around town. I've been gone so long and talking about all the old places I used to hang out really got me thinking about how much I've missed this city. And how much I want to see all my old local haunts again...and maybe some new ones. Really get to know New River again."

"You want me to be...like a tour guide?"

"Kind of...I guess?"

I don't know what kind of facial expression I'm making, but I can only imagine it's saying something along the lines of *"what the hell are you talking about?"* or maybe *"I thought you were trading subs for sex."*

He lets out a laugh. "Does that sound dumb? It sounded better in my head."

"Why me?"

"Why not?"

"Don't you have friends that can show you around?"

"Can't I make new ones?"

Well, he's got me there.

"I don't have a lot of friends in town anymore," he says. "The very few that do live here are busy with their own lives."

"And I'm not busy with my own life?" Everybody sure seems to think I don't have enough of a life, now a stranger is telling me the same damn thing.

"I didn't mean it like that. I just meant..." he trails off.

"Meant what?" I push.

He looks at me as if debating what to say, how much to say. "I don't know. We're both single adults in this city. All my friends are paired up with significant others."

This I understand. These words strike a familiar chord. We could pair up, he's telling me. We could be friends and go out and enjoy each other's company. So, he didn't offer sub sex, but maybe this isn't a terrible second option.

"I realize I'm not speaking very well right now. Maybe I'm a little nervous," he says.

"Nervous about what?"

"You." His eyes meet mine.

"Me?" My eyebrows lift.

He wipes his hand down his face, taking a deep breath almost as if he's resetting. "I have enjoyed your company today. I enjoy your company any day, really. I know we don't know a lot about each other, but we could keep getting to know each other. We could be friends. And we would have fun together exploring this city that we both love, don't you think?"

I tilt my head, study him. The words echo a similar sentiment I heard many years ago, but this time it seems genuine. It seems like he's looking for connection and friendship. Do I think we would have fun together? Yes, I do. This isn't dating. It's friendship. And it's a compromise I'm willing to make, one I can handle for now. I notice I've been silent too long when he speaks again.

"You can say no. It won't hurt my feelings. It was just an idea." He looks down at what's left of his sandwich. One bite and he's done.

I would love to, I think. *Let's do it,* I want to say. The words are about to bubble up out of me, right there, breaking the surface, when the door to Harry's opens and Gray casually looks over. His eyes light up in surprise as he stands to greet whoever has just come in.

"Holy shit, what are you doing here?" I hear him say, a smile in his voice.

The other person lets out a laugh and I feel a shiver of familiarity course through me. I turn around in my seat to peek at Gray's friend that has just come into the shop and my heart stops. The symphony of loud noises goes silent like a record scratching. Like tires screeching and skidding to a stop on hot asphalt.

He's just as handsome as I remember, looking just like his social media pictures. His light brown hair a mess on his head, golden eyes that can still spear me right through the heart. He's still tall, his muscles lightly filling out his shirt. He still acts like he's the most important person when he walks into a room - like the one he's just walked into now.

Because he's here.

Ben fucking Sadler.

Eight

Sabrina

"Gray!" he says. At least I think he says that. For a moment, time has stopped.

Ben comes over and once he locks eyes with me, his smile falters.

"Holy shit, Sabrina?"

"Wow. Ben. Hey." My throat is so dry it's about to catch fire.

God, how many times have I envisioned running into him again? How many speeches did I plan out in my head? How many times did I practice them in front of my mirror on mornings when I was particularly angry? The rage turning my voice into a growl.

"You two know each other?" Gray asks, voice laced with curiosity.

"I've known Sabrina for years!" Ben says. He turns on the charm so well when he has to. Yes, *of course*, we're old pals! I want to punch him in the throat. He comes over to me and envelopes me into a hug, but this one is just an act. It's void of emotion or care or *anything*. A bland excuse for a hug. This hug is a white saltine cracker and I want to smash it with my foot.

It takes everything I have in me not to tell him to go fuck himself in the middle of Harry's.

"Yeah, we've known each other since high school," I say, scratching the back of my head. This exchange is incredibly awkward, and I would love it if the earth could swallow me up right now.

But I dare myself to look at Ben. Ben, who stands in front of me in the most bizarre form of coincidence. Ben, who I have not seen since he ended things with me all those years ago. Ben, who tore out a chunk of my soul, a chunk of me, and kept it so tightly wound in his fist that I had to fight to break free.

And then I look at Gray.

And I see it register in his face: the realization that I am *the* Sabrina. *That* ex-girlfriend. The one that had her heart broken into a million little pieces. That tried like hell to make them all fit together again, but whose heart was never the same after that.

I keep my eye contact with Gray like a dare, keep it like an acknowledgement.

"Wait. You two know each other, too?" Ben asks. He must see that we're sitting together at a table eating lunch.

"Not really," I answer.

"We're friends," Gray answers at the same time.

Ben narrows his eyes at us. I refrain from shooting Gray a death stare.

"So, this is crazy, huh? How do *you two* know each other?" I ask, trying to keep my tone playful.

"Oh, Gray and I met in college," Ben says. He places his hand on Gray's shoulder, gripping it lightly.

"He's uh…he's actually going to be my groomsman."

And the earth shifts.

Go ahead and swallow me up now please.

"I'm going to get in line and order. I'll be right back," Ben says. He heads over to the line and Gray and I sit back down.

I turn to him, "We're friends?! I don't even know your last name!" I'm trying to speak quietly, because if I start screaming I might just vomit.

He chuckles. *Chuckles!* "It's Forrester."

"Forrester?! Gray *Forrester*?! Are you a soap opera star? Honestly!" I practically hiss.

I'm losing it now. Maybe it's the proximity to Ben after so many years. Maybe it's the proximity to Gray. It could very well be a mix of both, this disastrous cocktail of these men and me.

Gray looks at me and must see my distress because he leans over and places his hand on mine. The act is so jarring, I almost snatch my hand away. But it's warm and it's comforting, the weight of it settling right over and grounding me somehow. It's comforting in an incredibly uncomfortable moment.

I look up, caught off guard.

"You okay?"

"I'm good."

He tilts his head and lifts an eyebrow. *Are you really?* he's asking.

I remove my hand from his just as Ben pays for his sandwich and I watch Gray ball his up into a fist and keep it on his lap. Ben makes his way over to our table. *Is he joining us for lunch? Oh, Jesus.*

"Mind if I join you guys?" he asks. He doesn't wait for an answer, just pulls out a chair and sits down. I notice he's got two sandwiches in his hands as he sets them down. "Monica should be here any second. She'll be happy to see you, Gray," he says.

Lightning, strike me now. Somebody hit me with a sandwich. I will take a *chair* to the *face*. Somebody do *something!*

Wait - I drove here. I can just leave, can't I? I can let Gray and Ben catch up on whatever the hell they need to catch up on. Maybe talk about wedding party duties with Monica. I can absolutely leave.

I reach over to grab my keys from my bag. From the corner of my eye, I can see that Gray is staring at me.

"I just remembered I have some other things I need to do today," I say, stumbling through it slightly. Just as I get the words out, a waft of floral perfume hits me in the nose and I know before I even look up that Monica has arrived.

She's as gorgeous in person as she is in the pictures I've seen of her. Dark hair like silk cut bluntly just above her shoulders, big, brown eyes, her lips painted a delicate shade of pink. She smiles her million-dollar smile as she says hi to Gray and then kisses Ben as she sits down. She's wearing a romper for crying out loud. Nobody looks good in a romper.

"Hey baby. I ran into Gray when I came in here, isn't that funny?" Ben tells her.

"Small world. Good to see you Gray." She sits down in the chair Ben has pulled out for her.

"And this...is Sabrina," he says, almost hesitantly. But he is nothing if not a ball of charm and charisma and he can tell you

"This is garbage" with a smile on his face and you'll love every word.

Except maybe I underestimate her because her eyes turn sharp and her smile becomes tight, so tight I worry the tension might snap.

"Hi, Monica. So nice to meet you." *I guess I can turn on the charm, too.*

"You, too," she says quietly, probably trying her best to stay neutral in this mess. Gray's focus is on me, I can feel it. I look up and meet his eyes. I don't know what exactly I see in them, but there's a warmth there; there's a kindness.

"I was just heading out. I have so many things to do today, you know how life is..."

"You still baking, Bri?" Ben asks. His question is a curveball I didn't expect.

"Uh. Yeah, I have my own shop over on Second."

"Your own shop? With these rent prices?" he chuckles, taking a bite of his sandwich. The question is another shot, whether anybody notices or not.

"I got a good deal."

"Ah, makes sense."

Of course, it does. I roll my eyes.

"Sabrina used to bake me blondies and bring them over still warm from the oven," he tells the table, motioning to me with his sandwich. "They were so good. We'd lay on my bed and eat the whole pan while watching TV or something."

Honestly Ben, can you make this anymore fucking awkward? Monica's smile has grown almost impossibly tighter and I'm turning various shades of pink.

Gray clears his throat. "Her shop is fantastic," he chimes in. I give him a small smile in gratitude. I don't need him to defend me, but I find the words are nice to hear.

"I've been there about four years now. Mostly cakes at this point," I tell them.

"Cool. Birthday cakes and stuff?" Ben asks.

"Wedding cakes, actually. For the hotels on the Mile." So, he never read the write up in the local paper. So, he doesn't follow me on social media like I had secretly hoped.

His eyebrows lift a little at that. A surprise. Because my little baking hobby was only ever just a hobby. Nothing serious. *When was I ever going to be serious?*

I could have asked him the same fucking thing.

"The hotels on the Mile? We were looking at some of those hotels for our wedding, weren't we baby?" Monica chimes in, her voice rich and delicate, with a strength around the edges. If she were a cake, she'd be vanilla bean. Classic, crowd-pleasing, my least favorite – no matter how much the rest of the world likes it.

"Oh, yeah. Yeah, we were looking at some of the higher end ones," Ben speaks around a mouthful of sandwich.

Our wedding. My heart bottoms out at the statement, at the realization that they are planning a wedding here.

"Well, they're all pretty high-end and they're all great. It's called Luxe Mile for a reason," I laugh quietly at that, the bitterness weaving its way through. "You can't go wrong."

I see Monica wrap her hand around Ben's arm, snuggling closer, the ring in my direct line of sight.

Don't worry, I want to tell her. *You won.*

The table falls into silence, so I plan my exit.

"It's been great to see everybody, but I should head out now. It was nice to meet you, Monica. Thank you for lunch, Gray."

Gray stands just as I do. "Let me walk you out," he says. Ben looks back and forth between us, a question in his eyes. Monica eats her small turkey hoagie on wheat and the irony of that is certainly not lost on me.

"Nice to meet you," she says, not quite meeting my eyes.

All I can do is nod as I turn and walk out the door, Gray behind me.

"Sabrina, wait up," I hear Gray call out as I am hauling ass to my car, trying to get away as fast as I can. I'm trying to breathe in through my nose, out through my mouth, messing up the order and just hyperventilating instead.

I turn and I don't know what I expect to see - or feel - but what I see is Gray, jogging to catch up with me. And what I feel is Gray on my side.

All these feelings are so muddled and messy right now; I just need to get back home.

"Hey. I didn't...I didn't know."

"What? That I was *Ben's* Sabrina?" I laugh, but there isn't one ounce of humor in it. "Of course, you didn't know. There was no way for you to know. And had you known, you probably wouldn't have come near me with a fucking ten-foot pole."

He opens his mouth to respond but closes it just as abruptly.

"Just like I didn't know you were Ben's groomsman and best buddy."

"We're not best buddies."

"Oh, no? Could have fucking fooled me." My words are coming out a little harsh, a little emotionally charged. My personal MO. I take a deep breath. "Sorry. That was just a little rough in there."

"You don't need to apologize. Especially not to me. That must have been a lot for you in there, you're right."

There he is again, kind and understanding Gray. In-my-corner Gray.

"What is he doing here? Does he live here?"

"No," he shakes his head. "He drives down every now and then, but they want to have the wedding here so maybe they're planning?"

I nod, trying my best to wrap my head around that.

He studies me for a beat, a deep exhale from his mouth.

"Probably not the best time to do this again, but we didn't get a chance to finish talking in there. My offer still stands." He looks back at Harry's where we were just inside eating. "Be my tour guide," he shrugs, the line of his mouth curved slightly. "Be my friend. What do you think?"

I think so many things. I think about how my initial reaction was yes, but now something ugly is taking over and it has to be a no. No, we can't do this. You are guilty by association and that association is a messy, heartbreaking one to be a part of.

And I think that even then, how much I still want to see you. How much my heart might be starting to long for it.

He looks me over, almost like he can hear the gears in my brain grinding, the overthinking I am almost always guilty of.

"Today was nice," I begin, and I know he knows where this is headed. "But that...that was a punch to the gut." I look at the ground, the keys in my hand. Anything but his face. I'm too much of a coward for that right now. "I can't do this, Gray," I say softly, words caught by the wind.

"Sabrina," he says, and I wish it didn't sound so perfect.

I meet his eyes then. Mine are burning, the tears threatening, a lump the size of the sandwich I just ate lodged in my throat. I swallow around it as best as I can. "I'm sorry, but I can't."

"It's okay," he nods, a small smile tucked into the corner of his mouth, a line forming in the space between his brows. Empathy, understanding. "Drive safe, okay?"

"Okay." My answer is barely a whisper, I'm not even sure he hears it.

I climb into my car and drive home, tears running down my cheeks the whole way back.

NINE

GRAY

Sabrina pulls out of the parking lot, backing up and merging into traffic, leaving me standing there. I feel like I've just been hit by a truck. I turn and head back into Harry's, Ben and Monica whispering among themselves as I step inside and walk back to the table.

"Hey, sorry. Just uh…just wanted to walk her out," I say, taking a seat.

Ben and Monica nod in tandem, quietly. Soon after, she gathers her purse.

"I had a couple of errands to run, so I'm going to get going. Good to see you, Gray." She reaches over for a hug. "Love you, baby. I'll see you later." She kisses Ben goodbye and makes her exit.

Now it's just us and one very large elephant gracing this room. Ben finishes chewing his sandwich, I take a small sip of my Birch beer.

"She looks good," Ben says then, breaking the silence.

I look up at him. *Does he mean…?*

"Bri," he adds.

I don't like it. I don't have any right to not like it, but I don't. I don't like that he's talking about her, commenting on her appearance, doing so after Monica has been here with us.

I clear my throat, give a non-committal "Um, sure."

I saw the change in her immediately when he came over to us – her stilling, the tense lines of her body. How she quickly shut herself down, body caved in, making herself smaller. Not the openness, the lightness of minutes before. The door was locked, and the key thrown out.

And lunch had gone so well. Surprisingly well.

"So, you guys know each other?" Ben asks, a look on his face I can't quite figure out.

"Yeah," I answer, one syllable words in this painful conversation. This must be like pulling teeth for him.

I don't know how much to even say here. There is very clearly a history between them – one that I only know in bullet points - but the Sabrina I heard in stories is not the Sabrina I know.

I say this like I even know her.

But I also wonder what there is to say. I'm not sure what we are. Barely friends – no matter that I would like to be and she shut me down. And yet, this feels a little sacred somehow. Like something I should keep close to me, not something Ben needs to be made a part of.

Ben and I did meet in college, both of us in the same dorm hall. He was full of personality, funny, a magnet for all things social. He invited me out one night with a group of other friends and we all hit it off, as well as college friends do, bonding over classes with tough professors, campus parties, beer.

He was always somebody I could talk to easily, could have a decent conversation with. He was somebody I could count on during the confusing and heartbreaking years of Moriah. He was a friend that extended an invitation to come spend the holidays with his family during winter break.

Throughout the years we shared stories of past relationships, Ben laughing about them, his friends laughing with him about his exes.

Remember Sabrina? She was nuts.

Remember Sabrina? She was so obsessed, wasn't she?

As we got older, the social obligations changed. Yes, we lived in the same city, but we had careers, other commitments. He had Monica.

It definitely came as a surprise when he asked me to be his groomsman. Surely, he had closer friends than me. But even then, I felt elated to be part of his chosen group, happy to belong. It almost kept me from leaving. Almost.

It's still been hard to be here without my social circle, just like Pop mentioned. Seeing Ben today is a reminder of how much I need those social interactions in my life.

And yet, I'm starting to wonder if I enjoy hers a little more than his.

His sandwich is finished, the butcher paper crumbled up on this table. My cup is empty, the ice rattling around.

"Well, I should probably get going, too. I've got to get back to work," I tell him.

"How's the freelance going?"

When I told Ben I'd be moving back down here, he was supportive of it and of my plans. He even made some calls to get me a couple of clients.

"Good. Busy, but trying to pick up some more clients when I can."

"I might know some more people. I could send their information your way."

"That would be great, man. Thanks."

We clean off the table, throw away our remaining garbage and walk toward the exit.

"Sabrina Moss," he says again, mostly to himself, as he laughs quietly and shakes his head. "What a small world."

"Well, she lives here, so maybe not entirely unexpected," I say, my tone not as friendly as I would have preferred it to be.

His eyes meet mine, narrow slightly, and then he slaps me on the shoulder. "Good to see you, Gray. We'll talk soon."

I nod as he gets into his car and drives off, going who knows where.

This converging of my past and present lives is not something I expected. Not at all.

By late afternoon I'm huddled over the computer, working on client's proposal, eyes squinting from exhaustion.

A text from my mom pops up on my phone. ***"Hope you're having a good day."***

I expel a breath, exasperated. I was having a great one, but now I'm not so sure. I feel like I'm keeping secrets now – from Ben, who has been a good friend, good support. From Pop –

"Hey, how was lunch?" he says, leaning against the doorframe as if I somehow just summoned him.

"Good!" I respond a little too quickly, a little too enthused.

"Good." His tone is curious.

"Went to Harry's."

"Oh yeah? They still throw the meat around?"

This gets a chuckle out of me. "They sure do."

"Where's mine?" he asks, teasing.

"You know the doctor would never allow Harry's on your diet," I tell him, and he groans. "Alright, maybe I'll sneak you an Italian next time."

Next time. Like I told Sabrina she could get the bill next time. Like I hoped for more *next times* with her.

"How's work going?"

"It's going." I run my hand down my face, stretch a little. I really need to buy a new desk chair.

"Not working outside today?"

"No, no. Just took a lunch break, but wanted to stay inside, keep an eye on you." I look up at him with a smile while he rolls his eyes.

I haven't been to Amelia's in a while, opting to stay home and check on Pop more. Do the thing I came here to do.

"You're a pain in the ass, Gray," he says, turning to walk away.

"Right back at you, old man," I laugh.

"Don't work too hard," he calls out from the hallway as he leaves me alone – with my thoughts, with a growing mountain of work, with this shitty chair.

I groan and get back to it.

TEN

SABRINA

By the time I get home, I'm mentally drained and my phone is continuously buzzing from the texts I'm receiving from both Liz and James in our group chat.

James: "Details!"

Liz: "Did you get yourself a meat sandwich? Wink wink"

I throw my bag on the floor and fall onto the couch, sinking into its cushions and pillows. I pull my phone from my pocket and text back: *"All the dirty details to whoever comes over with wine first."*

Liz responds almost immediately: *"Done."*

James responds: *"Give me thirty minutes!"*

I fall back into the cushions and close my eyes, attempting to relax, silence my mind, until I hear the knock on my door.

Liz stumbles in with bright blue hair pinned back and a bottle of wine outstretched to me.

"Nice color," I tell her, taking the wine and heading into the kitchen to grab some glasses.

"Thanks," she responds, closing the door. "Isn't it a bit early for wine? Not that I'm judging here."

"Oh, it's never too early for wine."

"I think some might disagree with that statement. So, I'm going to assume lunch with Gray didn't go too well?"

"Well, Liz," I begin while I pour two glasses of wine. "The thing is...lunch with Gray was really nice. We talked, we laughed, he's great company. I feel comfortable around him."

Liz takes the wine I hand her and sits on a stool at my kitchen bar, waiting for me to continue.

I take a big gulp of my wine because I'm not exactly sure how to continue. I'm still trying to wrap my brain around what happened myself. Liz lifts one eyebrow slightly and then I spill it out.

"I ran into Ben."

She just stares. "Um. What?"

"Gray and I were having lunch and right in the middle of our conversation, Ben walked in."

"I'm confused. He doesn't even live here. Is he in town?"

"They want to have the wedding here. And surprise, Gray knows him."

"No, he doesn't!" Her eyes widen.

"Turns out he's Ben's groomsman."

"Holy shit." Her eyebrows shoot up past her hairline.

"You know, in his *wedding*. That he's planning on having here."

"Oh my God," she almost laughs, but catches it.

"They've been friends since college."

"And he saw you there with Gray? Did he have a fit?" Her mouth turns into a mischievous smile at that.

"Nope. No fit. He did join us, though."

"I'm sorry, what?" she almost chokes on her sip.

"Yep. Just sat his ass right in a chair. And guess what, Liz? He didn't have one sandwich in his hand. He had two. I'll give you one guess as to who that other sandwich belonged to."

"No!" she gasps.

"Oh yes. Monica walked in smelling like an angel's butthole and sat down to join us."

This time she lets out a loud cackle. "Oh my God," she says again.

"Is this funny to you? Because I am not laughing, Liz! She wore a romper!"

"Nobody looks good in a romper," she shakes her head.

I take a nervous sip. "He asked if I was still baking."

"That motherfucker knows damn well exactly what you're doing. He was probably trying to play dumb in front of Monica."

I consider this, like I considered so many other things before. I drove myself crazy with assumptions and scenarios and wishful thinking that maybe, just maybe he meant something else instead. But his words were clear, I just didn't want to hear.

"Doesn't matter. I did some small talk and then I bailed."

Liz takes a large sip of her wine just as there's another knock at the door. James lets himself in, holding more wine, and I grab a glass for him.

"What's up ladies?" he says, reaching for the wine I just poured for him and setting down the bottle he brought on the counter next to me.

"So, turns out Gray is friends with Ben and is going to be his groomsman in the wedding," Liz supplies.

"Shut the fuck up." James sits on a stool, mouth open, trying to hold in his laughter.

"This isn't funny James," I chime in.

"And she found this out because Ben walked into Harry's and then they all had lunch together!" she continues.

James is full-on laughing now, practically doubled over. "That's amazing."

"Amazing for who, James?!" I practically shriek.

He clears his throat and drinks his wine.

"Well, it sounds like he ruined the date for you," Liz says.

"It wasn't a date. And he didn't ruin shit. Gray walked out with me when I left," I tell them.

"What do you mean it wasn't a date?" James asks.

"What do you mean he walked out with you?" Liz asks.

I take a breath to answer. "Gray...proposed something."

"Please tell me it was sex," James says.

At least I'm not the only one who went there then.

"He wants to hang out...as friends," I look at James pointedly. "Check out the old places everybody used to hang out at and new ones. Stuff like that. And then he walked me out to make sure I was okay."

They both look at me, not saying anything.

Finally, Liz speaks up. "He – he wants to hang out with you? But as a friend? Is that what he said?"

"He said it would be nice to explore this city together. We're both single adults and he has fun with me." As I repeat the words back to them, I realize how they sound. I realize the familiar tone of them will send warning signals to Liz, will make James question the genuine nature of them.

"Huh. Okay, well he can certainly work on his delivery." Liz scrunches her face.

"Doesn't matter. I told him no."

"Probably because his delivery sucked," James mutters.

"You said no?" Liz asks.

"Of course, I said no! He is Ben's *groomsman!*"

"Are you kidding me Bri?" James asks, almost incredulously.

"Fuck Ben. Go get some Gray. Let the shoe be on the other foot for once."

Liz lets out a gasp and I look over at her. "James is right. Ben does not win this. You want Gray, you go get Gray."

"Okay, thank you both for the pep talk, but a couple of things here. One - I don't want Gray." Judging by Liz's snort she's either buzzed or she doesn't buy it. Maybe both. "And two – Ben isn't winning anything."

James looks at me pointedly. *You're letting him win this*, he's saying.

"What happened to saying yes more?" Liz asks.

"I did say yes. To this lunch. And it bit me in the ass."

"So, what? You're done?"

"I had to sit there in front of him and Monica, watch them kiss and hold hands, call each other baby. I had to pretend that my heart wasn't breaking all over again. And I'm supposed to say yes to hanging out with Gray? To the potential of seeing Ben again? Or hearing about him or his wedding?"

They both sit in silence.

"So, yeah. I told him no." I take another large gulp, my hands shaking as I lift the glass to my lips.

"Did you want to say no?" Liz asks, almost hesitantly.

I fiddle with the cork in front of me, looking down at my kitchen counter.

"Doesn't matter."

"Did you want to say no?" she asks again, in a firmer tone.

I shake my head at her question, a dejected, slow back and forth. *No, I didn't. I wanted to say yes so much.*

Liz must hear that tiny voice because she puts her hand over mine. It brings me back to lunch when Gray did it. His large warm hand right over mine. So jarring, so comforting. Just so *good.* "What are you smiling about?" I hear Liz ask.

I look up at her, caught. I didn't even realize I was smiling. "Oh. Just...Gray did the same thing at lunch when he saw how flustered I was about Ben being there."

She looks over at James briefly before responding. "He held your hand?"

"Ben was ordering his sandwiches and he could see that I was probably a mess. And yeah, he just...placed his hand right over mine. Asked if I was okay."

"And he wants to hang out as friends?" James asks under his breath, taking another sip of wine.

"Let's not start with the assumptions. My brain cannot handle assumptions. My brain can, however, handle that when somebody says, *'let's hang out'* they mean that as *'let's hang out'* not *'let's go bang in my car after eating large meat sandwiches'.*"

"The latter sounds fun though," Liz says.

"No, it doesn't, Liz. It sounds like heartburn and muscle cramps. You can't even sleep on a couch without waking up with neck pain."

"It's a lumpy couch!"

"And it still doesn't matter because I said no." I enunciate every word.

"You keep saying it doesn't matter, but you're not acting like it doesn't matter," James says then. "You didn't want to say no."

"She definitely didn't want to say no," Liz says to him.

I take my glass and move out of my kitchen to the couch in the living room, taking a seat in the corner against a mountain of pillows. They follow and snuggle up with me. I bring my knees up to my chest and sit quietly, slowly sipping the wine, twirling the stem between my fingers.

"I wonder if you get branded somehow when you realize your father has been cheating on your mother for years," I say then. Liz and James stay silent. "Are you destined to have fucked relationships because of it? Are you bound to be the grown up with too many daddy issues to work through?"

The silence lingers for a moment, and I take the time to gulp my wine instead. "Sorry. Wrong topic."

"Perhaps not," Liz tilts her head.

"We've all got daddy issues," James shrugs, drinking more wine.

I huff out a laugh. That was my first fight. The first time I held onto something so fiercely in the hopes that the decision could be swayed. My father packed his bags and moved in with a woman he'd been seeing for years. I begged him to stay, I begged him to give us a chance. I thought maybe, just maybe, I could change the direction of it. Surely, he still loved us; he could still come back.

I turn on the TV, channel surfing, drowning in my thoughts and the silence. I don't know why I'm thinking about my father right now, but he comes to the forefront when I wonder about my relationships in life. When I think about how my first friend, my first favorite person, decided I wasn't worthy enough and up and left.

When somebody finally speaks, it's Liz, her tone quiet. "Back to Ben," she clears her throat. "I can respect that you want to say no to something, but I think in this instance you're depriving yourself of something you would like to do because of some fuckwad that has unfortunately wedged himself into a place he doesn't belong. And he doesn't have to belong if you don't want him to. He doesn't need to have any part of this."

"What if Ben had never shown up?" James asks. "Let's pretend Ben never even went to Harry's. What would you have said to Gray then?"

I look up at him, thinking how funny it is to assume Ben could be so forgettable. Just a blip I can erase from my memory, from my life.

But maybe...maybe, I can rewrite the memories.

"Yes. I would have said yes."

"Okay. Tell me why."

A smile tugs at the corner of my mouth. I know what he's trying to do. "I want...to go out and do things without feeling like the third wheel or a burden or out-of-sorts. We enjoy each other's company and I think it could be a good thing," I tell them.

"Tell me more," James says quietly, his voice like a thread pulling at my vocal cords, coaxing the words out. I take a small sip of wine, hands touching the throw blanket I have on the couch, busying my fingers to calm me.

"After Ben, things were so hard. I didn't know who I was without him. I was always..." I take a deep breath, exhale long and slow, seemingly trying to expel all of this out of me. "I was always Sabrina, the one who loved him. Sabrina, the scorned ex. What about just Sabrina? I finally got her back and I want to go live life with her now, you know? She deserves that, too."

I think about how I can rewrite these memories in the city, claim them as mine again. This is my city, too, and there is so much more beyond the association of Ben. Beyond the loss of him embedded into every corner. I want those feelings left behind.

"She really does," Liz says.

"We love you, Bri. All the versions of you," James says. "And because we love you, we want the best for you."

"And I think the best for you here would be to say yes," Liz offers. "He shouldn't get to keep you from dating and living your life."

"Not dating, Liz. Nobody is dating anybody here," I correct her.

"Okay, he shouldn't get to keep you from making friends, then."

I inhale, one deep cleansing breath in. The anger is rising back up like the tide.

He shouldn't. He shouldn't. He shouldn't.

There's a blip of a feeling brewing in me, making me feel like maybe my no was too rash, too sudden. Another blip of a feeling making me feel like I deserve to do the things I want to do, regardless of anybody else's input. Or maybe in this case, regardless of a past presence making themselves known. And then one more blip, but this one bubbling up like possibility. Everything together to make something big brew inside of me, too hard to ignore.

"Okay. Okay." I nod now, the wine probably making me braver than I should be. "I'll talk to Gray tomorrow."

Liz, James, and I clink our glasses together, wine sloshing around them while Liz stands up to get the bottle for refills.

"Baby steps," Liz says, pouring more wine into our glasses. "And can I just add that you are not a fucking burden, Sabrina. Not even a little bit."

"Cheers to that," James adds, lifting his glass high. He snuggles into my side, arm linked with mine. "But for the record, he is really hot," he adds, a giggle past his lips.

I snort. "You are not wrong," I sigh, resting my head on his shoulder. If James were a cake, he'd be spiced orange. Warm like cinnamon, bright like citrus. Comforting, cozy, a big hug.

We snuggle into my couch under my throw blanket and watch some of the *The Witching Hour,* laughing and heckling the whole way through.

Eleven

Sabrina

Ben Sadler and I met sophomore year of high school. The very first day when I had been struggling with my mess of a schedule - new classes, new teachers, and my old friends from freshman year in separate classes far away from mine.

I'd already been to the registrar's office once that morning, trying to frantically fix my schedule errors. I was at my locker, fumbling with the lock that had to be turned just so in order to unlock, cursing the day under my breath, when he came up next to me. He started to open his locker and must have heard my curses when he let out a light laugh. I looked over, embarrassed, and he smiled.

"Rough day?" he'd asked.

"It's the first day and it already sucks," I'd responded.

He smiled at that, those rich golden eyes lighting up as he did. "Hope it gets better for you."

He was so cute. Like popular-boy-in-school cute. With bed-head brown hair, and dimples, and a charming smile he probably gave everybody, but it made you feel so special when he gave it to you.

"Hey Ben!" I heard somebody call out, walking past in the hallway. "See you around," he'd said to me and then turned and left.

That was the unremarkable, benign beginning that turned into years and years of my life.

The school year got better as it went on. And I did see him around. Our interactions were short at first - simple hellos while at our locker - and then they got longer, conversations growing within them.

"How was your weekend?"

"You ever go to the Glow Bowl?

"You should check out that wooden rollercoaster."

He was so sociable, so well-liked, and I couldn't help but follow suit and like him, too. Smile a little brighter when he was around, my body wanting to dance and sing with the giddiness he filled me up with.

We were friendly enough, up until I opened my locker and a folded note came floating out, slowly twirling to the ground—one with a phone number and a scribbled name: Ben.

After that, we spent hours talking on the phone after school, growing a friendship through late night conversations, developing a closeness through shared stories. And as these conversations went on, my heart grew fonder, and I wondered, maybe wished, if he felt us growing closer, too. If he felt something more, like I did.

But he spent his time dating all the popular girls, a new fissure on my heart with each one, and I spent my time resenting my lack of strength to ask for what I wanted. And yet some nights he'd be in my driveway, asking if I wanted to take a ride around town. The 24-hour Walmart, Taco Bell, the local park late at night, sneaking in through a hole in the chain link fence. My mother would still be up by the time I got home, reading in her recliner. "You're nobody's second best Sabrina. Start acting like it," she'd tell me. Mending her own broken heart, dealing with her own anger, watching her daughter fall into this hole.

But then one day he looked at me and it felt like he finally saw me. Late at night, driving around town, he'd reached his hand over the center console and took mine in his, fingers intertwined. My heart jumped into my throat, my body jolted, all my cells had come alive – blinking Christmas lights running through my body.

I fell for him then; I couldn't help it. I fell like falling into water, suddenly immersed with no way to breathe.

Maybe all I did in the later years was spend my time chasing that high, that feeling he gave me at the beginning. The one suffused with teenage hormones and emotions, first love and the first taste of independence.

That night when he dropped me off at home, he got out with me, and he kissed me. I kissed him back, greedily, eagerly. I gave that kid the messiest, sloppiest kiss he'd probably ever gotten.

"Let's be friends, Bri," he'd said to me then in the dark of night, the moon illuminating our faces and his heart-stopping smile. "Let's have fun."

And I couldn't lose him. Not when I just got him, not when we just took this leap, so, I'd answered, "Okay, let's." And that was that.

We kept our late-night car rides; we kept stolen kisses and secret smiles. I kept my desire for more, falling deeper and deeper with each passing day. I held on to my laughter, my loudness, but I started to notice that it was better to keep them inside, too.

"Tone it down, Bri," he'd tell me on occasion. I was too much.

"Let's do these things," he'd say. *But not like that,* he'd mean.

Soon enough he'd grown tired of me, too, finding *friends* elsewhere and I was left to pick up the pieces of sadness, embarrassment, a broken heart.

"This was just fun, Bri."

We went our separate ways after high school. He went off to college and I stayed home. Whenever he would come home to visit for holiday breaks or the summer, he would still reach out, still want to see me. When I would feel that I was maybe moving on, getting over him, casually dating other people, he would come back into my life. Charm his way back in, like I was most appealing when I was unavailable. Or maybe like nobody else could have me. Even if he didn't want me, not really.

So how convenient that he would come along and disrupt a lunch with Gray. That he would find his way back in.

He was twenty-two in my driveway, that ceremonious fucking driveway, asking for me back. He was so *charming* and I missed him so, so much that I couldn't say no.

"I miss you, Bri," he'd begged. I didn't know what to make of it. "I want this to work. You know I was young and stupid, but I'm here now. I want this, I want you."

I wanted it, too. I wanted him to love me. I needed him to love me. It was a longing, a pain so deep that it warped my insides and, in the process, I lost me.

Our relationship was different the second time around. One where we could spend nights wrapped in bed sheets, making plans, planning trips, opting to spend every second we could together. He was animated and romantic when he spoke, painting me a vivid picture, letting me fall into the dream with him. One where he'd whisper to me in the dark of his room, "I want to be with you forever. I'm going to be with you forever."

His stuffy lawyer parents were always unimpressed with me. The first time I met them, under the dim glow of an upscale steakhouse, they had asked, "What are your plans for after college, Sabrina?" What they meant was, "Will you be good enough for our son?"

"I want to bake," I had answered. It was always my answer. I wanted to bake. I knew it then, so whole-heartedly. It always fell flat when I said it to them though, like even I was doubting my plans. Even I was doubting the thing that brought me the most joy.

"Oh, that's nice," they had answered, their condescending tone ringing through it.

"She also mentioned going back to school," Ben had chimed in. "Majoring in something else, too. You know, just to have another thing in her pocket. Right, Bri?"

I didn't know how to respond, this comment out of left field, so I just nodded, replied simply, "Yes. Always good to have a back-up plan."

I wanted to confront him then, behind closed doors, when it was just us. But he took me in his arms, a surefire way to silence the rest of the world, and told me so easily, "Don't worry about them. I love you and that's all that matters."

I wanted it to be all that mattered. And for some years it was, until even that wasn't strong enough to hold us up. His actions started to depict somebody that wanted distance, not connection. I was the nuisance; his words were pitying.

It was another fight, another moment where I was begging somebody to stay. What was wrong with me? Why couldn't I be enough?

So, I went crazy, to hear everyone else tell it. The thing about feelings is that they're always inconvenient – especially coming from a woman. But I just couldn't let it be. Not when all I heard was the sound of my heart shattering in the places it never fully healed. And all I felt was the caving in of my insides, one painful inch at a time until there would be nothing left. And that was close. I had already shrunk myself so much to fit his perfect mold that there was barely anything left of me. And he still left me anyway.

So, I grabbed hold of the anger, the resentment and the embarrassment and I yelled and kicked and screamed. I let all those uncomfortable pieces of me come flying back out because I could not cave in.

Liz and James would come pick me up and drive us around town. Cheeseburgers from The Burger Shack, margaritas at Don Julio's, the beach late at night where I could scream at the waves, throw fistfuls of sand like an angry toddler.

I was fucking angry. I was so heartbroken. I felt so cheated.

I packed up my things that I kept at his place – some clothes, some toiletries. Eight years of a life now reduced to a couple of boxes, the evidence small and practically unimportant. I could have been any other girl.

I spent the years after that strategically avoiding places we used to spend time, avoiding places I thought I might see him, feeling almost trapped in my own city. But time lessened the blow. He moved away and I dove into my work, making it a goal to have my own company, to build something involving my baking. To be a success. I worked tirelessly, day and night, seven days a week. I would sweat in my one-bedroom apartment, balancing mounds of baked cakes on any surface I could find. I would move around my tiny kitchen, decorating and packaging and delivering them to whoever would order from me all while still working full-time at a bakery nearby. I started Sabrina's Sweets and I got that brick-and-mortar on Second Street and let myself remember who the hell I was. Who I am, who I can be. And that I would never compromise it again for somebody who could so easily get up and walk out.

But now here I am, weakening my compromises. Struggling in the depths I've been thrown back into, a hold on me that is gripping, frustrating. Suffocating.

My laptop is balanced on my knees now, *Dateline* on in the background. I'm looking over some contracts, sketching some cake ideas. I set everything to the side to take a small break. While I have now been able to give myself days off, I don't really take them – always working on something at home.

I look at my phone, think about my conversation with Liz and James the day before. The wine made me brave, but now sober I second-guess my decision to talk to him. Toying with the phone in my hand, I pass it back and forth, considering worst case scenarios.

He says no. That's totally fine. He can say no.

Maybe he tells me he was just kidding. Am I really that desperate to meet people?

Maybe he says he talked to Ben after I left and he changed his mind. He doesn't need that kind of drama in his life.

Or maybe he says yes. Maybe he says okay. And we do this.

I take a fortifying breath, one I've been taking for what feels like hours now, and I give him a call. It's only after the first ring do I realize I'm *calling* him, not sending a text message like normal people do.

I am absolutely diving into this and may spectacularly crash and burn, but it's too late now. I stand up and pace my living room, trying to rid myself of this nervous, frantic energy. Wiggling my fingers, flailing my hands to...I don't even know what.

He answers on the third ring, a tentative, almost confused "Hello?"

"Hey! Hi. Gray?" I clear my throat. "It's Sabrina. The uh – baker," I add in case he has no idea who this is. *Why am I acting like I've never spoken on the phone before?*

I hear his laugh on the other line, that joyful, hearty sound, rough around the edges. "I know who this is," he says.

"Oh."

"Yeah. I saved your number. Besides, there's only one Sabrina." I hear the smile in his voice.

"Oh. Okay. Well." My mind draws a blank.

"How's it going?"

I will my nerves to subside. I can have a conversation, for crying out loud.

"I changed my mind," I say, matter of fact.

"You....?" he trails off.

"I've spent years working so hard to build something, but in the process I left the rest of life behind," I tell him. "I want to live my life differently. Get out and explore. I want to see the places everybody else talks about. I want to see the old places again, too. And I don't want anybody to keep me from it. We can be each other's tour guides, how about that?" *Okay. Maybe that was a bit too much.*

I can't see him, but I can feel that gorgeous smile, that scrunched up nose over the phone. I can picture it, eyes shining bright blue right at me. "That sounds perfect," he says. Deep voice, breath of relief, smooth like bourbon.

I remember him in the parking lot at Harry's: radiant, warm, and kind Gray, and I think you're bringing out something in me that's ready to fight again.

"Alright. Well, that was all I had to say."

He chuckles at that, something soft. "I have to finish some things for work, but we'll talk soon, okay? See you, Bri."

My heart swells at the sound of my nickname on his lips. The familiarity of it, the closeness of it. How he's taken to using it, like any of my friends would.

"See you, Gray." My smile grows impossibly wider.

My phone lights up on the coffee table later in the evening, an incoming text from Gray.

"You know where you could always find me on a Friday night in high school? Bowl-O-Rama. They still do the Glow Bowl. Nine o'clock on Friday?"

Of course, he used to go to the Glow Bowl.

I guess this is really happening, isn't it? Maybe I could jump off this moving train, but I think I'd like to see where it takes me this time.

I type out a response and send it. ***"You're on."***

Twelve

GRAY

"I DIDN'T KNOW THIS place was still here," Sabrina says as I park the car.

One of the lights on the sign is out, advertising Bow-O-Rama, and the red paint on the building has faded, leaving it a rather unpleasant pink.

I had offered to pick her up and drive us this time and she'd agreed, standing outside her house as I pulled into the driveway. It felt a lot like seventeen, picking up friends, picking up dates and heading to the bowling alley.

The drive over was comfortable. Windows down, music playing. She let the breeze flow through her open fingers as her hand wandered outside the window into the humid air. I would look over at her occasionally, catching her eye and smiling, the warmth of tonight mingling with the warmth I feel from being near her.

I did a double take when her name popped up on my phone on Tuesday night. And when I answered and she let me know she'd changed her mind, it felt almost too good to be true. Thank God she couldn't see me on the other line, fist pumping in the air like an idiot, overjoyed at the thought of spending more time with her.

"My friends and I spent many weekends here," I tell her, opening the door for her to the bowling alley.

"I'm not surprised," she says.

This was one of the more popular hangouts when we were in high school. Kids were often dropped off to meet up with their friends for Glow Bowl. The popular crowd congregated outside or by the arcade on weekends, spilling out of their cars in droves.

We step inside and the familiar smell hits me like a gust of wind to the face: musty carpets, stale beer and fake cheese poured out of a dispenser and onto bagged tortilla chips.

"Wow, it even smells like 2006 in here," I hear her say.

"Nostalgia is an acquired smell, you know?"

She snorts, looking around. "This definitely takes me back though."

The Glow Bowl is in full effect: bright neon lights, loud music, music videos playing on a jumbo screen. High school kids still come here, but the numbers are smaller. There must be cooler things to do.

"Did you hang out here a lot, too?" I ask. "Were we in the same place at the same time without knowing?" I act distressed, my palm moving to my chest. My question pokes fun, but the thought stops me a little: what if we'd been circling around each other for years?

"Not a lot. Every now and then, but I didn't care for much of the crowd." We start walking over to the counter. "It wasn't until we graduated that Liz, James, and I began to hang out here during weeknights. Smaller crowds, a bit more inviting."

Once at the counter, we pick a lane and grab our shoes, Sabrina pulling out her wallet to pay.

"I've got this one," she says, and I try to protest, but I think she wants to keep this fair, even, friendly, so I thank her, and we head to our lane.

She sets her things down and puts on her shoes, while I sit at the computer to add in our names.

"I haven't been bowling in years. I'll probably make an ass out of myself, so you're welcome in advance," I turn to her.

"Ha! I haven't bowled in a while either, but here goes nothing," she says, as the screen indicates that it's her turn first.

"Like riding a bike!" I yell out behind her.

She rears the ball back and lets it fly, my eyes definitely not watching her bend over to release the ball. We then watch it slowly make its way to the gutter.

"Wow, you're terrible."

"Unbelievable," I hear her mutter. "This is just a warm-up!" She calls out while the pins get ready for a second turn.

She rears the ball back again, lets it go more gently this time, and watches it very slowly take down two pins.

"Well, it's an improvement," I say, slow clapping with an amused smirk on my face.

"Why don't you show me how it's done then Lebowski?"

"Gladly." I give her a wink as I grab a ball and walk up to the lane.

I rear the ball back, let it go, and watch as it curves and makes a strike, the *crack!* sound of the ball hitting the pins reverberating throughout the building.

I turn around to find Sabrina's jaw hanging down to the musty carpet.

"Are you a bowling shark? Is this a ruse?! You said you haven't bowled in years!" she practically shouts, her eyes wide and bright.

"Like riding a bike," I shrug, smiling the whole time. "I did spend a lot of time here in high school."

Her mouth is still agape as she says, "You sneaky asshole."

I'm laughing full-on now, the sound bubbling out of me. It feels good to laugh like this, with her, out in the world. "Sabrina, are you competitive?"

She laughs with me now, a grin from ear to ear. She stands up with conviction, smooths her shirt down, and says, "Well, if by competitive, you mean determined to kick your ass, then yes."

She walks over to retrieve the ball and on her second turn, she manages to knock down four pins. "And by kick your ass, I mean do that."

On my second turn, I manage a spare.

"Should we get something to eat? Maybe a drink?" I ask.

"I could drown my sorrows in some cheap beer. Maybe a mozzarella stick."

"The way to a girl's heart is always through a mozzarella stick."

"Are you trying to get to my heart?" she asks, a quick rebuttal, a joke. But it catches me off-guard.

"Uh..." I smile, clear my throat, feel my face heat unexpectedly.

"Kidding. I was just kidding," she spits out and she's so adorable when she's flustered, I can't help but laugh.

"I'll be right back."

I come back with two pints of draft beer and a tray of bacon cheese fries, balancing them on my hands, slowly setting them down on the table.

"They were out of mozzarella sticks, so I figured this was the next best thing."

"It'll do, I guess," she sighs dramatically. But then quietly adds, "Thank you, Gray," and I try not to think about how her soft words settle right over my heart.

"You should see the menu here. It looks like they've revamped it, made it more like... what's the word? Gastropub?"

"Mm," she nods, grabbing a fry from the tray, the melted cheese pulling as she goes. "Very common these days. Throw some truffle oil on anything and suddenly you're a gastropub."

I grab the flyer from the center of the table and read, "'Now featuring our world-famous truffle mac-and-cheese'".

"See?" She waves her hand in the direction of it as if making her point.

"We should get some. The flyer says world-famous."

"I bet it is. We'll get some next time, how about that?"

"Please. We're not going bowling next time. There's a whole city to see out there."

"There is definitely a whole city to see out there." Her answering smile is shy, almost.

"Cheers," I say, lifting my glass to hers. "To new friends." Our eyes meet above the rim, a quick second and then she looks away, but I see the smile she's trying to hide.

I lift my glass to take a sip, the beer souring as it goes down. "The food might be gastropub, but the beer is not. How did I ever drink this stuff?"

She mirrors a sip and winces as she swallows. "I guess nostalgia is also an acquired taste." She sets her glass down and picks up another fry from the tray. "How is your grandfather doing?"

"He's doing well," I answer, my heart warming at her question.

"You mentioned doctor's appointments," she starts slowly. "Is he...is he okay?" she asks almost nervously.

"Yeah," I nod, picking at another fry. "He's got high blood pressure, and no desire to take his medication. He's got high cholesterol. I get to be the enforcer."

After college I stayed in the northern part of Florida, working and living a solid, quiet life. One that didn't require moving every six months, one that could be stable for me. "Pop and I always had our weekly phone conversations, but when I called him one night, he seemed...off, and I found myself missing this city. I just found myself missing him. So, I decided it was time to make the move back. I want to make sure he's okay. I want to be close."

She nods, listening, her eyes set on mine.

"And now look at me, having the time of my life." I chew on a fry, laughing to myself, but she smiles, too.

Sabrina picks up another fry, the cheesiest of the bunch, and asks, "Alright so, what would be next on the agenda to add to the time of your life you're having here in New River?"

"Hm. Well the Grand Prix death trap rollercoaster is unfortunately out. Really crushed my dreams there. Is The Downtowner still a moldy dive bar with pricey beer?"

"It sure is."

"Put that one on the list then."

"Now we're talkin'."

"Stick with me, Bri, and you'll go places."

We snack away on the fries, taking turns to bowl. The conversation continues effortlessly: quick quips and laughter, straight-forward dialogue, an all-around good time being out with her like this. It's like we've done this so many times before, a comfort and a trust like it's been living between us forever.

Our lane is adjacent to a group of high schoolers, way cooler than us, boisterous and loud. She smiles almost to herself.

"This feels like Never Been Kissed."

"Like...the movie?"

"Yes, like the movie," she laughs. "Like I'm getting a high school re-do and it's way better the second time around." She chews on a fry, a blush blooming on her cheeks. I love it so much.

I think of what her high school experience must have been like, the crowds she hung out with, the cliques she made herself a part of – if any. My thoughts are running through my head, one after the other, until I think them out loud and say then, "I'm sure Ben spent plenty of time here."

Her body stiffens and her chewing stops for a moment. *Shit. I'm an idiot.* The last thing I wanted to do was bring up that unfortunate topic, the one that caused her to originally shut me down, tell me no, but I find myself wanting to set a record straight with her.

"I'm sorry. You probably don't want to talk about him – "

"I don't," she cuts me off, voice firm.

"But I can't imagine that it was easy."

She stares at me for a beat, finishes chewing another fry. "No. It wasn't easy. And now that I know he'll be in town planning the wedding, it's even harder for me to go about my life, wondering when the hell I'm going to end up running into him again."

"You hadn't seen him around here?"

She shakes her head. "It's been years."

I nod at that, begrudgingly taking another sip of beer.

"Anyway," she says, a statement of redirection, wanting to move on from this topic that I dragged her into.

I meet her eyes, go for broke as I tell her, "I'm glad you changed your mind. I'm glad you're here with me."

She looks surprised, but the small smile forming is soft and warm. "I'm glad I'm here with you, too."

Our fries are done, my beer is undrinkable, and that sudden exposure of myself has me feeling too many weird emotions. Our game is over, me winning by a landslide. The music is still playing at full volume – current pop hits that I don't even know.

Just then, my phone rings with an incoming call. I pull it out of my pocket, looking at the screen that is lit up with the name

Mom. I decline the call and notice that Sabrina is looking at me curiously.

"Should we get going?" she manages.

"Oh. Sure," I say, coming back to the present, like she took me out of a daydream.

We gather our belongings, return our shoes, and head to the car.

The drive home is silent, maybe a little uncomfortable. Did I overstep? I know we're friends here. I know we're just hanging out. This should be so PG; we're practically running errands together. That's an idea. Maybe next time we can just go to the grocery store and keep it simple. As I pull into the driveway, she unbuckles her seatbelt to get out.

"Hey, Bri," I stop her, hand lightly on her arm.

She looks over at me and those hazel eyes bore into mine.

"I know there might be some tension between us because of...him, but that's not what I want. You didn't want to talk about him, but I did anyway and I'm sorry about that."

"Thanks," she says quietly.

I'm recognizing a feeling in the center of my chest, growing slowly, but surely. An infatuation. I think I like her. Hell, I know I like her, but this budding friendship can't have that right now.

"Next time, we'll pick something you don't suck at," I grin.

She laughs softly at that, stepping out of the car. She closes the door and leans in through the window. "Night, Gray."

Illuminated by her porch light, she stands there, leaning in as the light filters through the strands of her hair. It shines lightly on her eyes, making her face glow. The words almost get caught in my throat at the sight of her. It's like I'm seeing her for the very first time. "Goodnight, Sabrina."

I watch her go to her door, make sure she's inside, then reverse out of the driveway. I don't know where this will take us now, whether we'll continue to hang out. But what I do know, in a confusing and surprising turn of events, is that I've never felt so alive in my life.

Thirteen

Sabrina

My phone rings early Saturday morning and I fling my arm over to answer it, wrestling with my bed sheets I'm burrowed in. James is on the other line, frantic. His sister, thirty-eight weeks pregnant, has gone into labor early and he wants to hit the road to go see her, keep her company at the hospital in her city about three hours away.

"Keep me posted, James, and drive safe," I tell him over the phone, groggily.

I roll out of bed and get moving, knowing there's a busy day ahead of me and a lot I'm going to need to juggle.

Liz and I find ourselves in the bakeshop an hour later preparing for a big delivery. About a year ago, Jess, an old friend from elementary school had reached out, wanting me to make her cake. It's one hell of a cake for one hell of a party. In addition to the five-tier wedding cake, she also wanted a dessert bar set up with three other dessert options: key lime tarts with swirls of toasted meringue; chocolate truffles dipped in chocolate dark like midnight; and light rose French macarons with brushes of gold. Her wedding is being held at the Regency on the Water in its incredibly lavish ballroom.

I am in the process of boxing up the tiers of wedding cake when Liz gets a call on her phone.

She looks down at the screen. "Oh, it's Jeff," she says. "Hey babe...you *what?*...when?...what happened?...where are you now?...oh Christ, hang on."

I hear the one-sided conversation from my end, but she sounds stressed. It sounds like bad news and that stresses me out, too.

"What's up?" I ask.

"Jeff fell off the ladder truck." Jeff is the clumsiest firefighter in his department in an outer suburb about twenty minutes away. He's hurt himself so much on the job, but even this - falling off the truck - seems serious for him.

"What?" My panic starts to match Liz's.

"Well. He fell getting *out* of it." She rolls her eyes so hard they go to the back of her head. "He said something about broken bones...bruised ribs...Shit. He's at the ER right now." She's typing frantically on her phone.

"Go, Liz." I tell her firmly, a frown on my face.

"We've got this cake to deliver, Bri. I can go after."

"Are you kidding? I can manage. He needs you now."

"No way you can manage. It's five tiers for the Regency! Plus, all the extra desserts. You know what a nightmare it is to maneuver that place."

She's not wrong, but she needs to be with Jeff now, not here. "It's fine. I can figure it out, I promise. Maybe get Julian from reception to help."

She thinks it over, pacing back and forth. "What about Gray?"

"Gray?"

"Yeah. He can be an extra set of hands!" Her eyes are pleading.

"I don't know about that. I don't need to bother him for work stuff."

"Can you just ask? I would really feel so much better if I knew you had some help before I headed over to the ER."

I sigh, consider it. "Okay fine, I'll ask, but if he says no, you still have to leave."

"Deal."

I pick up my phone and call Gray, listen to it dial on the other end while I play out what I'm going to say in my head. How can I sound indifferent? Calm? Not pushy?

"Hey Bri," he answers.

"Gray, help us!" Liz yells into the phone.

"Is everything okay?" Now *he* sounds panicked. Great.

"Hey Gray," I drawl. "Yes, everything is fine." I glare at Liz. If looks could kill, she would be way past dead. "I'm sorry to bother you like this, but I'm stuck in a bit of a work situation."

"What's going on?"

I explain the dilemma. Jeff's fall, James' sister, the cake, the wedding delivery. "I was wondering if you would be able to offer a hand? If you can, that is! I know you've got stuff with your grandfather, maybe work things, I don't know."

"No, no. I'm not busy at all." I hear him shuffle some papers around. "I can be there in about half an hour. Is that okay?"

We'll be pushing it for time, but I can certainly make it work. Especially since I absolutely did not expect him to say yes. "That would be perfect. Thank you so much."

We hang up and Liz breathes a sigh of relief.

"Gray is a hero!"

"Go see Jeff. Tell him I hope he feels better."

She grabs her bag, walking towards the door, then turns and winks, "Tell Gray I said thanks."

"Did Jeff even break his arm or is this a ploy?!"

She cackles. "That ding-dong definitely broke something, but damn I should try something like this again." She waves on her way out the door.

As promised, Gray is at the bakeshop thirty minutes later. I let him in, the bell jingling as the door opens. He stands in jeans and yet another perfect T-shirt, his stubble a little more grown out, his hair a little bit longer, almost falling into his eyes.

"Thank you so much for coming to help. It was last-minute, I know, so I really appreciate it," I tell him.

"Don't worry about it. Pop's neighbor stopped in today and work is a little slow for me right now."

I give a brief explanation of how deliveries work and have him help me load the tiers and extra desserts into our delivery van, taking extra care each way. Once everything is loaded up, we head out.

The drive over reminds me of a wedding I went to at the Regency once for a friend of Ben's. It was a beautiful wedding and I had gushed about it to Ben, my voice probably taking on that swoony dreamlike quality. *"Did you see her dress? And those flowers! The venue was so gorgeous."*

When it was over and we had thoroughly enjoyed the open bar, we took the elevator up to our room, opting to stay in the rooms blocked out for the wedding guests for the night. Again, I gushed, "That was a beautiful wedding," perhaps the champagne getting to me a little bit, making me a little fuzzy.

Ben answered with a laugh, "It was alright, but I'd never want to ruin my life that way." His comment sobered me up. I probably should have left then, but I rallied on, not wanting to hear what he was saying. Not wanting to take a hard look at it. Instead, I opted to try harder, force myself into his mold some more, push to fit into it.

I'm brought back to the present when I hear Gray's voice beside me: "What's going on over there? You look constipated," he teases.

"Hilarious." I roll my eyes. "I'm thinking shitty thoughts," I tell him. I don't know why I say it, but I do. Maybe I'm looking for somebody to talk about it with. Maybe I'm tired of always answering *"It's nothing, I'm fine."*

"Like what?"

"Like when I went to a wedding at the Regency once. With Ben."

"It was a shitty wedding?"

"Oh no, it was a gorgeous wedding. Have you ever been to the Regency?"

"Actually, no."

I sneak a glance at him. "Really? You're in for a treat then. It's a stunning venue."

"So, then what was shitty?"

"The company."

"Ouch. Got it. Hope I don't end up falling into that category."

"Of shitty company? I hope not either." I smirk.

He smiles at that. "I think I'm doing okay so far."

I maneuver through the vendor entrance to the Regency and park the delivery van in the parking lot. I unbuckle my seatbelt and look over at him. "You're doing okay so far. Now let's go deliver some cake, newbie."

Once the boxes are placed on my cart, we begin the very slow walk to the ballroom where the wedding will take place. The Regency on the Water is, in fact, on the water. They have their own private beach, as do most of the hotels on the Mile, and ballrooms to host whatever you could possibly want to host. But their most popular wedding room is the most lavish and hosts up to three hundred guests. Crystal chandeliers hang down draping the room in a gorgeous glow that makes it seem like gold is dripping from the ceiling. The room has what appear to be windows on the far wall, giving you a perfect view of the ocean, but they are doors that can be opened up entirely to let you out onto a large balcony that wraps around the length of the room. It's indoors, it's outdoors, it's the best of both worlds.

As we slowly make our way inside, Gray's mouth forms an *O* of shock.

"Wow. You weren't kidding," he says. "This is intense."

The tables have been set up already: printed menus in gorgeous gold calligraphy, plate settings, silverware, champagne glasses. The chairs are tufted, upholstered cream, the tablecloths have accents of gold and lace on them. Joining the chandeliers decorating the ceiling are rows and rows of gorgeous flowers, raining down like you're in paradise. Arches of them, bouquets of them, mountains of them cascading down. It is stunning.

"This must have cost a fortune," Gray says, still in shock as we slowly walk.

"Definitely was not cheap. Jess's family is loaded though, so this is apropos for them." I locate the cake table and dessert bar along the far wall.

"First things first, we need some insurance." I take out my apron and then pass him Liz's apron that she had packed for herself to put on. He mimics me, twisting the strings behind his back and then bringing them to the front to tie them in a bow and *damn, what is it about a man in an apron?*

I busy myself with the cake boxes. "We're going to unbox the largest cake tier and place it on the table first. Then we're going to work our way up. The dowels are already in place so everything should stack easily."

"Sounds good, boss," Gray says.

My mouth lifts at one corner. I place the largest tier on the table and then Gray holds the second tier to stack on top. While I hold my thin offset spatula in place, I have Gray very slowly bring the cake down onto the spatula. I check that it is level and centered, moving the spatula just so to adjust, and then I very slowly slide the spatula out.

"Good job, newbie. Only three more to go."

Once the cake is stacked, I begin the decorative process and work on any touch ups. Nina, the florist from a popular wedding vendor Everbloom, is nearby with her crew finishing up final touches on arrangements. She comes over to hand me the flowers that will be added to the cake to match the flowers in the centerpieces.

"Hey Sabrina. These are all washed and ready to go."

"Great. Thanks so much, Nina."

"New help today?" She's barely looking at me.

"Ha. Yeah. Liz and James had some emergencies come up, so I called a friend. This is Gray. Gray, this is Nina. She owns Everbloom Florals."

"Nice to meet you." He shakes her hand cordially. It doesn't escape me how Nina checks him out.

"Well, I'll be over here if you need any extra help."

"Thanks again," I tell her.

"She seems nice," Gray says once she's walked away.

I laugh.

"What?"

"Well, for starters, she never asks to help me with anything, but were you really that oblivious to her checking you out?"

"Checking me out? Really?" He turns back to find Nina staring. "Oh shit, she's looking at me."

"I've got her number if you want it," I say casually. Maybe I should put some distance between us. These outings have been building up, making me want things I have no business wanting right now. There was a compromise, an understanding. Besides, the last thing I need is a romantic distraction and a rejection. I can already picture Gray telling me, *'We're just friends, Sabrina. You know that,'* and it's enough for me to throw Nina's number at him. Hell, I'll throw Nina at him if it means I can keep my sanity.

"Her number? I don't want her number. I mean, she seems nice, but no, I don't want her number." He looks at me, confused, as he says it.

"Oh. Okay," I shrug, trying not to show how elated his answer makes me.

I continue to touch up the cake, smoothing the frosting so that everything appears seamless. Once done, I'll start adding the fresh flowers.

"Okay, the florals are next. Can you pass me the floral tape?"

Gray passes me the roll of green tape and I show him how I put it together, twisting the tape around the stems and then arranging and placing the flowers right where I want them.

"A little tape goes a long way. We're going to make a cascade of the flowers down one side of the cake, curving and ending up on the other side." I make a sweeping motion with my hand, showing him the trajectory of the flowers. I've marked it lightly on the cake and so we will very slowly fill in the bits and pieces with them.

"Be gentle with the flowers. The tape helps hold them up, but we still want everything to look perfect." I delicately add a flower onto the cake, slowly pushing into the buttercream and stepping back to examine it.

"It's fascinating to watch you work," he says.

And it makes me stumble just a bit, makes me almost lose a flower.

I laugh to make up for the blush I can feel coming up over my chest and face. "What makes you say that?"

"It's just the truth. You're confident and you know what you're doing. It's cool to watch," he says.

If I didn't know any better, I'd say I caught a blush coloring his cheeks. If his words didn't already knock me down, that blush might as well put me on my ass.

"That's really kind of you to say, Gray. Thank you. I don't feel very confident in other aspects of my life most days, but cakes I know. And I know them well. So at least there's always that."

"You're confident in other parts of your life, too, you just probably don't see it."

I look over at him. "I think you just make me feel so comfortable that my comfort translates to confidence," I tell him, hoping he doesn't catch my heart beating so hard against my chest, it might jump out any second.

"Confidence is comfort."

"You're confident."

"You make me feel comfortable, too." He's still fumbling with floral tape on a flower, but he looks at me then and I feel the weight of those words on me, feel them settle on my shoulders.

I don't even know how to respond to that comment, so I just power through. *Focus on the cake, Sabrina.*

I clear my throat. "Okay, you're going to wrap the tape around like that and then you can hand the flowers to me, and I'll place them on the cake."

We work in silence for a couple of minutes, getting into a rhythm that would make any stranger assume that we've been working together forever. It's always so easy with him.

"So, what would your ideal wedding cake be?" he asks, looking down as he wraps tape around another stem.

I take a minute to answer. "Hm. Hazelnut, probably. A hazelnut cake. Praline...chocolate. Something rustic, small. Semi-naked layers. Fresh flowers just like these. I'd like a small wedding. This is gorgeous, but it's not really me."

"I like that."

"Not that I've thought about it or anything," I mutter. "What about you?"

"Me? I don't know. You're the expert. What kind of cake should I go for?"

I chuckle at that. "I get that question more often than you'd think." I study him for a beat, thinking. I watch him wrap those stems in green floral tape, strong hands delicately holding them, forearms flexing as he does it. I see him stand there like I've seen him all day - focused on each task, listening to every direction I've given him, jumping at the chance to help however he can. I see him stand there in perfect fitting Levi's that hug his hips, a dark grey shirt hugging his biceps and the deep blond hair he's been running his fingers through all afternoon. Ocean blue eyes, scruff along his jawline, those full lips smiling at me. If Gray were a cake, he'd be chocolate on chocolate. Sinful and rich and decadent. You know you shouldn't do it, but it's so tempting and so damn good that you do it anyway. A classic. Rewarding, satisfying, desired.

"Let me get back to you," I tell him. *Let me think of something else so I don't give away all my secrets.*

"You must be quite a hopeless romantic."

"That's a hell of an assumption," I say lightly.

"The care you take in making these cakes, in meeting with these couples…it's like you're rooting for them from the very beginning."

"I am rooting for them, but I don't know if I could call myself a romantic, let alone a hopeless one."

"What – you don't believe in love?" he jokes.

I shrug. "I believe in cake."

He stares for a beat. "You're serious."

"About cake? Absolutely."

"No, about love." He looks a little hurt.

I swallow then. "I don't *not* believe in love. I am rooting for these couples because I believe in *them*. I believe in the power of them." I look down at a stem in my hand, twirling it mindlessly between my fingers. "As for love, yes, I believe it is out there, but I wonder if it's out there for me is all." I say that last part a little quietly, surprised to be revealing such a vulnerable part of me to him.

"It's out there for everybody," he says, looking right at me, right into the very center of me, that familiar furrow in between his brows.

"I definitely didn't take you for a hopeless romantic," I say, an attempt at a joke to break free from this odd moment between us.

"Not hopeless," he shakes his head slowly.

I hold his stare then look away, taking a step back to examine the cake. A couple more flowers and it will be done and delivered.

"Wow. This really is a work of art," Gray says, looking at the cake with me.

"Well now you're just sucking up."

"Honest, Bri. This is a beautiful cake."

"Thank you for helping today. I couldn't have done this without you." I look over at him, offering this gratitude for help and support that has been both unexpected and heartwarming.

"I'm glad you called. I'm always here if you need help."

I can't help but practically swoon at that, this selfless, kind offering. "I guess I should return the favor. Let you know that if you ever need help, you can call me, too."

"I'll hold you to it," he teases. "So, what happens now?"

"Now we move on to the dessert table." I point to a table that's nearby.

"Oh shit, I almost forgot about that."

He follows me over to the table, pushing the cart with boxes and décor.

The next hour is spent arranging the different desserts on the table. The wedding planner adds some special touches, and we all take steps back, considering, and then diving back in until everything looks perfect.

"Alright. Now we're done."

"Amazing," he says, shaking his head in disbelief like he's never seen a dessert in his life.

I pull my mouth to the side to keep from laughing at how adorable he is. "We'll take some pictures, pack up our things, and then head out."

He nods once like he's gotten the order and then he moves, starting to pack things up in their respective boxes as I take out the camera to snap the pictures. I step back to look for anything that needs to be touched up, fixing some flowers here and there. Gray comes up beside me and I put up my hand. He high-fives it, an elated grin forming on his face.

"You did good, Gray," I tell him, mimicking the phrase we use when we deliver cakes.

"You did good, too, Sabrina," he replies, and it makes my heart melt. Just the tiniest bit.

"Let's head out," I motion to the exit. Just then I notice Jess come into the room, stunning in a blur of white satin, lace, and tulle. "Oh my *God*, Bri, that is *gorgeous!*" she screams.

I walk over to her, whispering to Gray just as she comes barreling down toward us, "She's a hugger!"

"Jess, you look absolutely beautiful! Congratulations." She envelopes me in a tight, strong hug, rocking side to side in joy.

"I don't know how you did it, but you made such a perfect cake!" She looks over and sees Gray. "Hi! I'm Jess. Are you new?"

I can't help but smile. "This is Gray. He's a friend, but he's just helping me out today. Liz and James ended up having to tend to some emergencies."

"Congratulations and very nice to meet you," Gray extends a hand, which she promptly ignores and wraps him in a hug, too. He awkwardly pats her back while I bite the inside of my cheek to contain my laughter.

"Thanks again Sabrina. And Gray! I love it so much!" she tells me.

"You're so welcome, Jess." I hug her goodbye and she walks out.

"She is a hugger." Gray looks a little startled as I laugh behind him.

"Come on, time to go."

We make our way out of the ballroom, onto the service elevators, past reception and outside to the delivery van. Once loaded up, I feel a seed of an idea start to blossom in me. It's growing and growing and soon enough I can't sit still with the thought of it.

We're in the van now, seated and buckled in, ready to back out and go back to the bakeshop. But I don't want to yet. I don't want this day with him to end just yet. I turn to Gray.

"Want to know what I used to do on Friday nights?"

"Definitely," he answers.

"Follow me." I unbuckle my seatbelt and get out of the van. I lock it and walk us back to the hotel.

"You used to spend your Friday nights...here?" he asks, pointing to the Regency.

"Not all of them, just some. But yes. Come with me."

We walk past reception and the lobby where I lead him to the guest elevators.

"This feels a little like déjà vu," he says.

I chuckle. "Maybe a little."

Once in the elevators I push the button to the top floor, and we watch it go up in silence.

"Alright, you've got me curious," Gray says, looking at the numbers go up and then at me.

The elevator dings and the doors open. We step out and I lead him past the rooms to the end of the hallway with the door labeled STAIR ACCESS.

"This just keeps getting weirder."

"It's not that weird, I promise."

I open the door to the staircase and lead us upstairs. Because even though we've gone as far up as the elevator will take us, the stairs can still take us just a little higher.

At the end of the stairs is another door, this one labeled very clearly: ROOF ACCESS. EMPLOYEES ONLY. ALARM WILL SOUND.

"The roof? You hung out on the hotel roof on Friday nights?" Gray says behind me.

"Not all Friday nights, I told you. Just some."

"And...how are we going to get up there without sounding the alarm?"

"Oh. That. Well, they never actually used to put the alarm on. It was always too much of a hassle for employees so they would just leave it off."

"That is...not at all reassuring."

"There's always the risk that today will be the day they finally set the alarm, but it's a risk we're just going to have to take."

"Uh."

I place my palms flat on the bar on the door, feel them shaking slightly as I lean my hands against them just so. This was always the exciting part: will it sound, or will I get up there undetected?

"What about a camera? There's gotta be a camera here," he says as he looks around.

"It's a live feed," I respond without a second thought, then notice the look of concern on his face. "Oh. This sounds bad. I swear I'm not a criminal."

I lean my hands against the bar again and count to three. *One, two, three*...push. The door opens and all you hear is the wind gusts twenty-two floors up.

"Today is your lucky day, Gray."

We step through the door and walk into the warm evening, the concrete ledges surrounding us, the air conditioning systems scattered throughout. We reach a set of small steps and walk up, holding on to the handrail. I remember the first time I took these steps. Liz showed me this rooftop first. She found out about it through some guy she was dating at the time. She dumped him but kept this spot. We spent weekend nights here together, sometimes apart. But the first time – I wish I could bottle up that feeling.

I took those steps and as I walked up each one, another part of the picture emerged from behind the ledge and showed itself to me. A high-rise here, a glowing light there, until I reached the very top and I was standing on the highest part of the roof, the one with a clear view of this beautiful, beautiful city. Not facing the ocean but facing New River itself. Bustling downtown, cars on the streets, high-rises reaching toward the sky, and lights coming from windows. The whole city on display. What an incredible view.

I walk these steps now and reach the top, waiting for Gray. Once he reaches the top next to me, all I hear is an inhale. And then the slowest exhale.

"This is amazing," he says. And the wonder in his voice tells me he means it.

"This is my little part of the city," I say. "It's no Glow Bowl, but..." I trail off, laughing quietly, not wanting to ruin this moment.

"How did you find out about this?"

"Liz. A long time ago," I say. I have always loved it up here. And even though I loved it here with Liz, I always hoped to share it with somebody else, always hoped for that fairytale romance. I envisioned rooftop dances and kisses atop this city, but when Ben and I came here for the wedding, he didn't want to come up and I was too tired to try to convince him to do something I wanted to do. Once he was asleep, I came up alone, but it was even lonelier than it had been when I was single. So, I went back to the room and back to bed.

Here with Gray, this doesn't feel lonely. It feels...new. Like I'm showing somebody a little piece of me and they're accepting it. Taking it for what it is and enjoying it.

"The city looks incredible up here." He put his hands on his hips, leaning over the ledge to take a good look. "And I know that we're on a rooftop and it shouldn't be that remarkable, but it really is."

"I know how you feel." I smile. "And you know the best part?"

"What's that?"

I curve my hand around my ear, leaning slightly over the ledge, listening for what I know will be coming soon.

The music wafts up to where we are and all I can do is smile, letting it fill my soul with glee. "You can hear the wedding reception from up here."

Gray's answering smile is the one I dream out. The one that takes up his whole face, a crinkle in his nose, the light in his blue eyes, the one that screams joy. Sometimes I think it's all I'll ever need. It's certainly one hell of a memory to keep.

The rhythm starts and I begin to move with the beat, tapping my toes here, swaying my hips there, my hair dancing with the wind. I spin and spin, moving and tapping, swaying and laughing. Gray just watches, the grin overtaking his whole face.

Here it is, all I've ever wanted to do and I'm getting a redo with him. It feels so right, I don't even know how to proceed.

How do I handle this? Because this right here is starting to run deeper than friendship.

Still dancing, I feel Gray's eyes on me and I look over to meet them. I stop moving, try to catch my breath.

"I love it up here," he says, not breaking eye contact.

"Me too," I whisper.

He takes a step closer to me. Another one. I think I'm holding my breath now. He stops inches away from me and we stand like two statues staring, until he very carefully reaches out to tuck a loose strand of hair behind my ear, his fingers lingering on the spot just below it.

Kiss me, I think.

And maybe he's about to. Maybe he's about to lean in and kiss the shit out of me. But just then the rooftop door swings open and a flash of light beams across the roof.

"Who's up here?!" a voice yells.

"Ah shit," I say, palm to my forehead. "I think I forgot to mention that this is also a risk factor."

"What?" Gray looks panicked, ready to start running for the hills.

"Just walk behind me," I tell him. Once we make our way down the steps, I notice who it is.

"Marv? Hi! Long time no see!" Marv is one of the Regency security guards who has worked here for many years.

He squints, adjusting his eyes. "Sabrina Moss? Seriously?"

"I got lost on my way to the bathroom."

"Aren't you a little too old to be up here doing this?"

"You're never too old Marv! And look!" I motion to Gray beside me, who has lost all the color on his face. "Even brought a friend this time."

"Move it along guys. *I'm* too old to be chasing you two."

"Always a pleasure, Marv."

"Sir, I am very sorry," I hear Gray say behind me and I chuckle so hard I snort.

We walk back into the hotel, down the stairs, and into the hallway corridor that will lead us to the elevators.

"Sorry about that. You looked really scared for a minute there." I bite my lip keep from laughing.

Gray shakes his head, smiling, and looks at me with an expression I can't decipher.

"What?" I ask.

"Just you, making friends with Marv, the resident security guard," he says.

"Too much?" *Am I too much? Was that too much?*

"Never."

I feel his eyes on me all the way to the elevators, hands swinging in tandem as we walk, occasionally brushing fingers and setting all my nerve endings on fire. Once inside the elevators he reaches over to push the button, but instead of pushing ground floor he pushes 18, the floor that the ballroom is on.

"Where are we going?" I ask.

"You ever crash a wedding, Sabrina Moss?" he asks, mischievous smile in place.

This is turning out to be the best night I've had in a very long time.

Fourteen

Gray

"So first we need a backstory," I tell her as we're walking down the hallway that leads to the ballroom doors.

"Have you done this a lot?" she asks.

"Maybe a handful of times."

"A handful?" she asks, incredulously.

"Maybe more than a handful, but definitely less than ten."

"Gray!" She laughs and the way she says my name sends my heart right into my throat. "For somebody that has crashed that many number of weddings, you sure seemed concerned about Marv."

"Wedding crashing won't put me in prison," I reason.

She tilts her head back, letting out a loud laugh, and it's my favorite thing she does. That exposed line of her throat letting out a vibrant sound of pure joy. "Marv won't send you to prison either."

"Says you."

Still laughing, she asks, "Okay, so what's our backstory?"

"Alright, so we're with the bride – "

"Well, I actually do know one of the brides so how is this going to work? Also, we're not dressed for a wedding," she says, gesturing to her black leggings and yellow Crocs, this time with socks that have cupcakes on them.

I look down at my jeans and plain T-shirt. We've reached the entrance to the ballroom, the sound of music and conversation heard from just outside. I grip the handle, open it slightly to take a peek and close it again. "Okay, new plan. We're with catering. Grab a tray and just go with it." I open the door again and push us in.

"Wait – what?" I hear Sabrina say next to me. Just then I notice some trays being set down, so I walk over to them and grab one.

"Here we go!" I whisper.

There's a garbled sound that comes from Sabrina as she scrambles behind me to grab a tray and then pass one around. I almost lose my tray laughing, but move through the crowds easily, passing out the main course as guests are deep in conversation, laughing. She's following behind, her movements just as graceful as anybody else's here. The plates are set down quickly and efficiently and then she moves on to the next table, never lingering too long, trying not to get caught.

It makes me laugh how she takes on this role so quickly, almost as if she's as concerned about being here as I was about getting a flashlight shone on my face by Marv on the roof. She seems to prefer the background, the shadows. Working in the quiet and slipping out just before the noise, letting her cakes get the praise instead. I wasn't kidding when I said she seems so confident in what she does. She is, and her confidence shines even in the darkness. Even when she's silent in the background, the rest of her speaks volumes.

We move through the tables, working alongside the rest of the catering until the main courses are passed out and then step back, lingering against the wall in a darkened corner of the ballroom.

"Do you usually crash weddings just to offer free labor?" she whispers beside me.

"Can I tell you a secret?"

"Maybe."

"I've actually never crashed a wedding," I whisper back.

Her mouth hangs open as she turns to look at me.

"You're the only hardened criminal between us," I tell her.

She snorts and then covers her mouth just as quickly. I love it so much it makes me laugh, too.

"You have no idea what you're doing, do you?" she asks.

"Not even a little," I tell her. "But I'm having the best time doing it anyway."

She smiles and it takes over her whole face. "I think the point of wedding crashing is to actually enjoy the wedding." Sabrina nods to trays of champagne being passed around for a toast, scooping up two glasses and handing one over to me.

The mother of one of the brides stands, the *clink-clink* of the fork on the side of a glass echoing through the room. Silence falls as she addresses the guests.

"Thank you all so much for coming to celebrate our darling Jessica and her beloved Alejandra. We are so happy that you are here with us for this joyous occasion."

I turn to Sabrina, toasting my glass with hers and taking a small sip, my eyes meeting hers above the rim. I don't know what's happened tonight – maybe it's the adrenaline in doing something so unexpected, so out of character for me. Crashing a wedding, trespassing onto a hotel rooftop. Maybe this started when Sabrina called me asking for help. I jumped at the opportunity to spend more time with her, to revel in her orbit.

And now here I am drinking fancy champagne out of some fancy glass in a hotel ballroom with her.

I fidget with my glass, wanting to turn to her and tell her all these things: how great this has all been, how much I enjoy being with her, how much I want more of it, more of *her*. But Ben pops into my head and the words get caught in my throat. Ben shouldn't have anything to do with this, I try to reason away. It's not his fucking business, but there he is anyway, the dead weight we've carried around everywhere we've been together.

I'm starting to get tired of it, feeling my knees buckle from it, but I worry about overstepping boundaries with her. I initiated this as friends; I need to keep it that way. I need to at least try.

The toasts continue: stories about Jess, about Alejandra. Some funny, some sweet, some heartfelt. Toasts about love, finding your person and letting everything else fall away.

"When Jessica first met Alejandra, she was so scared. Scared of her feelings for her, of how quickly everything seemed to be moving," the maid of honor speaks. "I remember when she told me about Alejandra – how her eyes lit up when she talked about her. And when I saw them together, I knew this was the real deal. Love is a risk, but it's always worth it. It's been such an honor to see Jessica bloom with Alejandra by her side, to witness her finding this rare and wondrous love, holding on tight to it through all the ups and downs. I can only hope we are as lucky as the two of you."

I listen quietly, some foreign feeling stirring in me. I take a sip of champagne, try to wash it down, but it stays. And if I didn't know any better, I'd say that it's only bound to grow bigger.

"I love weddings," I whisper, turning to look at her.

She smiles, a small one like it's meant only for me, and whispers back, "You're not shitty company."

It's only bound to grow bigger, and I don't think I can stop it anymore.

We keep staring, seemingly unable to move, until we notice the guests getting up and heading to the dance floor. The DJ starts up again and "Cake by the Ocean" starts blasting, the poppy beat thumping through the speakers.

"Want to dance?" I ask her.

"Always."

I follow her to the dance floor and take a second to watch her move. The pure joy of it, the way the music just flows through her. I see her spin and laugh, tilting that head back again, like she's having the most fun out of everybody here. There she is radiating an energy I'm so desperate to hold on to.

I want to kiss you, I think. *So much.*

"Let's go Gray Forrester!" I hear her yell over the song. So, I make my way over and dance with her. My two left feet and all her spirit. And even then, she moves with me, makes me look like I somewhat know what I'm doing.

Aunt Jill, who also made a toast, zooms by us, twirling in a sequined jumpsuit, raving, "How fitting is this song?!" I think she's been hitting the open bar a good bit, though most of the guests have at this point.

"I thought this song *wasn't* about cake by the ocean?" I ask Sabrina under my breath.

"Oh, it definitely isn't, but it's been a popular song choice for beach weddings in recent years anyway," she tells me. She sends Aunt Jill a thumbs up.

"So, are you with the Jess or Alejandra?" she asks, still moving next to us.

"Jess," Sabrina answers.

I manage to mumble something resembling Alejandra at the same time and I see Sabrina's smile tighten.

"I just love how weddings bring people together!" she shouts over the music and twirls away.

We continue to move together, in our own kind of rhythm, Sabrina laughing with me. This feels oddly like a middle school dance. Me, nervous. The girl, oblivious to me and having the best time. And just like a middle school dance, the pop song ends and a slow one begins.

"Should we..." *leave the dance floor,* I want to say. I don't know where these nerves are coming from suddenly, like I don't know how the hell to act with her right now.

But she says "Sure" and comes in closer. Oh. Oh, we're going to slow dance.

We've never touched like this before. I wrap my arm around her waist, and she steps forward, bringing her hand to my shoulder. I grab her other hand and we sway gently, maybe awkwardly. This is the closest we've ever been. Even closer than earlier on the roof when I wanted nothing more than to kiss her then. I love how she feels in my arms, all her curves fitting like puzzle pieces in my hands, against my own body. The dip of her waist, the softness of her belly. It's like she's belonged here her whole life.

There's a pink shade blooming on her cheeks which makes me think she's nervous, too. She's looking around at everybody but me and yet I'm finding it hard to look away from her. Her hair high up in a ponytail, those bangs falling around her eyes and framing her face. From this close I can see the tiniest freckles scattered across her nose; I can see the fullness of her lips. God, how desperately I want to taste them. Fuck, this is about to get really inappropriate. I should probably keep a slight distance so I don't embarrass myself.

Maybe she feels me staring, but she turns to me then and whispers, "I think they're catching on to us."

It takes me a beat to break out of my trance and I realize she means the guests at this wedding that we are absolutely crashing. I look around and some are staring, whispering.

We slowly sway to the end of the dance floor, then as stealthily as we can, walk through the tables and lingering guests and right out the door.

Sabrina and I lean against the wall tucked into a small alcove in the hallway, her giggles filling up the silence.

"This is the best night I've had in what feels like forever," she says, her grin lighting up this whole corridor.

"I agree," I say, smiling with her. My eyes slip to her mouth. She notices and her eyes move to mine. Adrenaline courses through me, what feels like electricity zapping between us.

The universe is giving me a push here and I need to just take it. I want to bury this dead weight between us, I want it to just be us, even for a second. I start to lean in, the slightest inch forward, and I see her bite the corner of her bottom lip. *Fuck, let me bite it.*

"Bri," I start.

And then, right on cue, my phone rings. *This fucking phone.* A loud shrill sound that I chose so I would make sure to always hear it, because this specific ringtone is for Nancy - *Shit, Nancy!* - who I told I'd be home in a couple of hours.

I stop, panicked, reaching for my phone in my pocket. "Shit! Sorry, it's Nancy. Pop's neighbor," I tell her.

She looks a little panicked, too. Maybe a little dazed from what was just happening.

"Hey, Nancy. Is he alright?...Yeah, I'm so sorry, I got tied up with some things, but I'll be on my way very soon....Thank you so much, Nancy." I hang up and tuck the phone back into my pocket.

"Is everything okay?"

"Yeah, she was just worried because she hadn't heard from me, and I told her I'd only be a couple of hours."

"Oh shit, I'm so sorry, Gray. I asked you to help and then I held you hostage."

"I was a willing participant." I laugh softly. "It's alright, but I need to head back now."

"Yes, of course." She grabs the keys from her pocket and we start walking toward the elevators. Once inside, the silence is loaded, the air tense with questions. I keep my distance, trying to digest what just happened and how I can get it to happen again. She stands on the opposite side of me, looking down at her keys in her hand, at her shoes. We head out of the elevator, and through the double doors into the parking lot where the delivery van is.

Once seated and secured in the van, I look over and tell her, "This really was the best night."

"I know," she says, smiling.

I grin, reveling in her perfect orbit, the whole way back to the shop.

FIFTEEN

SABRINA

I STUMBLE INTO WORK the next morning, getting in early for another busy day filled with deliveries and finishing orders.

Liz follows behind an hour later, a mound of messy green bun on her head.

"Morning. Oh no, did the blue turn green?"

"Does it look like pond scum or can I pull it off?" she asks, running a hand through her hair.

I tilt my head to look at her, considering. "You can pull it off. How's Jeff doing?"

After the delivery last night, Gray and I came back to the bakeshop and he quickly drove home, wanting to get back to his grandfather. I felt bad for keeping him out, assuming he had all the time in the world, running after my own fun. *But the wedding crashing was his idea,* I tell myself.

I was tired, both physically and mentally, drained from trying to work out what had happened between us, so once I headed home, I went straight to bed, only managing to reply briefly to the group chat: Liz and her updates about Jeff - he's okay. A couple of bruised ribs, a fracture on his leg. And James's pictures of his beautiful baby nephew.

"Jeff is fine! Who cares? Tell me about the delivery!"

I snort at that. "And did you hear? James's sister had a beautiful baby boy!"

She huffs out a breath. "Yes, yes. It's wonderful. Now stop holding out on me!"

"It was fine," I tell her, trying to hold in my smile. "We delivered the cake, everything got there in one piece, Nina eyeballed him like a piece of meat, and then we were done."

"Ugh. Dammit, Nina." "He's a good listener," I say, going through notes on my clipboard.

"Is he now? Hm." Her eyes are boring into my head. "And so, you set up the cake and just left?"

I look down at my clipboard, staring at one word so hard in the hopes that she'll believe I'm actually looking through these notes.

"Spill it, Bri." She's onto me.

I look up at her and take a deep breath. "I just – I took him up on the roof," I rush out in an exhale.

Her eyes widen comically. "The roof?"

"Aaaand then we crashed the Veracruz wedding."

"You...you *crashed* the *wedding* that you delivered the cake to?"

"To be fair that one was his idea."

"Oh my God, this guy is a goner."

"What?"

"I mean, you are, too, honestly. The roof? You took him on the roof!" She swats my arm.

"Ow!"

"Please tell me you took him home, too."

"No, his grandfather's neighbor called and he had to go back home."

Her eyes widen again. "But you wanted to!"

"Of course, I wanted to! Are you kidding?" I exhale, exasperated. "But..." I trail off, shaking my head.

"But what?" she presses.

"I don't know if this is the smart thing to be doing Liz."

"Why the hell not? If your home is a concern, you could have just gotten some on the roof," she supplies.

"Marv caught us."

She laughs at this, that loud cackle that erupts from her whenever she finds something particularly amusing. "Caught you doing what?!"

"Nothing!" I laugh with her. "We were just...dancing...but he had leaned in. I don't know, maybe he was going to do something?"

"Okay. Listen to me, Bri."

"Crap." I know what's coming.

"You are not seventeen anymore. You are thirty-two, you are successful, you are beautiful. You can make the moves you want to make. And - brace yourself for this one - but he's not Ben. He's also not seventeen. He seems like he's got a good head on his shoulders, and I don't know how you're oblivious to it, but this guy is in it with you. 'Let's hang out as friends?' Please. That was one hell of a pick-up line if I've ever heard one."

"You mean I'm thirty-two and still falling for pick-up lines?" I joke.

"I'm going to punch you."

"I don't know," I sigh. "What if I'm reading this wrong? I've done it before. What if this is a risk I take and it doesn't pay off?"

"The Sabrina I know deep down wants to take those risks. It's not easy, that's true, but what if the risk does pay off?"

"Maybe that's even scarier."

"I know," she whispers, hand over mine. "Stop denying yourself the things you want."

"It's not that easy." *Is it?*

"Isn't it?" She echoes my own thoughts.

I expel a breath. "I'm taking an Amelia's break. Want anything?"

"The usual," she answers. As I grab my wallet and head out, I hear her voice. "Love you, Bri."

I smile. "Love you, Liz." If she were a cake, she'd be lemon, no question. Tart, sweet, a pick-me-up when you need it.

I enter Amelia's quickly, planning to be in and out. It's a busy Sunday, locals quietly reading the paper, friends chatting over coffee. She spots me and I let her know the usual for Liz and me.

"I haven't seen you in a while. Been busy?" she smirks.

"Work has been busy if that's what you're asking." I give her a knowing look.

She laughs at that. Once the coffees are done, she places them in front of me. "He's nice," she says, leaning against the counter.

"He is," I agree.

"Tell Liz I said hi." She winks as I grab the coffees and wave goodbye.

As I'm heading out, I see the local news bulletin near the door, brimming with flyers and business cards. One catches my eye: Brewery Bike Ride. A bike ride through downtown ending at the local brewery this Tuesday starting at seven o'clock. The past couple of years has seen an influx of not only high-rises and restaurants, but also craft breweries. James, Liz, and I have been to a couple, but this could be a fun thing to do. A fun way to really see the heart of the city and then hang out with a cold beer and some casual conversation. This could be good.

I snap a quick picture of the flyer and before I can change my mind, send it off to Gray in a text.

His response is almost immediate: ***"Let's do it."***

Let's do it, indeed.

Sixteen

Gray

"Hey Pop, I'm heading out tonight. Nancy should be here soon." I check my watch. "You need anything before I go?"

"You've been going out a lot lately, Mr. Popular," he says, a smirk on his face.

"Just been getting out like you told me to." He's playing sudoku in his *Sudoku Everyday!* book, looking up at me, glasses perched on his nose. "Uh-huh. And you've been doing this alone?"

I laugh at this. He's wanted me to go out and meet people, sure, but Pop has never been shy about making it a point to have me go out and meet "a nice girl", whatever that means.

"I've been going out with a friend."

"A lady friend?"

"Her name is Sabrina." I lift an eyebrow. "She's a baker."

"Sabrina," he repeats, sounding the name out. "She make wedding cakes?"

"Yeah, actually. How did you know?"

"Lucky guess. I read a write up about her in the Sentinel years ago and it always stuck with me," he shrugs. "Beautiful cakes. I love cake."

I'm surprised by this, a little bit of Sabrina extending and reaching the residents of this town. "She does make beautiful cakes," I agree.

"What's she doing hanging out with you? She's certainly out of your league," he jokes.

"You're not kidding," I laugh. "I don't know why she's hanging out with me either." Even as a quip, I realize how much I feel some truth in that. My hope is that she enjoys my company as much as I enjoy hers.

The doorbell rings and I go to answer it. Nancy steps in, greeting me and then Pop. "Hey Nancy, good to see you. I'm not sure when I'll be home if I'm being honest, but I'll keep you posted."

"Hot date?" she teases.

"You guys are a tough crowd today." I smile, shaking my head. "See you both later. Love you, Pop." I squeeze his shoulder before I go.

When Sabrina had texted me about the brewery bike ride, I figured we could share a car there instead of driving. Downtown traffic and parking can be a nightmare. The car pulls up and I get in, giving the driver Sabrina's address. Once we arrive at her place, I open the door for her and scoot over so she can get in.

"Hey. Nice khakis, is there a golf tournament later?"

"What's wrong with my khakis?" I look down at my shorts. I didn't really know what to wear to this thing, so I opted for some khaki shorts and a casual Henley. She's wearing some athletic leggings that flatter every curve and a T-shirt with a picture of a mixer and words that read *Whip it good!*

"Nothing, I'm kidding," she giggles. "I feel way underdressed compared to you, though."

"I think I might be overdressed. We're going to be riding bikes. You've got the right idea."

"We'll find out soon enough," she shrugs. "Nice to see you by the way." Her smile is bright, her cheeks are tinged pink.

"Nice to see you, too" I smile back, taking an unexpected punch to my heart.

The drive to the brewery is a mostly quiet one. If she feels any awkwardness from our night at the Regency, she doesn't show it. We talk a little about work, how our days have been. It's an enjoyable conversation, always relaxed with her, always flowing. It makes me realize how I've longed for this for some time. Some stability, sure, but the consistency of seeing one person, talking to one person every day. Getting to talk about your day. The familiarity of coming home to one person, who is waiting up for you to talk, to listen. I'm taken aback by where my mind wanders to - the vision that pops up in my head of getting to see her every single day and the desire that burns for how much I want it. Her energy, her laughter, the way she gives you her attention, the way she lights up a room. *I could get used to that around here.*

The car pulls up to the brewery. We give our thanks to the driver and spill out onto the curb, joining the group standing around by the entrance in a mix of shorts, sweatpants, and leggings. New River Brewing is set up in an old warehouse so the ceilings are high with exposed rafters. The open door is wide like a garage door, letting in the breeze. Café lights are strung up along the walls inside making everything fall into a glow. It's a cool spot, one I could see myself frequenting. This brewery is one of the newer additions to the downtown nightlife. It certainly wasn't around when I was in high school.

There's a table set up inside right as you enter with a young hostess passing out clipboards with waivers that need to be signed.

"A waiver? This is getting serious," I mumble, extending my hand out to grab a clipboard.

"If you go flying over the handlebars, you're on your own, Forrester."

"This isn't a competition, Moss. Can we enact the buddy system here?" I feign outrage.

"I'll think about it." She signs her waiver and passes it back to the hostess.

"And who's to say you won't be the one flying over the handlebars?" I hand my waiver over.

She laughs at that as we walk over to join the group. For the bike ride, you can bring your own bike, or they provide some you can rent. We opt to rent them, picking out our bikes and helmets and moving along to the start area.

"These bikes have seen better days," she mutters, the squeak of her handlebars getting louder as she pushes it toward the start area where everybody is gathered.

"No wonder they made us sign waivers."

A man with very large biceps and a full beard stands in front of the crowd and speaks then. "Good evening, everybody! My name is Greg and I'll be your tour guide for tonight."

A couple of people shout back "Hey Greg!".

"Oh shit, I know him," Sabrina whispers.

"Who?"

"Greg. Vanilla bean on vanilla bean."

"What?"

"He's marrying Evelyn."

"Do you always refer to your clients by cake flavors?"

"Sometimes," she answers. "Okay this is kind of adorable. I wonder if Evelyn is a bike enthusiast," she mutters mostly to herself, looking around the crowd.

"Thank you for joining us! We started doing these bike tours almost a year ago and they've been a big hit. I've got a couple of rules for tonight: we will be biking on the roads, so I ask that you bike two-by-two. Stick to a 'biking buddy' if you will."

"Will you be my biking buddy?" I whisper to Sabrina next to me.

"I was really hoping for that guy." She points to some random person in the crowd. "But I guess you'll do."

"This bike tour will take about thirty minutes. If at any time you don't feel well or you have bike troubles, let your bike buddy know and get off the road. Then you can just call out to either me, Marcus," he points to another man to his right wearing one of those sleeveless gym shirts, "or Chet," he then points to a man on his left wearing a New River Brewing T-shirt. "Chet is one of the brewers that initiated this bike tour idea."

Somebody else in the crowd yells, "Yeah Chet!"

"Chet sounds like he *would* be a brewer at a downtown microbrewery," I murmur in Sabrina's ear, and she huffs out a laugh, but I don't miss the goosebumps that rise along the back of her neck.

"And please remember to drink lots of water. We have bottles of water for everybody here so feel free to take one." He points to a large cooler then motions to another bearded man in the group. "Eric, take two."

Eric grabs two and we hop onto our bikes to get started, lining up in two rows.

"Let's do this, friends!" Greg shouts from the front of the group, clapping as we head out, Sabrina's squeaky bike and mine with an odd rattle.

We turn slowly onto Fifth, the small side street New River Brewing is on, biking past some small offices, an art gallery, and some apartment buildings. We then turn onto a busier street, biking past a juice bar, a coffee house, and an arcade bar. A quieter, older crowd.

All the while, we hear bits and pieces from Greg up front: "You can see local businesses on this street. If you have the chance, check out the arcade bar. They've got a ton of games and the world's best truffle mac-and-cheese." Sabrina locks eyes with mine and we both try to hold in our laughter.

"I call bullshit," I say to her. Eric turns around then and gives me a weird look which makes Sabrina laugh louder.

Following the group, we turn onto the busier, trendier part of downtown. This must be where all the young kids are these days then. Large, loud groups spill out onto the sidewalks from the bars, drinks in hand. Tables outside of restaurants are full, diners talking and laughing. The sun is just falling below the horizon and everything here shines. Streetlights, high rise lights, twinkling café lights from the restaurants and bars. I look to the sky, following the windows of the corporate buildings up. There are larger chain restaurants here, too, but not many. I peek over at Sabrina and see her do the same, looking up to the sky, taking everything in.

I'm too busy not paying attention that I don't realize there's a curb up ahead I need to watch out for until it's too late. Next thing I know I am tumbling down on my side, my arm shooting out to catch my fall.

I hear Sabrina yell "Oh shit!" then come to a stop next to me. She huddles down on the ground where I am laid out, my khakis now streaked with dirt.

"Are you okay?!"

"Yep. Just hurt my ego, I think." I groan as I sit up and examine my hands, the palms red and a little scratched from the pavement, tiny bits of gravel stuck to them.

"Should I call Greg?"

"No, no." I wave her off, but I realize everybody else has stopped to check on me, too. I wave hand my hand in the air weakly, saying "I'm good!" and get back up.

Sabrina is biting the inside of her cheek, trying not to laugh, and I can't help but crack first, laughing at myself and then her joining in.

We get back on the bikes – her jumping right back on, me very gingerly lifting my leg over the seat and cautiously sitting down.

"You gonna be okay, Lance Armstrong?" she says beside me, eyeing as I adjust in the seat.

A laugh bubbles up out of me as my face heats. We start to ride again and continue the trek through downtown – museums, the theater, more office buildings – turning down a side street to head back to the brewery.

I hear Sabrina beside me, huffing louder than usual. "Who the hell told me cardio was a good idea?"

I'm starting to huff, too. "Do you think we need to pull over and inform Vanilla Bean Greg?"

"Speak for yourself, Forrester." She pedals forward.

"Maybe we can call over tall, dark, and handsome Marcus?"

"Oh, now you're on to something."

"Maybe Chet the brewer?"

"Maybe," she puffs, out of breath. "Maybe they can massage my legs and feed me sips of cold beer and bar food," she says dreamily. "Damn, that sounds like the dream."

I know she says this all in fun, but it still eats away at me, nudging me as a reminder that I don't like it. I don't have any horse in the race here, I know that. There's no reason for me to be feeling this ridiculous jealousy, but it doesn't stop me from saying to her, "I'll massage your legs and get you an ice-cold beer, Moss. How about that?"

"Now we're talking, Forrester," she says enthusiastically. "I'll hold you to it." Her eyebrows lift as the corner of her mouth tilts into the sexiest smirk.

Visions of the night of the wedding crashing pop up again - strong, bold, and demanding. I saw something in her eyes that night, and I'm seeing it again.

I want to keep seeing it, the thought pushes through.

We bike up to the brewery closer to seven forty-five, out of breath and sweaty, and grab a table by the open doors. There are sounds all around us – conversations, laughter, the cacophony of plates and silverware. There's chatter, people mingling, beer glasses clinking.

"How are your hands?" she asks.

"They're not bad."

"Will you be able to hold a utensil?"

"Don't think so. You might need to cut my food up into tiny little squares and then feed them to me."

We sit down in our seats across from each other while the host provides us with menus.

In front of me Sabrina stays quiet, admiring her surroundings. She turns back to look at me, a sheepish look on her face. "It's been a long time since I've been out like this. Most nights I find myself at home working on cakes or shop work for the week," she tells me.

"Do you and Liz or James ever go out?"

"We do, but we all spend so much time together at work that sometimes when we have days off, Liz wants to spend it with Jeff and James wants to spend it with Marc. We go out as a group, too, but I just become the odd one out."

"I'll join your group," I say, in a rush.

She looks over at me, a hint of a smile in her eyes at my outburst.

"Just an offer. I seem to throw lots of offers your way. What's one more?" I smile, mostly to myself.

She's about to respond when our server comes over to introduce himself and talk about some beers on tap. Sabrina orders something light with citrus while I pick a sour-style beer. Once our server leaves, we open our menus. I peek over it, studying her as she studies it, never tiring from looking at her. Her cheeks flushed from the bike ride, sweaty hair in a messy bun on her head, tendrils falling around her face. Those deep, warm eyes browse the menu in front of her. *God, she's beautiful.*

"Alright, what looks good?" she asks, looking up at me.

I try to look down quickly, but I'm caught.

"What?" she asks. "Do I look like a mess? Am I sweating profusely?" She lifts her arms to check.

I smile at that. "No. Well, you are sweating, but we all are." I lean closer and whisper, "I think Eric's got the pit stains though." I nod in the direction of the table next to us.

Her answering laugh makes my smile grow bigger. This night feels so alive; I feel so alive with her.

"You have a great laugh," I tell her and watch her cheeks turn an even darker shade of red, followed by the tips of her ears and spreading like wildfire down her neck.

"Thanks," she responds quietly.

"Okay, what looks good," I clear my throat. "The goat cheese croquettes? The hangover fries with beer cheese and a sunny side up egg? The short rib grilled cheese?" I recite some menu items to her. "Have I mentioned I love cheese?"

"Cheese is my love language," she agrees. "Maybe we can order a bunch of things and just have a free-for-all?"

"I like the way you think, Bri."

When our server returns, we order the croquettes, the fries, a truffle flatbread, deep fried brussels sprouts - "A vegetable to balance it out," Sabrina says - and short rib meatballs.

Once the food arrives, a smorgasbord covering the table, Sabrina thanks the server, skewers a piece of meatball with a fork, and brings it to the direction of my mouth.

"For my injured biking buddy," she says, pouting, a giggle bubbling up out of her mouth.

I maintain eye contact and bite the meatball off the fork, loving how intimate it feels. Her smile lingers, blush deepens, and eyes darken. I see her teeth bite the very corner of her bottom lip again and I take another bite of the meatball, my eyes fixated on her mouth.

Shit, what are we doing?

"I can use a fork," I mumble, even though I'd rather she feed me all night. "I was just kidding."

"I know." She grabs another fork and digs in.

We're scarfing food down as if we've never eaten in our lives when my phone rings, this time my mom's name popping up on the screen.

I decline the call quickly and she watches, her stare shifting between me and the phone.

I look back at her, a small smile in apology.

"You can answer that. I don't mind."

"Don't want to," I tell her, shrugging as I bite into a croquette.

There is silence for a beat, then she says, "My dad left us when I was thirteen."

I look up at her, taken aback. "I'm so sorry, Bri."

"Don't be." She shakes her head and leans in, elbows on the table.

"What happened?"

She takes a deep breath and a minute to answer. "He was having an affair with another woman, left to go be with her. He married her, according to social media."

"Shit."

"Cynthia." She looks a little lost as she says it, a little surprised. "I've never said her name out loud before." She swallows. "I tried to get him to stay. I begged, I fought for us as a family. I was *thirteen*. Why was I doing that?" she frowns. "My dad tried to keep a relationship with me - behind my mother's back no less - and I allowed it for a while. But I was so angry at him, I gave up. I didn't want to anymore. I guess what I'm saying is I understand that desire to avoid," she tells me then.

I still, listening.

"And I had a right to be angry, but I wonder if I could have put everything aside and just accepted what it was? If a relationship with him would have been better in the long run?

I don't know." Her shoulders lift slightly, her eyes look down at her plate.

"He's an asshole," I blurt. The beer's loosened my tongue.

Her head pops up, looking at me with her mouth pursed, trying not to laugh.

"Sorry," I wince. "Stop apologizing." Her mouth is a smirk now.

"I just think…" I start slowly, "you deserve people in your life that stay."

Her wide eyes, full of surprise, stare back at me. Like she's never been told this, never even thought about it herself.

"Gray…"

I shrug, shift the conversation back while my heart tries to skip out of my body. "Pop always tries to make sure I talk to my mom regularly. It's just been a little bit harder lately."

"It usually is," she says, a kindness in her eyes that I don't quite know how to handle.

We eat in silence, the ambient noise surrounding us.

I change the topic then. "Speaking of, Pop knows of you."

"Oh yeah?" She spears a brussels sprout with a fork, runs it through the balsamic drizzle on the plate, and then stuffs it into her mouth. She licks any residual balsamic off the fork and I could watch her do this for the rest of forever.

I clear my throat, check if I'm not drooling. "Yeah. He said he read about you in the Sentinel once. Some write up years ago."

Whatever I said stops her, her fork frozen mid-air. She keeps going like nothing happened, but I saw the glitch. I saw something. "Wow. I didn't realize anybody had read that."

"He said it always stuck out in his mind and that you make beautiful cakes."

It takes her a minute to process, but then I see the evolution of it: the glitch, the barest quiver of her bottom lip, and then the smile, big and bright. It goes right to her eyes, a little glassy, like she's glowing from the inside out, and I can't look away. "Tell him I said thank you. That means a lot."

"I will."

***

"Well, I have no regrets," she says. We are practically slouched over the table scattered with empty plates and glasses. My stomach will probably hate me tomorrow morning, but for now I am blissfully satisfied.

"Definitely not. Top ten best decisions I've made."

"The bike ride, the beer, or the food?" she laughs.

"The company," I say. "Always the company."

"I agree," she grins, chin resting on her hand, a blush starting to spread. "I've had so much fun with you, Gray."

"Me too," I tell her, words almost caught in my throat. "Should we get dessert?"

"Nah, nothing good on the menu."

"What? Did you even look?"

"I'll have you know it is the first thing I look at on any menu and these desserts were nothing to write home about."

"Alright, then what do you recommend?"

I see her fidget, like she's working up the courage to say something. She bites that corner of her bottom lip again. Is that a tell? Something is brewing in her mind.

"I have a perfect idea for dessert as a matter of fact, if you're interested."

"I am definitely interested."

"How about...how about I bake you my all-time favorite dessert?" she asks, leaning into the table, slightly closer to me. My eyebrows shoot up, surprise probably all over my face. I did not expect her to say that. "Uh. Yes. Definitely. Yes. That sounds great."

Her answering laugh is little shy. We pay the check, and she orders another car.

Walking out of the exit and into the night, I turn to her and ask, "So, should we head to the shop or...?"

The car pulls up then and Sabrina opens the door, answering, "Oh, no. We'll just head to my place. Is that okay?"

I'm struck dead as she hops in and scoots all the way over to make room for me. I see her lean forward to me. "You coming?"

"Absolutely."

This whole night can fall under top ten best decisions I've ever made.

Seventeen

Sabrina

My body was tingling the whole drive over here, filled with the kind of electricity I've only been feeling with him, and I worried if I should change my mind and stop this now.

But I can't stop now. I don't want to stop now.

We pull up to my house and get out of the car, Gray following behind as I reach for the keys in my bag.

"Please make yourself comfortable," I gesture dramatically as I open the front door. I flip on the light switch and he steps inside, studying everything. I feel as exposed as I did when he was checking out the bakeshop, but maybe less so. I can't tell. What am I feeling? Excitement? Anticipation? Indigestion? Who told me ordering all that food would be a good idea?

I walk in after him, closing the door behind us.

I live in a small two-story townhouse in a suburb about twenty to thirty minutes away from the bakery, depending on traffic. It's quiet and homey, affordable, and perfect for me.

Walking into my house, I take my shoes off by the bench near the door. Gray copies me, setting his sneakers right next to mine.

He walks through the entryway and into my kitchen off to the left. My kitchen is small but has a breakfast bar with stools on the opposite side. The living room is just beyond it with my big blue comfy couch and the stairs which lead to my bedroom and guest room.

While Gray looks around, I preheat the oven, grab some bowls from the cabinet, some eggs and butter from the fridge, and set everything on the counter.

He comes over and sits on a stool, facing me across the bar. "So, what kind of cake will you be making?" he asks.

"Who said anything about cake?"

"Didn't you say you were making your favorite dessert?"

I wince a little. "I hate to break your heart, but I actually don't like cake all that much."

His eyebrows shoot up to his hairline. The look on his face is the one I imagine he must have had when his parents sat him down and told him Santa Claus wasn't real.

"Are you serious?"

"They say never meet your heroes," I shake my head. "Listen, cake is good. It's fine. Other people love it so that keeps me in business, but is it my all-time favorite dessert? No. Though, to be fair, my all-time favorite dessert is kind of like a cake."

Gray looks at me expectantly.

"Chocolate soufflé," I say, leaning in, with a smile. "A warm chocolate soufflé right out of the oven is my favorite thing. It's so rich, so decadent, but still lighter than air. And don't tell the soufflé gods about this, but I like it best topped with a big mountain of freshly whipped cream. The soufflé is warm and gooey, the cream is cold. It mixes and gets all melty. It is the best thing in the world," I sigh.

I realize I might be drooling. Gray is staring at my mouth, hanging on my every word.

"So...you're going to make me a chocolate souffle and then make me homemade whipped cream to go with it?" The tone of his voice is a little bit incredulous, a little bit awe.

"Well, you're actually going to help me," I tell him.

The words surprise even me. As much as I bake for the rest of the world, I'm notorious for not really baking for the men in my life (except for that one). And having those men in the kitchen with me? Absolutely not. It's my sacred space that I like to have to myself. I don't even know who this Sabrina is right now. She is out of control.

I kind of like her.

Gray eagerly stands up, walking around the breakfast bar and into the kitchen with me. "Learning from the master. I like it."

I never realized how small my kitchen is until now, and with the two of us standing in the middle of it there is not a whole lot of room to move. His tall frame takes up most of the space and I have to think of how we're going to bake together without being on top of one another. Maybe this wasn't the best idea.

"My kitchen is really small," I say apologetically, moving around him to grab the container of sugar that sits on my counter in a corner. In the process, my elbow bumps into his back and in stepping out of the way, he steps on my foot. Part of me is a little embarrassed, but the bigger part of me is laughing, snorting as it happens.

"Okay, stand over here." I grab his upper arms and position him next to me. He stands still adjacent to me, his delicious warmth radiating and making my heart beat faster. "Have you ever baked anything before?" I ask him.

"Do slice-and-bake cookies count?"

"Oh, you're in for a real treat today," I say with a smile. "A souffle is not as hard as it looks. It's more about technique than it is about a recipe. Let's start with the eggs first," I tell him.

I grab an egg and quickly tap it on the counter. The shell cracks and I break it open, letting the egg fall into my hand. I spread my fingers out and let the white fall through into my mixing bowl. The egg yolk remains cradled in my palm, and I place that in a separate, smaller bowl. He watches as I do this, the same concentration as the cake assembly and floral tape. The same focus as when I talk to him about rooftops and bicycles.

"Your turn." I pass him an egg and watch as he grabs it and taps it so hard on the counter that he ends up splattering egg bits all over.

"Shit," he says, trying to hold in a laugh.

"May I?" I giggle. Wiping the egg - and sweat - off my hands with my kitchen towel, I take his in mine to help him crack and separate the egg. "What you want to do is tap it on the counter gently, but firmly, with one quick flick of the wrist."

I move his hands to demonstrate the motion, then grab another egg for him to try again.

I hold my hands above his, touching them ever so slightly, watching as he taps it on the counter just hard enough to crack it. This proximity to him is sending shocks through me, right down my middle all the way to my toes. His hands are large and strong. I can't help but wonder how they'd feel all over me.

I watch as he cracks open the shell and separates the yolk from the white with his hands. The white falls through and he places the yolk delicately into the bowl with the other one.

"Perfect."

He turns to look at me, his face inches away from mine, shining with pride. I take a breath and move over to the stove where I've placed a small saucepan. I pour cream into it and let it start to heat up gently.

"Can you grab some chocolate from that cabinet?" I ask Gray, pointing to the one behind him.

He passes me the bag of bittersweet chocolate and I add it to the warm cream, letting it slowly melt in. I hand Gray a small spatula and turn off the heat. "Stir that gently until the chocolate is all melted. Once it's done, we're going to whisk in the egg yolks and a little pinch of salt."

Gray whisks the chocolate mixture as I slowly add in the egg yolks and the mixture immediately turns luscious and rich, the chocolate flowing so thickly off the whisk like ribbons of silk. The silence is comfortable, as it always is with us, but something is charging and about to break the surface.

"So do you bring home a lot of guys to bake with them?" he asks, still looking down at the saucepan as he whisks.

"I don't bring anybody home to bake with or otherwise, if that's what you're asking."

"I was just...curious..." he mumbles.

"I don't bake for guys either," I tell him, whipping up a meringue in my mixer.

He turns to look at me and I know exactly what he's going to say. "Not even warm blondies right out of the oven?"

I roll my eyes at that. "He was the unfortunate exception."

The Sabrina that's emerging wants to take the bait and tell him he's the exception, too. He's even better than the exception. But we're in the middle of making souffle and I really want some, so I rally on.

"The trick is to not overmix your egg whites," I tell him, shifting the conversation back. "You want a shiny white cloud of meringue."

"You're so serious when you bake," he says, smiling over at me.

"I just love to do it," I shrug. "I love to talk about it and teach people about it and make people happy with it."

"I can tell."

I look at him. I wasn't planning to continue this topic, but maybe it's the comfort of being in my kitchen, and the comfort of him, and the comfort of making souffle that lets the words come out anyway. "I got into baking during very formative years when everything else around me was falling apart. It was something steady to hold on to when everything seemed to be changing or leaving.

"I loved to make chocolate chip cookies anytime I was feeling particularly blue," I tell him, reminiscing. "There is love and happiness behind every warm chocolate chip cookie straight out of the oven. There's probably world peace, too."

He smiles, listening.

"It's nice to hear when it shows; when people appreciate what I do."

He nods, whispering, "I see it."

But what it sounds like he's saying is *"I see you"* and that's a kind of steadiness I never imagined.

"We're going to fold the meringue into the chocolate now," I blurt, grabbing another spatula. I show Gray how to fold it in - the delicate curve of the spatula, the twist of your hand, the turn of the bowl. I stand beside him to help, my hands itching to touch his again, desperate for that contact.

Once mixed, we pour the mixture into the baking cups. "Now this is the best part," I say, taking my thumb and running it along the edge of the ramekin, making a little souffle moat. "It helps the souffle keep an even shape as it rises in the oven and as an added bonus, you get a taste test."

As quickly as I hold my thumb up coated in delicious chocolate goo, Gray's mouth covers it and I watch as he sucks the chocolate right off. My mouth falls open, the rest of my body screaming for more.

"You're right. That's delicious," he says, a twinkle in his eyes and a cocky grin on his lips.

My panties are absolutely on fire right now.

I turn to place the souffles into the oven, stumbling ever so slightly, my burning hot face subject to the open burning hot oven.

"Okay, now we wait." I fidget, starting to gather up the dirty dishes on the counter and load them into the dishwasher.

"Let me help you with those," he says and scoops up the rest.

We work in tandem to get the small kitchen cleaned up, maneuvering our way around each other, already figuring out how to get around without landing on top of one another.

Once everything is away, he wanders off to my living room, walking over to where I've got a vintage *Sabrina* film poster on the wall.

"Your namesake?" he teases.

"Yes, actually. It was my mom's favorite movie and then it became mine. The Julia Ormond and Harrison Ford remake is also acceptable, but this one has my favorite movie quote ever in it."

He looks at me expectantly, eyebrows raised.

"Audrey Hepburn goes away to Paris for culinary school. She's heartbroken and it's souffle day. Once it's time to present them, she realizes hers is still raw. The chef looks at it, clearly not happy with her result. A student beside her then tells her, 'A woman happily in love, she burns the souffle. A woman unhappily in love, she forgets to turn on the oven.'"

Gray smiles at that, meeting my eyes. "Very apropos."

The timer dings then so I head over to the kitchen and crack open the over door to take a peek. They are perfect, rising well above the rim of the ramekin. I carefully take out the tray and set it on the counter to cool for a minute.

"Wow. Who knew I could bake?" he jokes, sitting back down on a stool and eyeing the souffles out of the oven.

"Practically an expert," I tease as I open the fridge behind me to grab a bowl of whipped cream I had left over from another dessert.

Gray sits across from me and watches as I dollop a big spoonful of whipped cream on top of the souffle and then shower it with powdered sugar. I grab a spoon from my silverware drawer and pass it over while placing the souffle directly in front of him.

He studies me first, a look in his eyes I can't quite decipher, then looks at the souffle.

When he finally speaks, it's quiet, a little bit nostalgic. "Whenever it was my birthday, Pop would always take care of the cake. He loved to bake and would make me whatever birthday cake I wanted. It was my favorite thing, the one thing I looked forward to more than anything else every year. I always felt lost in the shuffle so being taken care of like that? I longed for it. What a wonderful thing to do for somebody. Kind of like giving somebody a little piece of your heart," he says, looking down at the dessert in front of him. "This souffle reminds me of that."

It's a compliment I didn't see coming, his words cracking me open, breaking me apart to pull out this deep hidden part of me that has been yearning to see the light of day for so long.

I look over at him, heart beating thunderously in my chest, unable to move while he takes a bite of the souffle, spoon digging into the mountain of cream, right through the gooey chocolate surface, and then directly into his mouth. He eyes me thoughtfully for a beat.

"Wow. That is...wow." He looks back down at it like he's speechless, a furrow between his brows.

"Yeah?" I practically whisper, frozen in place, the muscles in my body twitching from the desire to move and fidget, from the need to run over to him.

He takes a larger bite and watching him lick the chocolate goo off the spoon is the best thing I have ever seen. He's watching me more intently now.

"You're a surprise in all the best ways, Bri."

In my head all I hear are Liz's words like a mantra: *You can make the moves you want to make. Stop denying yourself the things you want.*

"Everybody needs a baker friend like you," he tells me and it's the push I need to send me right over the edge.

I really hope I'm reading this right. I hope this jump I'm about to take doesn't leave me with a broken heart. Or worse.

"I have enough friends," I tell him, the words tumbling out of me before I can grab them.

His spoon freezes mid-air as he looks at me. His eyes could probably burn a hole into me; I stare back. "So, I can't be in your friend group?" He says it softly, lightly like a joke, but the weight feels like a ton.

I don't want to do this again. I don't want a repeat of past mistakes. But what I didn't do then was ask for what I wanted, so maybe all I did was break my own heart instead.

You can make the moves you want to make. Stop denying yourself the things you want.

"I want more from you."

He swallows, asking, "What do you mean?"

"You know what I mean."

"I need you to spell it out for me."

"I don't want to just be friends with you, Gray. Not sure I ever did." The words spill out and I want to hide. My body is vibrating, but I'm determined to stay still, to keep my focus solely on him.

His brilliant blue eyes stay on me, processing my words, releasing what seems like a breath of relief. Then he punches me in the gut with his one-word answer. "Good."

I see him stand and walk around the breakfast bar over to me, everything moving in such slow motion that by the time he's in front of me I am a tightly wound ball of desire, just waiting for him to pull that one hanging piece of thread so I can unravel and come undone.

And maybe this started, little by little, tonight when I offered to make him chocolate souffle. Or maybe it was on the rooftop. Or the wedding. Or further back to Harry's. Or maybe even at Amelia's. Maybe this ball started rolling ever so slowly that very first time I saw him, a need building up in me until I was shaking with it.

He stands in front of me, his own hands fidgeting with a nervous energy I can feel so deeply. "I want more from you, too," he says, and those words send me careening right into the universe. He takes another step closer, leaning down slightly, his mouth inches from mine, the tension so palpable, and says, "Can I give you more now?"

"God, yes."

He kisses me, finally fucking *kisses* me, hands making their way to either side of my face. Those large hands and that perfect mouth I've dreamt of for so long. It feels like somebody flipped on a light switch and everything is so much clearer. Standing on my tiptoes, I grab onto his waist and kiss him back with all the energy I can muster. It is still not enough. He tilts my head up to kiss me deeper, his tongue decadently swirling with mine, and that elicits a moan right out of my mouth, one I didn't even feel coming, but I'm in too deep to be embarrassed. I hear a low rumble from his throat as he pushes me against the counter and I lean into it, giving myself some stability before my knees buckle.

His mouth is sinful, rich dark chocolate and sweet cream - a damn souffle seduction. Hands move down my back to my waist, holding it firmly, pushing me closer into him. Mine have taken hold behind his neck, moving up to finally – finally run them through his hair. I pull the strands with my fingers and feel him hum in approval. Our bodies are fused together, mine forming to fit his, his hardness between us.

God, it's been so long since I've been kissed like this.

Have *I ever been kissed like this?*

"Shit, Bri," he breathes out against my mouth.

I catch myself smiling as I break the kiss, taking a moment to catch my breath.

"That was better than a chocolate souffle," I say right against his lips.

He runs his thumb along my bottom lip, eyes fixated on my mouth. "Yeah, it was."

A line forms between my brows as I try to make sense of this. "And chocolate souffle is my favorite thing in the whole world," I say, speaking in a hushed tone to not disrupt the magic that I feel brewing here.

But maybe you are now, I think.

There's a silence that follows, but it's a loaded one. Like the calm before a storm. And then his mouth is on mine again, his teeth biting my bottom lip, my tongue slipping into his mouth. We are a swirling cloud of hands and tongues and teeth, moans and sighs, as he moves us out of the kitchen, making a pit stop against a wall. Gray's hands play with the hem of my shirt until he moves them underneath to touch my bare skin. It's the most delicious feeling, a live wire waking up every nerve ending. I want more. I want this all day, every day.

"Your hands feel so good," I say in between kisses.

"*You* feel so good," he tells me, fingers brushing at the softest parts of my belly, toying with my shirt like he's holding back from ripping this thing right off me.

So, I slowly reach up to take it off, pulling it over my head, tossing it to the side.

His eyes dart down, roaming along my body, making me feel more alive than I have ever felt with just one heated look. A penetrating gaze, a warm blush on his cheeks.

But then I remember that I spent an evening bike riding in leggings and a completely unsexy sports bra.

"Oh." I look down. "I dressed for the bike riding occasion, not, like, a hot make out session."

He laughs at that, a deep rumble in the back of his throat. "I don't care. God, I really don't care."

His mouth kisses across my jaw, down my neck, moving down to my chest. Every kiss is another little earthquake rumbling within me. His large hands move up my body, span the sides of my rib cage, and reach up to grab my breasts through the fabric of the bra, a stifled groan as he goes. His fingers maneuver their way under the straps, lightly teasing, caressing back and forth.

"Is this okay?" he asks.

"It's all okay," I blurt out before I realize what I've said, but his small laugh is kind and warm and the mischief that lies just below it makes me feel like a burning flame. His hands continue to make their way under my sports bra as he tries to get it up and off. But this completely unsexy sports bra is a tight sausage casing that I am awkwardly trying to fumble off my body, rolling and pulling and contorting. I finally manage to get it off and toss it as far as it will go.

His hands immediately replace it, kneading my breasts, thumbs grazing my nipples, teasing them, pinching them. It all feels so good, so deeply good, that I feel like I'm in danger of just turning into a puddle of overstimulated goo right here.

My fists are twisted in his shirt, matching his energy, his *want*, and I pull at the hem to take it off, tossing it into the pile of clothes we seem to be making on the floor. He is strong, broad shoulders and golden sun-kissed skin that I run my nails lightly down, getting to the button on his shorts, as his hips pin me to the wall.

"Is this okay?" I ask now, mimicking his own question, my hands pulling at the waistband.

"It's all fucking okay," he breathes out, a little laugh like I even need to ask the question, biting at my lip once more. But I do because I want us on the same page here. I need us on the same page.

My hand slips inside, groping him and eliciting a delicious groan from his mouth. Gray's lips continue to explore parts of me, lovingly, desperately, while I push his shorts down and he stumbles getting out of them. We're laughing, we're panting, we're like two horny rabbits hopping around my house.

"The couch," I manage to say between more kisses.

We continue kissing so deeply, walking, swaying, until we're right at the edge of my plush couch.

He falls first, keeping me at arm's length to tuck his fingers into the sides of my pants.

"Can I take these off?"

"Please do."

He pulls them down as I step out of them and stand in front of him in nothing but my underwear. Any other time I'd be finding a way to hide my body, my mind consumed with what the other person must be thinking. *Am I toned enough? Is my body okay enough?* But I stand in front of Gray and the look on his face is the only one I'll ever need for the rest of my life. Looking at me like I'm the only goddamn person that exists. Like he can't believe I'm real.

"You're so perfect, you know that?" he says, his voice deep and raspy, rough around the edges and forming goosebumps across my skin.

"I do now," I answer, my voice quiet and laced with so much desire.

He grabs my hips and pulls me close. I come crashing down on top, squealing in delight, my thighs on either side of his legs. His lips meet mine once more and they continue to work their magic, mine already swollen. I feel everything building within me, tumbles of excitement in my belly, lower where I'm now ridiculously wet.

I feel Gray's hands start to travel, grabbing my ass and then bringing them to the front, kneading my thighs with growing pressure.

Kisses travel down my jaw, my shoulder, behind my ear in rapid succession. I hear breathless mumbles that come from his mouth: "You. Me. Together like this. I've wanted it. I *want* it." Words that fill me up like a balloon. His hands continue higher and higher until his thumbs are right there between my legs.

"Is this a good enough leg massage for you?" He huffs out a laugh against the base of my throat.

"*Fuck.* Definitely."

He pauses, pulling away just slightly to look at me, eyes wild. His hair is a mess from my hands, his lips are tinged pink. His breath comes in short spurts and he looks dazed, like he doesn't even know how we got here. Maybe his expression matches mine because I feel the same way – practically naked on his lap on my couch, feeling every bit of him below me, rolling my hips to feel more.

His groan is low as I feel a slight tremor in his hands that hold me. "And is this okay?" he whispers against my mouth, referring to his thumbs grazing right between my legs, right where I want him the very most.

My body rolls forward toward his hands, and I repeat my previous words. "It's all okay, Gray."

I feel his fingers slide under my underwear, painstakingly slow, and delicately move them through my wetness, sucking in a breath as he does. He slips one finger, then another inside, and pushes them in deep as I gasp, this feeling like nothing I've felt in so long. His fingers push in and out slowly, over and over, and I watch him watch his fingers, eyes black and full of heat, the most seductive appreciative groan coming from his lips. I feel my body start to quiver with pleasure as I tilt my head back to take it all in.

"You are a goddamn wonder," he says reverently. He pulls his fingers out, the emptiness already too much, and I watch as he brings them to his mouth, licking them clean.

I sense every part of me shake, an explosion so imminent. "I need you inside me," I whisper, needy and rushed. I don't even recognize myself, my voice. These demands. I'm not used to being this vocal, but I think I like it.

His answering smile is a mischievous one, dirty and sexy. He grabs my hips once more, lifting me up with ease and setting me down on the couch, my back making contact with the seat cushions. Gray gets up to reach for his shorts, pulling out his wallet and a condom tucked inside haphazardly. Thank God one of us still has their head on straight.

He does away with his boxer briefs, tossing them into the ceremonious pile and he comes back over to the couch, kneeling over me. I take a minute to just look at him: the mountain of his hair, the scruff of his jaw, down to the muscles on his biceps, the strength in his forearms. My eyes cruise down his chest with a scattering of hair to his stomach, happy trail leading down to a very happy Gray.

He rips the condom wrapper open quickly like he's got no patience and I watch him roll it on, not wanting to miss anything. His hands find my underwear and he grabs them, running them down my legs and off. Gray comes over me, hovering just above, hands on either side of my head.

There's deep desire in his eyes, but there's a softness, too - one I've come to expect from him. He settles between my open legs, positioning himself just so, checking in with me once more as he has done this whole time. It's been a welcome surprise, something I never knew I needed: communication that expresses how much we both want this and how much we both want to be here.

I softly whisper *yes*, opening wider for him.

He thrusts in slowly, making me gasp, filling me up with a pleasure I didn't know existed.

"Holy shit Bri, you feel so good."

"I could say the same to you," I gasp again, breathless once he's in so deep. I look up and find him with eyes closed, not moving. "Okay, Gray, I need you to move now," I say, wrapping my legs around him.

"I know, I know, I just...need a second."

I don't know why that makes me giggle, but it does. And then the realization hits me that everything is fun with him no matter what. Everything is playful and fun and funny and if that isn't the best thing then I don't know what is.

Gray starts to move, eyes still closed, and I revel in his face above me as he slowly thrusts in and out. Eyes squeezed shut, mouth slightly open, the muscles in his shoulders bunching and releasing. My desire is starting to get the better of me and what I need is more, what I want is more.

I realize I must have been saying that out loud because I hear his gravelly voice break through and say, "Tell me what else you need."

Tell me what else you need, he says. Here is this perfect man asking for me to tell him what I need. And so, I swallow whatever reservation I have left in me, reach up and bring his mouth to mine again, panting against it, "Harder, Gray. I need it harder."

A curse slips from his lips before he responds, "Absolutely." And then he gives me what I ask for, making me feel like what I want matters and is deserved. His thrusts are hard and deep and all I feel is everything building up inside of me, filling up all the parts of me that have been empty for so long.

Gray bends down to kiss down my throat, nipping as he goes along. He kisses down further taking my nipple in his mouth, licking and sucking, his teeth grazing. The sounds coming from my mouth are making even me blush, but I can't rein it in. I don't even want to because all that means is that I have Gray here with me, making me feel this incredibly good. My hands run down his back, up over his arms, and right into that beautiful mess of hair. Nails scratching his scalp, fingers pulling the strands.

"Sabrina," he's chanting over and over, his eyes open and looking at me now. A piercing gaze into my eyes like he can see right through them. "This is...you are...." He shakes his head, unable to complete those thoughts.

I can't look away, the sheer intensity of his stare sucking me in while he continues his perfect thrusts into me. His fingers have joined in now, slowly working to bring me closer and closer to the edge. He's moved my legs, pushing down on my knees to open me wider to him, the possibility of me being split open from this insane pleasure very likely. I don't know that I've ever felt this. Was everything before just pretend? Have my memories been getting the better of me?

I keep my eyes on his, those dazzling blue gems, dark now like the deepest parts of the ocean, and I don't even try to look away when I feel the build up inside of me rattle and explode. He watches in awe as I come undone underneath him, grasping at his shoulders, shaking through it. He follows shortly after, tensing above me, my name falling from his lips in a gasp.

Gray collapses on top of me and we lay there for a moment, trying to catch our breaths, me trying to untangle the knot of emotions starting in my chest. There's a whisper of a feeling settling on my skin like a veil. Hope, maybe. Shock, possibly. I definitely didn't wake up planning on having sensational sex on my couch, but here we are. I feel him shift above me and he pushes up onto his hands, looking down at me, that perfect smile taking over his face and making his blue eyes shine brighter.

"Hey," he says.

"Hey," I smile back.

And then the reality of the situation slaps me in the face. We are naked. On my couch. Did that just happen? Did we just jump each other's bones? I clear my throat. I can be awkward in most dating situations, but this one is taking the cake. Probably pun intended.

"I'll be right back," he says, planting a kiss in the small space right above my collarbone. It's a simple act, but in the aftermath it feels extremely intimate and sends a shock right down through me. He stands and grabs his clothes, carelessly throwing them on while also managing to dispose of the condom. I find my clothes and get dressed, too, this part always vulnerable and odd. What was felt in the heat of the moment tends to dissipate when all is said and done. He comes back over to me and we stand in front of each other, an awkwardness starting to fill the void.

"That was one hell of a souffle," he says, making me laugh like he's so good at, making some of the awkward feelings fade.

Gray laughs with me and I respond, "You're welcome to stay for more," the double entendre not lost on me.

"I would love to," he says with a crooked smile, his hair mussed from my hands, his shirt stretched and wrinkled. And then the smile drops. "Oh shit, Bri, I can't – I can't stay tonight." His palm goes to his forehead. "Pop...I – I need to get back home."

I swallow, casually tell him, "That's okay. I understand." He doesn't owe me anything, I know this. This was some freak accident. Maybe a one-time bad decision that he's already regretting. *Maybe this is about Ben.*

"I feel like such an asshole."

"No, no. I seem to be the one that has a habit of holding you hostage when you need to go," I laugh lightly, the humor not really catching.

He shakes his head at that.

"Hey, Gray, honestly, it's fine. This was fun." As soon as the words are out, I feel like the asshole. This was fun, but it was more than fun for me.

He winces at that, but it's so subtle I almost don't catch it. "Yeah, it was fun." He grabs his phone, typing and scrolling, probably ordering himself a car back home.

I don't want to fall into this trap again, the one where somebody else leaves because I'm not what they want me to be. The one where I overestimate the role I have in this thing between us. But that open bottle that was spilling out all her desires just a little while ago is now corked up, closed so tight so that nothing else escapes.

He sighs, a deep, heavy exhale like he's been holding his breath for too long. "I really wish I didn't have to go, Sabrina. It seems to be that every night spent with you is the best night I've ever had."

I look at him so longingly, the knot in my chest growing. He kisses me once more, deep and rich and luscious, pressed against me, lingering, fingers trailing down the hollow of my throat. Then he turns to leave, the car he called for waiting for him outside my door. I walk him out and close the door once he's driven off, leaning against it still working to untangle this knot.

Shit, that was a mistake.

We've crossed over now, past the comfort zone of a friendship where my feelings stay in check. My stupid feelings never stay in check. I worry this feels like too much, too soon. I jump in headfirst and then I get cold feet.

I need to take caution; I need to keep a distance. I need to keep one foot just outside the circle so that my heart won't completely shatter when this is over. So that *I* won't break when this is done.

Because Gray and I aren't sustainable. We can't be.

Can we?

Eighteen

Gray

Holy fuck, what just happened?

I breathe roughly, unevenly as the car pulls away and takes me back home. This was just a bike ride and some beers. Some dinner, a good time. A great time, even. And then she asked me back to her place and she baked me a fucking dessert. *A souffle!* Jesus.

Why am I pretending like I didn't want this to happen? Of course, I wanted it to happen, but I thought a friendship was the safer alternative. I thought maybe she was still dealing with Ben.

What happens now? Do we keep hanging out? Maybe she just needs me to be a good time. She clearly let me know before I left that this was fun. I can be a good time; I can be fun. I can be whatever she wants me to be.

I'm getting ahead of myself here. I don't even know what she wants.

A souffle. A fucking delicious souffle. I watched her work through that kitchen and it was like a dance I never wanted to see end. All her moves, her twists, her hands that hovered over mine to guide me seemed to ignite something in me somehow. She was so comfortable there, not a second thought to anything she was doing. She moved with purpose, her face glowing in delight. And when she presented me with that dessert, expectantly waiting for my thoughts, I saw something in her that I couldn't let go of.

I would have figured out any way to kiss her, but she spoke her truth first. It's the weirdest case of amnesia – I don't even remember how everything happened, how I got up and kissed her and then we were naked on her couch, and yet I remember all of it. How her skin felt, the goosebumps that rose as I touched her. How we kissed like we had been waiting for it our whole lives. How she fucking tasted. How I realized how desperately I had wanted her and when I had her in my arms it was like learning to breathe all over again. It was like my heart started beating new.

And then watching her come underneath me? *Jesus Christ.*

The driver pulls up to the house and I thank him, getting out, and taking a big inhale of fresh air. When I open the door, I find Pop and Nancy sitting at the kitchen table playing dominoes. They both look over at me and I awkwardly wave, trying to look as normal as possible.

"Why are you guys still up?" I ask.

"Intense game of dominoes. Looks like you got some cardio in," Pop says, trying to keep in his laughter.

"Bike riding is a strenuous activity," I tell him, matter of fact.

"So is sex, Gray," I hear Nancy say. Pop lets out a bark of laughter.

My face turns hot. Am I really going to discuss my sex life with Pop and Nancy? "I'm thirty-three years old. I'm allowed to have sex."

"Of course, you are. Was it Sabrina?" Pop eggs on.

"Oh, the baker? Nice girl. She made the cake for my cousin's wedding. Beautiful cake," Nancy says.

"Did you make it romantic at least? You know you're out of her league. You need to bring your A-game."

"I – " I'm about to give him some half-assed rebuttal until I think about how we went from her baking me a souffle to sex on a couch. On her couch. Just a mess of clothes and limbs and sex...on a couch.

But she enjoyed it, didn't she? I think we both did.

And then I left. Then I stood up and had to leave.

Oh, fuck. That was probably a disaster, wasn't it?

"You doin' okay over there? You've got smoke coming out of your ears," Pop says.

"I'm guessing he didn't make it romantic for her, Ed," she says.

Pop shakes his head, a *tsk* escaping his lips. "You kids these days just want to mess around and then leave. Nobody wants to make it special anymore. Look at you, forgetting everything I taught you."

I take a seat at the table joining them, running my hand down my face.

"Well, I couldn't stay. I've got you to take care of," I motion to him.

"Me? I told you I'm as healthy as a horse! You don't need to worry about me."

"Gray, I can always come by and hang out if you need some time with your lady friend. Or for other things," Nancy adds.

I sigh, head in my hands.

"You okay?" she asks quietly, her hand on my shoulder.

"Just having an existential crisis, thanks."

She laughs. "I'm serious, Gray. I get it. You're allowed to get some time to yourself, too. You've done a lot moving back here. It's okay to take some time for you."

I lift my head up to look at her, take in her words. I nod at that.

"I'm sitting right here. And I am absolutely fine," Pop chimes in.

"Don't listen to him," she stage-whispers.

"Thank you, Nancy. I think I'm going to go to bed now."

"Nancy's better company than you anyhow." Pop winks.

I huff out a laugh, say my goodbyes and goodnights and shuffle down the hall to my room. Once in bed, I can't sleep, replaying the night on a loop in my head. Her laughter, the peeks of vulnerability I saw. I replay her moans and gasps, that breathless voice whispering "harder" against my mouth. Fuck, I'm getting hard again just thinking about it.

Pop makes a point; I know he does. She deserves better than couch sex, better than me getting up and walking out. She even opened up to me at dinner – the story about her dad, their relationship that is now non-existent. And I fucking left. What

I need to do then is show her that I can stay, that she is worth me staying. I should talk to Nancy.

I wasn't kidding when I told her that every night with her is the best night I've ever had. And I'm starting to think that if I had my way, I would see her every single night. I would bake with her in that kitchen every single night. Listen to her talk and laugh. And then I would give her all of me, worship all of her. Every single night if she'd let me.

Fuck, maybe I don't want to be a good time. I'm tired of it – being the good time, the fun. Falling in second behind somebody else. I don't know what is starting to form here, but she's starting to feel like home.

Home in my favorite town.

Nineteen

Sabrina

"You got laid! I can see it all over your face," Liz practically screams at me when we meet up on Wednesday morning. We're getting breakfast at the café, the usual banana pancakes, yogurt bowl, and coffees, when she delivers this accusation.

"Will you keep it down? People are trying to eat their pancakes, not listen to you talk about my sex life."

"You're not denying it! Was it amazing?"

"I do not kiss and tell. Thanks for asking." I sip my coffee, eyeing her above the rim.

"It *was* amazing!" she squeals, her light purple hair bobbing up and down in her ponytail. Her excitement makes me laugh.

"I...baked him a souffle," I tell her almost sheepishly.

"No, you did not!" She slaps the table. "Sabrina Moss bakes for no man."

"I did. And he loved it. And then he told me this story about how his grandfather used to make him every single birthday cake and how he loves when people bake for him. I don't even know what happened but you know how I get with those sappy stories and so I told him I wanted more from him and then we jumped each other's bones."

She listens as I tell her this story, gasping and swooning at the appropriate parts.

"I'd be lying if I said I wasn't looking for it to happen. I mean I invited the guy over and baked for him for crying out loud. But...I really wasn't expecting it to happen if that makes any sense. I'm trying to make sense of a lot of things right now." I sip my hot coffee greedily, the caffeine making me jittery.

"Mm."

"What if he feels like he's betraying Ben? Maybe that plays a role here."

"Ugh. Can I tell you how tired I am of hearing that stupid name?"

"He left almost immediately afterward, had to go take care of his grandfather. But what if he didn't?" I feel guilty as I say it. "I don't want to think that. I don't know him extensively, but still, I find that I trust him. If that makes any sense."

"Mm."

"Stop saying 'mm!'," I say, mouthful of pancake.

She sets her spoon down and looks at me, her head tilted, taking in my words. "Is Ben your concern?"

I swallow the pancake, think about her question. "I think the memory of Ben is my concern." And even as I say it, I realize how true that statement is. How the emotional damage left me so scarred that even the sound of his name makes me feel like I've swallowed lead. And yet, seeing him leaves me missing him, too.

"I believe that," she says, matter of fact. "But is Ben here your concern, Bri?"

I sigh, let it out. "What if Ben finds out?"

She shakes her head as if she was waiting for this question all along. "Who fucking cares? What do you owe him? Not a damn thing."

"Won't it be awkward?" I'm mad at myself for even asking, for even considering it. But the words tumble from my lips anyway.

"Probably. Too fucking bad for him. You don't get to dictate how your life goes because of him." Liz shakes her head. "And I know, I fucking *know,* you have been. Deep down in there somewhere you have been. But it fucking ends today. It has to end, Bri."

"I didn't realize I signed up for tough love today," I tell her, sitting quietly, letting everything she said sink in. Is Liz right? Sure, she is. It's embarrassing that she's even noticed how I've tried to make it so Ben will look at the success of my life and deem me worthy enough for his love.

And then I think of Gray, not only admiring my work but enjoying my company, enjoying *me.* He certainly seemed to be enjoying me last night. I never need to try with him, I just need to be. Being is enough.

And isn't that all I could ever ask for from somebody?

Her answering sigh softens her tone. "Talk to Gray. Get on the same page. You guys were having a good time together, no reason that needs to end just because of some souffle-induced sexy time." She takes a sip of coffee, shrugging as she does, and sets it down.

I nod at her words, a hint of a smile playing on my lips as memories of last night slip back into my mind. A souffle-induced *very* sexy time.

"Are you ready to head over?" I ask. "The Regency sent me an email late last night, asking if we could squeeze in a cake tasting this week. I told them today would be best."

"I thought you told them to stop doing that," she says.

"Camille was very apologetic about it. She was put in a tough spot, and you know I don't like to turn down cakes. We should have some tasting trays available. They didn't send any information yet, so once they do, we'll do what we can with it."

We pay our bill and head over, this familiar walk between her and I. Yellow Crocs and boots on the pavement, Liz continuing the conversation between us.

"Did you hear they renewed *The Witching Hour*? Listen to me – talking about this like I'm a fan."

"You are absolutely a fan."

"Literally the biggest fan. Unbelievable."

I laugh loudly at that, unlocking the door to the bakeshop and turning on the lights, ready to get the day started.

That warm feeling, the one I felt last night after Gray did delicious things to me, was still surrounding me this morning. Something light and almost ethereal. Glittering, but maybe a little fleeting. I feel it now, lighting me up from the inside. Maybe I really did just need to get laid. This could be the feel-good aftermath.

Or maybe this is the start of something more forming and I need to push it down as far as it can go.

We work nonstop for several hours, baking cakes and making buttercream batches, baking small batches of scones and madeleines for Amelia. I almost suggest an Amelia's break, but take a look at the clock and notice it's almost time for the cake tasting. I managed to set out some flavors from a tasting tray I had so we can work with it until I can meet the couple and get a better idea of what they would like.

I start heading towards the back office when I hear Liz coming up front.

"Hey Bri?" she calls out. "Camille just sent over the information for the tasting."

"Great. Can you bring it over?" I call back to her.

"Um. Sure," she says, an inkling of worry in her tone.

"What's wrong?"

"This was a last-minute booking?" she asks, the paperwork in her hands.

"Yeah. Something about how the couple specifically requested me and wanted to get in as soon as possible. Why? Who is it?"

A knock on the door breaks our conversation and I turn to find Ben and Monica just outside, this déjà vu most unwelcome.

I turn back to Liz who is holding the booking information, eyes wide as saucers. "Um. It's Ben and Monica."

"I'm sorry?" I grab the paper from her, looking over the information.

"Do you want me to tell him to fuck off? Cause I absolutely will."

"He wants me to bake his wedding cake? Is he out of his fucking mind?" There's a buildup of something brewing at the base of my throat. Not sure if it's rage or vomit, but I don't know if it's a risk I'm willing to take right now. So, I drink a sip of water then turn around and walk over to the door to unlock it.

"Hey Bri" he says, walking in past me as I open the door for them. Monica follows behind.

"Hey guys. Nice to see you. They just sent over your information so I didn't realize I would be doing your cake tasting today," I tell them, trying to keep the ice in my voice at a low level.

"Yeah, it was a last-minute thing, I know. But thanks for getting us in," he says.

I look over at Monica with her pale pink nails and cream purse and shiny dark hair perfectly brushed and I see something in her eyes. There's a cautious nature to them, like somehow it was not her idea to be here. I almost feel a pang of sympathy.

"Nice to see you again, Monica," I tell her. I remind myself she's not the asshole here. She doesn't deserve my hate.

I lead them over to the table where I've set out some of the trays, but I need to grab some remaining items.

"Would you like some water while I get some final things organized for your tasting?"

They both accept and I walk over to our small fridge and grab some bottles. My hands shake slightly and I will them to stop, taking a deep breath in and trying to recalibrate myself.

I walk back over to the table, sending Liz a glance, a sharp raise of the eyebrows that I hope conveys something along the lines of *what the fuck?*

Once back at the table, Liz brings over some remaining things – fillings, plates, and silverware – and helps me to arrange everything.

There's an insecurity rising inside of me, self-doubt creeping into the nooks and crannies. I love what I do and I like to think that my passion, my confidence shine through. But here I am face to face with somebody who belittled this very thing I love so much, who made me feel like it wasn't a valuable enough profession for him and now he's seeked *me* out. Ben sits at the table across from his fiancée after specifically asking for me to make his wedding cake.

The smaller part of me would like to think that maybe his feelings have changed. He sees my hard work and he acknowledges and appreciates it. The bigger part of me wonders if all he's looking for is for me to serve him again. Is he doing this to continue to keep me under his thumb? What if I do it and he still thinks I'm a joke?

"Elizabeth Garrison? Wow. It's been so long. Great to see you! I didn't know you and Bri were working together," Ben says, in a saccharine voice, but it's fake sugar. It's the charm he can put on so well.

She eyeballs him. "Yep," she curtly replies. Liz sets down the ingredients and walks away while I bite the inside of my cheek to keep from laughing.

"So, what made you guys decide to pick me for your wedding cake?" I ask.

"Ben has been raving about all the desserts you used to make for him. He says you're a great baker. And when we booked the Regency, we sat down with the wedding planner and got information on all their vendors, and you were on that list."

Monica surprises me by answering my question. She surprises me with her answer, too. One that implies that Ben liked my baking, remembered it, has now pushed his fiancée into it. I can't decipher her tone. It's very plain, matter of fact, but the look on her face is screaming something else.

"Oh. That sounds great," I reply because I honestly have no idea what else to say to that. "Okay, well, let's try some cake, shall we?" I move it along before some other nonsense comes out of my mouth.

I take a deep breath to steady myself then start with my explanation.

"Here on the platter you will find the cake flavors we offer." I point to the board set in the middle of the table. "I like to send out a small questionnaire before cake tastings so I can get a better idea of what kind of flavor profile the couple is interested in for their special day. This was a last-minute booking, so I took some liberties with the flavors if that's okay. As you taste, I can ask you some questions and then I can aim to get a better idea of what you would like or what you are interested in."

Ben smiles as I talk and Monica nods, occasionally looking at the cakes on the board.

"The fillings are here and our frosting options are over here," I tell them, pointing to the other platters set up with separate bowls. "The approach I always recommend is to take a mini cupcake, slather on a filling of your choice, add frosting, and then take a bite. Think about the flavors. Do they work? Would you prefer something else? Feel free to mix and match until you find something that works for you both. I am very flexible, so if nothing works for you today, we can discuss other flavor options. I always tell my couples, 'this is your day, and this is your cake.' So please, begin."

After I finish talking, I grab my clipboard and pen and sit on a stool with them while they taste and discuss their thoughts. Ben looks over at the cakes, going for chocolate for the first try. Monica takes a little more time to decide before settling on the hazelnut to start. They eat in silence at first, mixing and matching flavors.

Ben looks over at me occasionally, that familiar smile I always loved so much gracing his face. Then he looks over at Monica and gives her the same smile, reaching over to grab her hand and squeeze it lightly. It feels a little like somebody digging the knife deeper inside of me. I'm so lost staring at their hands that I almost miss when one of them talks.

"This hazelnut cake and chocolate ganache is very delicious," Monica says, a look of concentration on her face.

"Thank you." I give her a small smile.

"I love the chocolate cake, though. Don't you think the chocolate cake is a good option, baby?" Ben coos at her.

Her eyes meet his, a question in them. I take the opportunity to jump in – always the referee, never the bride.

"Hazelnut is a delicious option, but it is important to know about your guests and any allergies they may have. Chocolate is a classic so you can't go wrong. Sometimes I tell couples if they really love one flavor over another, they can pick it as a top tier just for them."

"Oh, that's a good idea. What do you think about that baby?" Ben asks.

Monica just silently nods, moving on to another flavor.

"You have interesting cake flavors," she says. "I've never heard of a spiced orange cake."

"It used to just be a fall flavor, but it was so popular that I offer it year-round now. It's something different, but nut allergy friendly."

"These cakes are really tasty, Bri," Ben says.

I know, I think.

"What about coconut?" he asks Monica, taking a bite out of a coconut mini cupcake that he slathered with key lime curd.

"I don't like coconut," she says. Then turns to me, "No offense."

"Oh, none taken," I tell her.

"I bet it's popular for a beach wedding, though. Maybe we could think about it for one of the tiers," he mentions off-hand.

I feel the hairs stand on the back of my neck then. "She doesn't have to compromise on anything, Ben." I look at him pointedly. *Not her laugh, not her passions, not her fucking wedding cake.*

Monica just stares, slowly spreading jam on a lemon cake, the tiniest twitch of her lips, so quick I almost miss it.

Ben nods, a tight smile in place. "Of course not."

If Ben were a cake, he'd be red velvet. Covered in fondant. Nobody likes red velvet, or fondant for that matter, they only pretend to. It's a cake all about appearances, but the inside of it, the taste of it? A mess.

We continue to talk - asking questions, discussing flavors - like this is the most normal thing in the world, when I hear the lightest tap on my door. I look over and it's the last person I expect to see right now. The missing ingredient in this nonsense cake.

Gray.

And he's not standing empty handed. He's holding coffees from Amelia's and if I had to guess, I would say those look an awful lot like Liz, James, and my regular orders.

"Is that Gray?" Ben asks, incredulously.

"Um. Looks like it." I stand and walk over to the door, unlocking it to let him in.

"Hey," he smiles and all it does is bring me back to last night. His smile when he kissed me, his smile as he hovered over me. I want to walk over and press my body right to his, press my mouth to his and fall into him.

So much for taking caution.

Then I remember we are not alone, that right on the other side of this door is Ben, for fuck's sake. I clear my throat and smile back as demurely as I can. "Hi."

"I couldn't wait to see you again." He speaks to only me and I take in the luxurious feeling of those words, of his warmth, of his presence.

"Hey Gray!" Ben yells from the table and I am harshly brought back to the present. "What the hell are you doing interrupting my cake tasting?" he laughs, but if I didn't know any better, I'd say there was a slight edge to his voice.

"Your cake tasting?" He looks over at Ben, then Monica, then me, then back to Ben. "I didn't realize Sabrina was doing your wedding cake?"

"Yeah, yeah. It was kind of a last-minute thing, you know how that goes. These cakes are awesome."

Gray looks over at me like he isn't sure how to proceed. I move my eyes to the floor. Suddenly the questions I asked at breakfast – what if Ben finds out? Won't it be awkward? – seem much more real.

"What are you doing here?" Ben asks.

"Oh," he says, realizing the question is directed at him and he needs to figure out an answer. "Sometimes, I do my work at the coffee place at the other end of the plaza. And I know Sabrina, Liz, and James need a coffee break every once in a while, so I just brought some over."

Liz comes over, grabbing her coffee and planting a kiss on his cheek. "This is awesome. Thanks Gray!" She turns and walks away.

Ben and Monica eye this exchange, eye Gray standing inside my bakeshop with my regular coffee order, and maybe wheels start to turn a bit.

"That's cool," he says, as if this is, in fact, not cool at all.

"James isn't here today," I say to Gray, wincing a little.

"Oh." He looks down at the cups in his hands. "No problem. I'll just...drink it, I guess."

"Oh, Gray," Ben says. "I got you that new client information by the way."

I see Gray freeze for a moment, a little unsure of how to respond. "Thanks, man."

"Anytime. You know I've got your back."

"Yeah. Thanks."

I feel that statement in the pit of my stomach. Maybe Gray does too, because we both manage to avoid looking at each other, me looking at the floor instead, while Gray just stands there with the coffee, nodding casually.

This is all totally casual!

Was that meant to show Ben's support? Was it meant to serve as a reminder of their friendship? Cause if I had forgotten before, I am certainly well aware of it now. I wish I could roll my eyes at how ridiculous this whole entire thing is, but I can't. I just stand and sweat profusely, silently panicking instead.

"We need to finish up this tasting but thank you for the coffee," I rush out, suddenly anxious at having both of them in the same room. I want Ben out of here, but he's unfortunately a client, so the panic has me pushing Gray away instead.

There's a little surprise on his face, maybe a little hurt, but he covers it up just as quickly. "Sure, sure." He nods and hands me my coffee. "It was good to see you guys," he directs towards Ben and Monica, waving as he walks toward the door. "I'll talk to you later," he says quietly to me.

I hear the door jingle and I turn back to Ben and Monica. "Okay, so what did we decide?"

"That's so funny. I keep running into Gray in random places around town," Ben says, mostly to Monica.

"Don't you guys talk and hang out?" I ask, curiosity getting the better of me.

"Nah, not really." "Oh. Why not?" I press further.

He shrugs. "Monica and I only travel down every couple of weeks. Between the wedding planning and his work, it's been hard to get together."

And yet, between my work and his we've managed to get together just fine.

"Do you guys hang out a lot?" he asks, and it catches me off guard.

"What?"

"You two just seem really friendly."

"Cause we're friends."

"How did you meet again?"

I don't know that I like where this line of questioning is going. "We actually met at Amelia's, the coffee shop in the plaza."

"That's so random."

"It was."

Monica sits quietly listening to the exchange, picking at a mini cupcake she's made for herself. I realize then how much I don't want him in my business, in any part of my life. He has no right. And how it seems like he's making Monica feel so small with these questions prying into my friendship with Gray.

"So, did we decide on a flavor then?" I ask, bringing the conversation back to the reason why we're all here.

"I'm not sure. What do you think, baby?" he asks Monica.

"I liked the hazelnut. The lemon was delicious, too. I'm not sure."

"Like I said, we can always talk about it a little more and schedule another tasting if necessary."

"I think we'll do that. It's so hard for you to decide sometimes, isn't it baby?" a condescending tone weaved right through it.

That's all it takes. There's a deep exhale and my words are thrown like daggers right to his face. "Don't be a dick, Ben. It's her day, too. She's allowed to take her time deciding what she wants. And you shouldn't get to sit on your ass and criticize her about it."

Once the words are out there's no taking them back. That feeling at the base of my throat was possibly rage. I tamed it, but it lingered. And if he says another stupid, condescending thing, it's going to burn even hotter.

Monica and Ben both look at me, eyes wide, but hers seem to be harboring a small glint of gratitude. Or maybe it's rage burning, too. Ben's dumb mouth tilts into the tiniest smirk before he responds with, "You're right. I'm sorry, baby," to Monica and then "You always were a firecracker," quietly, to me.

You won, I thought of Monica once. But now I wonder, *maybe she didn't?*

And when my eyes find the coffee Gray brought me, and the image of him pops into my head, surprising and unannounced, I consider *maybe I did, though.*

I walk over to the door, holding it open for them. "We'll be in touch. Thank you for stopping in today."

They gather their items and walk out, leaving me in a cloud of frustration. Liz emerges from the back just then, a shit-eating grin on her face, slow-clapping.

I roll my eyes. "He's lucky he didn't get hit in the face with a sheet tray," I say. "The fucking *nerve!* I cannot believe that whole mess just happened."

"I can," she laughs around her straw, sipping caramel cold brew. "James is pissed he keeps missing all the fun stuff."

"Oh my God. And Gray stopped by!" I motion to her cup, "With coffee!" My hands fly to my cheeks while Liz continues to laugh.

"I *know!* Bless him and his perfect timing!"

"He looked really thrown off about Ben being here. Ben looked confused, too, to be fair. Shit, I need to apologize to Gray for kicking him out like that."

"You really did kick him to the curb," she snorts.

I groan then pull out my phone to reach out to him.

Bri: Hey. I had no idea Ben would be here today. Sorry about kicking you out like that.

Gray: It's fine, I get it. Busy with work. Talk to you later.

"Dammit," I tell Liz. "This is too much bullshit for a Wednesday."

Twenty

Gray

I RUN MY HANDS down my face, stretching in this uncomfortable chair that I've been sitting on for hours. I really need a new fucking desk chair.

So, I was a little curt with the response. And after I sent it, I felt like an asshole, but I was caught off guard by seeing Ben, too. I felt like an idiot standing there with coffee while Sabrina kicked me out. I'm surprised Ben didn't even mention anything about having Bri do the cake. Not that it's my business, I guess.

I saw she was handling a cake tasting through the window, but their backs were to me. I almost didn't knock, not wanting to interrupt her work, but I didn't know what to do with the coffees I'd just ordered, so I knocked anyway. The look on her face was a mixed bag of emotions while mine was just one: *I'm so happy to see you.*

After leaving her last night, I couldn't wait to see her again so I headed out to Amelia's today and ordered their usuals, thinking it would be a nice surprise. Turns out I would be the one surprised, too. Shit, I don't even know what I was expecting. She let me know last night that *it was fun* and there I was showing up to her work like a lovesick puppy.

And then there I was running into Ben of all people, and it was probably written all over my face: I SLEPT WITH SABRINA. Seeing him there with Monica while they both curiously looked at me...I know they know something is up. It'll only be a matter of time.

But what's the problem with that?

He's engaged. Sabrina is an adult and she can make her own fucking decisions. I can make my own decisions, too. We're not doing anything wrong, and yet I feel like we're sneaking around, keeping secrets, harboring a big lie. I put my head down and continue to work until the sun sets.

It's getting dark outside when I head to the kitchen to start on dinner. I'm definitely no baker, but I do okay with cooking. Pop is in his favorite rocker, reading his James Patterson, when he peers up at me.

"Nice to see you've emerged from your cave."

"It's been a busy day," I say, a weak response and he can probably tell.

"How's Sabrina?"

"Don't know."

"Didn't you go see her today?"

"How did you know that?"

"You said you were going to that coffee place, but I know Sabrina is nearby."

"You're too smart for your own good."

"So they tell me," he smirks. "What happened?"

I sigh, sitting down on the couch across from him. "I figured I would bring over her favorite coffee," I tell him. "But she was busy with a cake tasting, so she kind of kicked me out."

"Well, she was busy. That's understandable. You can't mess with women and their work, Gray."

"The cake tasting was for Ben, my friend who I'm the groomsman for? They used to date. It was pretty serious, too, from what I understand."

"Mm. Sounds a little messy." He sets his book down on the end table.

"Yeah, I think it was."

"I mean with you."

"Me?" Am I the messy part of this equation? Am I the messy part that doesn't fit? "Why me?"

His mouth tips up at the corner, and he levels a look at me. "I know you, Gray. So, I'd say your worry is coming from the fact that this wasn't just some one-off. I think this is a little more."

I stare. *I think this is a little more.*

"You think she still harbors some feelings for him?" he asks then.

I shrug in response. Do I think she still has feelings for Ben? I'm not sure, but I do think there's a history with Ben that might be holding her back. Maybe it was holding me back. And all I feel is competition.

"I'll take that as a yes," he says.

I grunt and walk over to the kitchen. I work in silence, grabbing a box of pasta from the cabinet and filling a pot with water for the stove.

"You know," I hear Pop's voice behind me. "Relationships are hard. Especially when they're serious. Memories linger. Feelings can be very hard to let go of."

"I know that." I know he means my relationship with Moriah, the years of on-again off-again until I finally let go.

"Maybe she's making his wedding cake as a sort of closure?"

I turn, back leaning against the counter, as I look at him. "I don't think she knew about it. She said she didn't know he was going to be there."

"That sounds odd."

I nod at that. "A little. I'm just a bit confused, I guess."

"It's called communication, Gray."

"I know, but there's something about her that's making me all tongue-tied."

"That's usually a good sign," he says with a smile.

"This whole situation is making me very tongue-tied."

He considers this for a moment. "It might be a tricky situation, but in scenarios like these, I think good friends can be understanding."

I watch the water boil, add salt, and dump in some pasta. "So, I talk to him?" The sheer thought of that gives me hives.

"I would start by talking to her. She's the important piece in this puzzle, no offense to your friend." I smile at that just a little. She is the important piece and maybe I'm noticing she always has been.

After dinner, Pop and I head to the couch to watch a little TV before he calls it a night. I make sure he is settled in and I head back to the living room, turning on *The Witching Hour*, barely watching as I scroll through my phone.

I decide to look up Sabrina on social media, scrolling through beautiful photos of cakes and beautiful photos of her with the beautiful cakes, the pride shining in her eyes with every work of edible art she makes. And I compare that to the face I saw today – one where she was confused and possibly frustrated. A similar look I saw in her eyes when we were at Harry's and Ben joined us.

I know things didn't end well with them. Their relationship seemed so fraught with tension, not to hear Ben tell it. He always preferred to keep up appearances, showing off that he was okay. He was not the crazy one. I shake my head at the memory of Ben talking about his past relationships in a bar one night. The messy aftermath, the sea of women he could swim in afterwards like nothing mattered, like nobody's feelings mattered.

We'd gone out to a local bar. Pitchers of beer lined the table, loud music played overhead, and I'd spotted Moriah cozy with somebody else. Painfully close, some mystery guy's arm around her waist, her lips against the shell of his ear. Clearly, she had been ready to move on and I was supposed to just let her go.

"Just forget her, man," Ben had said. "Look around," he'd smiled. Like, *look at all the women surrounding you. Look at how easy it can be to let go, to forget. Take one of them home. You can have the last laugh.*

But I didn't want the last laugh. I wanted Moriah. And I wanted to not have to watch her climb all over a new stranger, to watch her catch eyes with Ben.

Ben never deserved Sabrina. And it makes me angry to know he had her. But maybe I'm also grateful because I can show her how she deserves to be treated, how she deserves it all.

I look at my phone in my hand, the time showing almost midnight, and type up a text.

Gray: Sometimes, when I had a long day, I would grab some food from Luca's deli and head to the beach.

Bri: I should be done by six thirty tomorrow.

Bri: If that's an invitation.

Gray: It absolutely is. Should I pick you up at the bakeshop?

Bri: I'd like that.

Okay, then. Time to talk to her.

***

By the next day, I manage to finish work early to get ready to pick up Sabrina. When I pull up to the bakeshop parking lot, she's inside, looking over notes on a clipboard. I tap lightly on the window, waving when she looks up.

She unlocks the door for me and I step inside. "Hey," she smiles. "Sorry, I just need to finish up some notes for tomorrow if that's okay."

"Of course. Take your time."

I watch her jot things down on her clipboard, her mind working too fast for her scribbles, it seems. Always so focused, so deep into her work.

"Okay, all set." She hangs it up on a wall and turns off the lights, locking up behind us as we walk out the door.

We get into my car, secure our seatbelts, and drive east. Sabrina's shop is a couple of blocks from the beach so it's a quick drive, but I make a turn down one of the more popular streets where the deli is located.

"I love this place, by the way. Great choice," she tells me as I park the car in front.

We enter the shop and the man behind the counter erupts in greeting.

"Sabrina *bella!*" he calls, coming around the counter to give her a kiss on each cheek.

"*Ciao,* Luca," she responds, making me do a double take.

"You speak Italian?" I ask in disbelief.

She laughs softly at that, just a sliver of the laughs I usually get from her. "Just a couple of words here and there. I've known Luca for a while."

"You are popular around town, aren't you?" I say, a proud smile surfacing on my face. I love how embedded into this community she is. I love how much they all love her, and I wonder if she even knows it.

The deli is small but bustling with customers. It's always been a busy spot, even when I was living here as a teen, perfect for grabbing some food on the way to the beach. There are several glass cases to the left filled with meats and cheeses that are sliced to order, along with ready-made items that they make in house daily. There are shelves of Italian products to the right – pastas, oils and vinegars, pantry staples. This place, too, hasn't changed much – its old school look endearing and nostalgic. Banners of the Italian flag hang from the ceiling, soccer jerseys and memorabilia decorate the walls.

We place to-go orders for a couple of their most popular items – the antipasto salad, a semolina loaf, some sliced salami, a hunk of fresh mozzarella, and an order of their famous arancini.

"Cannoli?" I turn to Sabrina and ask.

"Definitely," she answers. I order four and we watch as they fill them to order, dunking each end in chopped pistachios and showering them with powdered sugar once in the container. He wraps them up and places them in a bag with our other items. "Oh. *E Baci, per favore.*"

Luca smiles, a twinkle in his eye as he looks between us, and nods, placing a handful of the hazelnut chocolates in a small bag.

We pay for our order and walk out, Sabrina giving Luca some more kisses and waving *ciao* to the employees. Once in the car, she balances the bags on her lap and I look over at her.

"You really can be a local tour guide," I tell her.

"Oh, stop it," she says, a laugh escaping her lips. *Getting warmer.*

"People love you."

"I don't know about that," she answers, the blush I love so much blooming on her cheeks.

"I do," I say. "This city really is yours."

Her eyes meet mine and I see something like longing and gratitude in them, because I feel just as much, but something deeper, too – something that gets stuck in my throat, the surprise of it, the realization of it almost too much.

"I've just lived here forever, Gray. That's all."

"You've got roots here, Bri. Everybody wants roots." *I want roots,* I think longingly. *And maybe I want them with you.*

"Let's go to the beach," she says, hazel eyes on mine. "The arancini are going to get cold."

"Yes, ma'am," I reply while a small smile plays on her lips.

The beach isn't too crowded, but the sun will be setting soon. We're on a strip further down from the touristy bars and hotels. A smaller, quieter stretch filled with locals out for an evening stroll – jogging, walking the dog, dipping their toes into the water. I've always loved the beach, a perk of moving in with Pop, but I started coming regularly to watch the sunsets in high school once I could drive. It was my favorite pastime. Just coming here to clear my mind, watch the sun sink into the horizon, feel the world start to dim.

I spent a lot of time here. Sometimes lumped in with a group of friends, or girlfriends, sometimes alone. And now, with her.

I think she's my favorite company so far.

We pick a spot in the sand and I lay down a blanket I brought. Sabrina unpacks the food and lays it out between us on the blanket. I toss off my shoes, and she follows, those Crocs and socks with strawberries on them.

Equipped with paper napkins and plastic silverware, we dig in, going for the warm arancini first.

"These are even better than I remember. How is that possible?" I ask, closing my eyes to savor the flavors.

She mumbles in agreement as she chews a mouthful.

"So, what's the story behind the shoes?" I motion to her Crocs in the sand.

She huffs out a small laugh. "Liz gave them to me as a gag gift one year. Turns out they're very comfortable for working in so I guess the joke's on her."

"Is it though?" I give her an exaggerated wince that gets a loud laugh out of her this time. My favorite sound, the one I play on a loop in my head.

We try to cut the semolina loaf with the flimsy plastic knife before settling on tearing chunks and pairing it with salami slices and forkfuls of mozzarella. This is not fancy – it's simple, the kind of casual that is easy, the kind of sharing that happens with somebody you feel so at home with.

It may be the best meal I've ever had. *Perhaps only second to that night at the brewery.*

There's a comfort between us that has always been there. And even after the other night, when I worried something would be compromised, it remains. She dips her fork into the salad container, taking bites, raving about how delicious it is, and then feeds it to me.

This. I want this. So much. All the time.

I clear my throat and will the words to form in my throat, but I hear her speak first. "I know you want to ask about him, so go ahead." She sets the salad container down, reaching for another hunk of bread.

"Am I that transparent?"

"No." She tilts her head. "Maybe a little," she says with a smile. "I know that yesterday caught you off-guard and my reaction wasn't an ideal one. I'm sorry about that."

"You didn't know he was coming in for tasting?"

"I didn't. It was a last-minute booking which isn't unheard of, but their paperwork wasn't sent through to me until they were knocking at my door."

She looks out at the ocean, the tendrils that have come loose from her bun whipping around in tandem with the wind. Her toes burrow into the sand and she rips off small pieces of bread, tossing them to the birds by the water.

"How did you feel?" I ask her, trying to get to the root of it.

"Confused," she tells me, a line forming between her brows. "I'm not sure what he's trying to do. And I know he's your friend, so I'm not interested in putting you in a tough spot."

"He is my friend," I answer delicately. *But I wonder if I'm starting to feel more of an allegiance to you.*

She nods at this, then wiggles her fingers over the cannoli container, wondering which one to pick. She picks one up and takes a bite, smirking as she says, "I'm sure you've heard plenty about me. Your face at Harry's was rather telling."

I want to tell her that whatever I heard was just bits and pieces of guy talk – descriptions that they got so wrong. She was the one so in love with him that she was needy, inconsolable, unstable.

But nobody needs to hear that. Nobody needs to be shamed for their vulnerability in heartbreak. Because I do think she was heartbroken and treated poorly at that. So, I just tell her quietly, truthfully, "It doesn't matter what everybody said."

"Our breakup was a messy one, I can't deny that. And it was publicly messy which makes things worse. Our mutual friend group didn't know which way to sway, but most stayed in his corner. It's easy for people to take sides when one person is so emotionally charged and one stays quiet, letting the other implode."

She takes another bite of the cannoli, toying with the napkin in her hand, staring out at the ocean. I look ahead with her, the waves rolling up to the shore and pulling back in, a mesmerizing push and pull.

"It was a mess of contradictions, of words that had lost all their meaning. He told me he needed more, but he had once told me how he wanted us to work. He wasn't the serious kind, but he had big plans. It was just fun, but I wasn't solid enough for him." She looks over at me, shaking her head. "I wasn't solid ground enough for him. Can't hold him back. He'd told me he wanted to be with me forever, but he was sorry if he had given me the wrong impression." Her laugh is small, bitter, nothing like the joy I hear from her when we're together. "It's like the only time he was ever honest with me was when he was breaking my heart."

She finishes her cannoli, wiping her hands with the napkin. "And so, I tried really hard to become that solid ground, but it cost me happiness. It brought loneliness; there were cracks in the foundation, you know?"

It's right then that I want nothing more than to bring her to me and hold her and simultaneously punch Ben in the face. I take her hand in mine instead and she welcomes it, wrapping her fingers around mine.

"I love my work. I truly do. But so much of it consumed my life. It was the choice I made, I know that, but I wonder who I did it all for. Was it for me? For them?"

"Bri," I sigh. I move the food and shuffle over to sit next to her, our sides flush.

She lets her head fall on my shoulder, fitting right in that space. She molds so perfectly to me.

"It's part of why I said yes to you, to...this," she motions vaguely with her hands. "I wanted to find myself again. Myself without my work, myself without Ben." She says the last part so quietly, the ocean swallowing up her words.

"And did you?"

"I think...I've been very slowly swimming back to her for a long time. But this time spent with you has made me swim faster. Do you like my beach analogies?"

I laugh around a mouthful of cannoli.

"Eating arancini on a blanket at the beach? This is living," she says, the wind carrying her words – and my heart – away.

With you, it's always living, I think.

I look down at our joined hands. "That day at Harry's you called yourself 'Ben's Sabrina'. I don't want to hear that from you. You are nobody's Sabrina but your own."

She sits up straighter, turns her head toward me and her answering smile is warm like the sun we're watching fall into the horizon, turning the sky striking hues of blue, purple, and orange.

"It's been so hard to break away. Years of still feeling tied to him somehow. I've gone out on dates, spent a lot of time comparing other people to him and how terribly unfair is that? I've felt imprisoned by my feelings for him."

I swallow hard, listening to the painful words coming from her lips. I feel stupid continuing to hold her hand, foolish leaning into her like she's interested in anything else with me.

She looks at the sky. "You ever have a Ben?"

"I had a Moriah."

"What was that like?"

"We met in college, dated for years, on and off. We kept coming back to each other even though we both wanted different things. It got harder and harder every time; it got to be painful. Eventually, we cut ties and came to an end. But feelings are hard to leave behind. I get that."

"Was that hard for you?"

"Very," I tell her truthfully. *But she doesn't even hold a candle to you.*

She nods at that, her thumb lightly caressing my fingers.

"I understand that this is a difficult situation. I'm not trying to make it more difficult for you. I know certain things happened last time we went out...and it was very enjoyable," I quickly add, a light laugh escaping me. I hope it doesn't sound as pained as I feel. "But we can continue to be friends." I push the words out with force. "We can keep hanging out as friends, if that's what you would like."

She looks at me, confusion in her features. "Is that what you would like?"

"I would like you anyway I can have you, Sabrina."

Maybe I imagine the breath of relief she expels, but I don't imagine the smile, the twist of her lips like she's just heard something she really likes.

"You've got me, Gray," she says, squeezing my hand. "He has no place here anymore. Not in my life and certainly not in the middle of this."

"And what is this?" I ask, barely above a whisper.

She turns to look at the ocean, watching a little girl scribble words and pictures in the sand by the water. A wave comes in and washes it all away leaving the girl practically in tears.

"When I was little, I used to love when the water would come up and wash away whatever drawing I had made in the sand. I always saw it as a blank slate, a chance to start new again." She turns to me, "This could be that blank slate."

I take a shaky breath and let her words sink in.

"You were never a comparison, Gray. You were only ever you. And I've never felt more like myself than I do with you."

We stare at each other for a beat before she reaches over and hands me a baci. She unwraps hers and we eat them together, reading the love notes tucked inside the wrapper.

"Mine didn't even come with one! Typical," she laughs. "What does yours say?"

I hold up the paper to read it. "'I only need you and the sunset.'"

"That's beautiful."

"Isn't it?" I say, looking at her.

"Do you have to go back home?"

I shake my head. I called Nancy and was able to have her switch her schedule around and come over later just in case.

"So, you don't have anywhere else to be?"

"I never want to be anywhere but with you." It's the truest thing I've ever said.

Twenty-One

Sabrina

THERE IS A SHIFT that has happened here, fueled by the beach and Luca's arancini, clearly. I started this outing with one foot right outside of the circle like I intended, but as it progressed, I couldn't just keep my distance like I planned to. I couldn't go back to just being friendly with him. I didn't want to. Gray's words in this conversation have seeped into me, digging deep into my bones where I feel them settle. How he's always made himself clear to me, always spoken his feelings.

Maybe this right here is falling into water. One big, scary jump off the high dive, completely immersed then shooting up to the surface to break through, breathing easier.

I look over at his deep blue eyes giving the ocean a run for its money, the scruff following the shape of his jawline, that sandy hair I love to run my fingers through. He is the beach and now the tide has come in and is wiping everything clean.

My eyes find his mouth. "You know baci means kiss in Italian?"

"Does it?" he leans in.

"Tell me something else in Italian," he says against my lips.

"Told you I don't know much. Just some words here and there. I also know how to say, 'you're an assface.'"

He laughs, a sound that I feel in tandem with my heartbeat. Then he kisses me, lightly, softly, exploring, hand cupped under my chin.

I've cried here, I want to tell him. *But now I've laughed here, too.*

"I missed this," he tells me in between our kisses.

"Missed kissing me?"

He hums in agreement as he continues to pepper me with light kisses that are slowly building a fire within me.

"You just kissed me two days ago."

"Feels like forever. I've been thinking about you for days, for weeks. I've been daydreaming of getting you back into my arms like this." He says this as he kisses my lips, my jaw, the palm of my hand that now rests on his chest. The fire is burning hot now.

"Maybe you should take me home then."

He smiles, all mischief. "I'd love to."

He kisses me one last time, full of promise, and stands. I stand after him and we gather up the food containers and throw them away in the garbage can leading to the parked car. He stops me before we get in, grabbing hold of my hands to pull me close, linking his arms around my waist.

"You know when I said earlier that people love you? They do love you, because of who you are. Your success is impressive and commendable, sure, but it doesn't make you anymore lovable. You're lovable all on your own. Just the way you are."

All I can do is stare at him dazed and dumbfounded, and let the words settle in my heart. If I don't get this man to my house right now, I will faint. I will just pass out on this sidewalk right here. "I can get my car tomorrow," I tell him.

Gray's answer is a cocky grin as he opens the car door for me. He turns on some music as he pulls away, the sounds of a guitar playing through the speakers, and he reaches for my hand, kissing it and holding it the whole drive through.

This car ride is much more different, this city is much more different as I watch it fly by past the open windows. It's brimming with new life, with hope, with possibilities. The beach, the bars, Luca's deli – which I have always loved so much – shining in the glow of new beginnings. And when I stepped in there, wrapped in the familiarity of it, a funny thing happened – I couldn't remember if I had ever been there with Ben, the thought that would consume me whenever I went anywhere in this town. It was like the edges of my memories had started to blur like a dream. I wonder if they even happened at all.

He pulls into my driveway and slows to a stop. It feels different this time. I'm nervous, I'm cautious. Maybe because last time wasn't even planned, but this time is. I unlock my door, Gray behind me as I do, and I open it to let us in. Do I play the host? Do I offer to bake something again?

My questions find their answer as he closes the door behind us and his hands find my waist, swiftly spinning me around to kiss me again. His kisses are rich and hungry, leaving me breathless and wanting more. His body pins me to the wall again like last time. My back arches and hips rise to meet his, to get as close as I possibly can.

I toe of my shoes, toss them in whatever direction I can. I drop my bag on the floor, a heavy thump sound echoing.

"You remember the last time you were here, when I said it was fun?" I say to him in between ravenous kisses. "It was more than that."

"For me too," he says as his hands do what they do best - explore all the dips and curves of my body. He kicks his shoes off, the two of us leaving a trail of footwear.

"Hey Bri?" I hear him whisper against the base of my throat. My hands find his mountain of hair; his teeth nip at my neck.

"Mm?" I hum the question into his ear, eyes closed as I feel his mouth work magic on me.

"You're my solid ground."

My eyes snap open to look at him, who looks back at me with a desire that cannot be contained.

And the strings that connected me to Ben, pulled so tight, frayed from all these years, finally snap. And I'm free. Free falling and crashing right into Gray.

He takes my hand and points to the stairs. "Your room is up there?"

I nod, dazed, and he walks us up, a tight grip around my fingers. He enters my room slowly, spinning to take it in.

My bedroom is simple, but my work manages to find its way into the corners of every part of my home. My bed is dark wood with matching nightstands filled with art and photography books, notebooks filled to the brim with cake ideas, and glasses of water scattered about.

Gray smiles as he looks around then brings me to him again. There's desperation in my hands as I grab him, kiss him, but his hands are slow, deliberate. Like he's savoring every part of this moment.

He walks me over to the edge of the bed, lifting my shirt over my head slowly. This time my bra is lacy – I picked it out in vain when he invited me out to the beach, but he still doesn't seem to care. He unhooks it gently and lets it fall to the ground. Every strip of clothing he peels from my body is another layer he's pulling away, getting to the very center of me. It's unnerving and addicting, how much I want him to shatter all these parts of me that are holding back. He's pulling me out of it so very slowly.

"I want you on this bed. I want to take my time with you," he whispers against my mouth.

I lie back and he kneels above me, running his hands down the length of my body and back up again. He tucks his fingers into the sides of my pants and pulls them down and off. Then he pulls down my underwear, past my ankles and off, leaving me naked on my bed.

"So fucking perfect," he says, eyes on every part of my body, the rumble of his voice lighting a fire under my skin. His hands continue to roam, down my legs and back up. They travel down my thighs, parting them and leaving me exposed to him. "I love the way you feel." He brings his hands right in between. "Especially here."

I feel his fingers tease me gently, barely touching, and then he slides one in slowly, deliciously. A small sigh falls past my lips as he pulls it out just as slowly.

"But I love the way you taste even more."

He dips his head then, planting small kisses along the inside of my thighs, traveling up and down and moving to the other side, leaving me aching and wanting, practically begging for his mouth on me.

And then there it is. Slow and sweet at first, then hot and wanting. I arch my back off the bed, reaching for purchase, holding on for life. I pull myself up onto my elbows to watch him, not wanting to miss a single second of anything, and I practically fall apart just looking at him. The muscles in his shoulders, his back, that bunch and show their strength. The veins in his forearms as he grabs hold of my legs, his mouth not stopping for a second. He grabs my thighs and pushes them even farther apart, placing them on his shoulders as he continues to devour me like I'm the best goddamn thing he's ever eaten. It's rough and needy, messy and liberating. I hear the moans and sighs that escape my lips, feel the growls that escape his as they vibrate through me. I feel his tongue thoroughly lick me, lap me up. I feel his mouth open as he sucks.

"Holy *shit*, Gray," I moan, breathless and aching. It's all so good; it's all too much.

My hands find his hair and they run through the strands greedily, putting pressure on the back of his head to keep him where he's at. To make sure he never fucking stops.

He slips one finger inside, pumping in and out slowly, as his mouth continues to explore every bit of me. His eyes look up to meet mine and it's that look – of desire and lust and fire - that sends me flying over the edge and I come, screaming, shaking, writhing on the bed as his mouth stays on me. My elbows lose their strength to hold me up and I tumble down.

He pulls away slowly and crawls up over me, kissing my stomach, my nipples, and all the way up to my neck and my mouth. I'm nothing but a puddle of lust on these sheets, looking at him through hooded eyes.

"I love to make you come," he whispers, grin gracing his face. "And I'm going to be doing it all night."

He stands to undress, reaching behind to pull off his shirt, then unbuttoning his shorts. He stands before me fully naked and I can't contain how much I just fucking want him. With me, next to me, inside me, all over me.

"I love how you look at me," he says.

"I'm thinking about how much I want you," I tell him, the desire taking center stage again.

He grabs a pack of condoms from his pocket, rolling one on and walking over to me.

"You can have me. All of me," he says.

He kneels on the bed and grabs me, pulling me onto his lap. My arms wrap around his shoulders, hands at the base of his neck, tangling in his hair again. His arms hold me securely at my waist as he thrusts in slowly and it's just as good as the first time, maybe even better. I let out a gasp and I feel his smile on my skin. He kisses every inch of me with reverence, periodically looking up at me to catch my eyes flutter closed. Delicious shocks course through my body. Everywhere he kisses is another zap of electricity, another racing heartbeat.

This isn't like the first time. It's slow, sensual. Intimate. Like he's got all the time in the world and no rush to do anything else but be here. We rock and sway together, my mouth hovering just above his, both of us gasping, panting, sighing. He grips the back of my neck, our bodies pushing and pulling. I feel his deep, slow thrusts that roll like waves.

"I want to go slow, Bri. I want to feel every little bit of you tonight. I want you to feel all of me," he tells me in between breaths.

"Yes, yes, yes," I hear myself repeat like I don't know another word. I've lost the ability to speak properly.

He lays me down, my body on display to him as he thrusts a little harder, a little deeper. One hand grips my hip with an intensity that makes me shiver while the other moves right between us, working in slow, maddening circles.

I feel it then, a slow burning thing. One that starts in my center and burns outward, spreading like wildfire and igniting my veins. Burning hotter and hotter, completely immersing me until I combust.

"That's it. Come for me. I want to watch you fall apart, Bri."

All I hear is his deep voice speaking those words and my cries echoing into the space between us. I worry I don't even recognize my body anymore. How I can continue to feel such immense pleasure, always, with him. It never ends; it leaves me wanting more.

"Don't stop," I manage to get out. But what I really mean is *don't stop touching me,*

don't stop kissing me,

don't stop making me feel this way – like I'm the only person in the world.

And then when I'm reaching new heights, climbing until I almost can't breathe –

don't ever stop making love to me.

I come crashing down, a spectacular ball of fire exploding in technicolor.

"I won't," he speaks through gritted teeth.

Maybe he knows what I mean, maybe he reads my mind, but he doesn't stop. He thrusts into me again and again, harder and harder, until he tenses and falls apart above me, a deep, guttural moan escaping his mouth. His eyes are wild, lips are parted, he's flushed and he's so perfect.

We take a minute to catch our breaths and then he leans down to kiss me, gently, delicately, lovingly. Just like the first time on my couch, when he kissed right above my collarbone. This kiss releases all the butterflies inside of me and I want to stuff them back in, but they're out. They're out and they are fluttering at a rapid pace.

So, this is what it feels like, I hear myself think.

And down into my bones, that feeling of hope and possibility emerges again. But this time the words are there. *I love you.*

I must look shocked, the feelings bubbling inside of me causing a torment of emotion, because I hear Gray's voice ask "You okay?"

I nod quickly, casually.

"Hey. Look at me." He takes my face in his hands, looking right into my eyes, studying me. "I'm not going anywhere, Sabrina," he says.

Shit.

I try not to think of the messy ramifications of his words. *They all say that. They try to promise it. But for one reason or another they never stick around.*

"Bri," he says, barely a whisper and a shake of the head, almost like he can't believe he's saying these words to me. But he says them anyway. "I'm here. I'm...yours."

Oh, fuck. I know he means it. I know he feels it, too. And that terrifies me even more.

He scans my face. What must I look like? My wild hair spread out against the sheets, face flushed, a mountain of concern and worry lining my features. He runs his thumb along my bottom lip and nods almost imperceptibly.

He takes my hand in his and brings it to his chest, laying it flush so I can feel his heartbeat, thunderous and chaotic.

I swallow and feel something brewing. There it is, I think. The feeling that I am finally being put back together. All the cracks are finally being healed, filled in, a river of glitter and gold running through them.

I never expected him.

If Gray were a cake, maybe he wouldn't be chocolate on chocolate. Maybe he'd be chocolate souffle, my favorite thing in the whole entire world and all mine.

Twenty-Two

Gray

I wake with a start, a little disoriented for a second, unsure of where I am. And then it comes back to me.

I feel Sabrina stir beside me. I feel my arms wrapped tightly around her, hands touching warm skin. Last night comes back in a tidal wave – holding her, making her come, making her laugh, just being with her.

She threw on my shirt shortly after the first time and went downstairs, emerging minutes later with a bag of Funyuns and a pint of some whiskey and pecan ice cream that was so delicious.

"This was all I had," she'd said, shrugging almost shyly.

We sat on her bed and watched *The Witching Hour* while she fed me ice cream and we talked and laughed. *I'm yours,* I'd told her and I could tell she panicked. But I didn't want to take it back, couldn't take it back even if I tried. Those words were out and they were my truth. I was hers, so completely.

After the pint was done, she took it and the chips back to the kitchen and came back with two cups of water to add to the three already on her nightstand.

"It's my bad habit," she'd laughed.

"I could live with it," I'd told her, probably blushing a little from the words that escaped my mouth.

And then she kissed me to shut me up. Leaned in and kissed me like she was starving and I was her sustenance. She fell right into me, and I let her come crashing down, both of us falling together. "There's nobody else but you," she'd whispered to me in the darkness.

And then I moved in between her legs again, making a home there, wanting nothing more than to spend my days and nights there. She fell apart again and again, the sighs from her mouth like secrets she was telling me, pieces she was revealing. I welcomed it, basked in it. And then she wrapped herself around me and fell asleep.

Now, I look over to check my phone – not even six o'clock yet. I feel her stir again beside me and then one eye opens, surrounded by a mountain of sheets.

"Hi," I hear her smile.

"Good morning," I whisper, smiling back.

Could this be every fucking day?

A loud alarm breaks through the quiet and she wrestles with the sheets to turn it off.

"Sorry," she mumbles.

She told me last night that she had to head into the shop earlier than usual today due to the orders she needs to get ready for the weekend. I have my own business to get to, clients to consult with, but I want as much time with her as I can soak up this morning. I'm dreading having to leave.

"Are you hungry?" I ask. "I could make you breakfast."

She looks at me for a beat.

"Or we could go get breakfast?" I add in a rush. I must sound like an idiot.

"It's not even six in the morning, Gray," she laughs, light and raspy, the sleepiness still in her voice. "How about we just lay here for a little while?"

"I could do that," I smile, bringing her closer to me, her leg wrapping around my thigh.

She dozes off again, for just a little bit, her breathing becoming quiet and rhythmic. I feel the lift of her chest and the exhale on mine and I lay still, honored to be her morning comfort. About twenty minutes later, she shifts again and awakens.

"Tired?" I ask lightly.

She snorts. "You wore me out."

"You're welcome." I grin.

"Mm. I could go for a coffee," she says, still bundled in her white sheets, my fingers grazing the softness of her skin. "I could also go for a shower."

She snuggles in closer and kisses me lightly.

"Come on," she says against my lips, and I watch her get out of bed and go into the bathroom. I follow immediately.

She turns the water on and steps in, moving aside to give me room. She leans her head back to wet her hair, the water running down her back, her legs. A rich lather of soap covers her body as she massages it into her skin. I watch, mesmerized, as her hands follow the curves of her own body, lower and lower, then back up. Her eyes are liquid heat as they watch me; her mouth is mischief.

She stands under the shower head to let the water rinse off the soap. Rivers run down her stomach, her arms, and I want nothing more than to follow the path of them and lick them up. I lose the battle with my self-control and lean down, my tongue mapping a line from her belly button up to her throat. She gasps, a little surprised, and goosebumps rise along her arms at the sensation.

I kiss just below her ear, then move to her mouth. She covers me in a lather of soap, suds covering my chest, my shoulders. I'm always in awe of how she takes care of me – the simplest acts carrying the most significance. Her hands move in circles across the top half of my body. Her fingernails lightly rake along my chest, stomach, then go lower to where she takes me in her hand, groping and stroking me.

I close my eyes and feel her stroke me once more, and then again. She continues the rhythm as I look at her now, lean in to kiss her, feel everything within me start to tighten. Her kisses are getting hungrier like she's got immense pleasure building up within her. I match her intensity, thrusting into her hand.

"Sabrina," I sigh, biting her bottom lip.

"I like to see you fall apart, too," she whispers, more secrets she's telling me.

"I'd rather fall apart inside you," I laugh, something pained as she grips me tighter, strokes me faster.

"Alright then," she says, a mischievous gleam in her eye as she lets me go, steps out of the shower, and walks backwards to the edge of the bed, smirking. I turn the water off and follow her, spinning her around to face the bed once I'm there.

Last night was slow and intimate, longing. Right now, it's want, it's *need*, a desire I feel burning in me. Loose, untethered, wild. Like I'm on a ride I can't break away from, like the second I leave her house I'll be floating around aimlessly through the world so I desperately want to hold onto her as long as I can, feel her ground me once more.

Our bodies fit so well in this tangled heap - her bent over the bed, body damp, smelling like lavender. My hands run down the length of her, digging into her flesh, while my body hovers over hers, and she arches her back for more.

I reach over to grab a condom – the pile we started with slowly dwindling – and roll it on, coming back to her. I kiss the side of her neck, the spine of her back. I move my hand between her legs, slowly, slowly, slowly bringing her to the edge. I bite her shoulder, watch her fists clench around the sheets. The sounds that come from her mouth keep me hungry as I thrust in and out – slowly at first, then hard, fast, out of control.

Her body starts to shake underneath me, vibrations moving through me, and I feel like I am absolutely going to explode any second. She falls just then, an earthquake below me, and I follow, my grip on her hip so tight I might have left a bruise, but I don't know that I ever want to let go.

We fall onto the bed, side by side, panting as we come down. She looks at me then, takes my hand and kisses my knuckles softly, sweetly. More secrets, more pieces that I'm obsessively collecting.

"Can I see you tonight?" I run my fingers along her thigh.

"You can see me whenever you want."

"What I want is to see you every day." I'm a desperate man, a greedy one at that.

"Okay," she tells me, my favorite smile painted on her lips. The one that lights up her hazel eyes, frames her face, reaches for my heart and squeezes.

"Okay."

***

We spend the next weeks together as much as we can – as much as her job or mine will allow. Some nights she stays late, and I bring her, Liz, and James coffee, chatting with them about life and cake.

"So, Bri doesn't like cake and Liz never wants to get married?" I'd found out. "This bakery is run by a bunch of rebels."

"And we're fun," Liz had supplied.

"Speak for yourselves! I love cake and I want to get married," James had said.

"It's true. James is the resident romantic. Liz has a thing about husbands and *Dateline*," Sabrina had said, Liz laughing in the background.

Other nights I work through the night, keeping an eye on Pop, trying to get ahead so I can spend my free time with Sabrina. And we always have Mondays and Tuesdays which she designates as her days off.

We dressed up and went to the casino one night, a staple hangout when we were in our early twenties. She suggested we dress for the occasion so I wore whatever button-down shirt I could find and a pair of pants. She wore some strappy little black dress with heels; she looked stunning.

We spent the night playing penny slots, people watching at the bar while I drank an old fashioned and she drank some fluorescent green drink in a martini glass that she used to love in her twenties.

"What in the world is that?" I'd asked.

"It's an apple martini, because I am *sophisticated*," she'd winked at me.

"You're definitely something."

I took her home shortly after that, dress thrown on the floor, arms on the pillow above her head, heels still on her feet as I tossed them over my shoulders.

Another night we ended up at that arcade bar by the brewery playing Pac Man and eating bowls of truffle mac and cheese, laughing and competing the whole night through.

One lucky Saturday night, I finally found out about that mysterious pastelón. Liz's mother made trays and trays of it, this incredibly delicious concoction of plantains, ground beef, and cheese, and I spent the night stuffing my face, meeting more people than I probably ever had in my life. There was loud conversation, louder laughter, even louder music. Sabrina spent most of the night by my side, introducing me to whoever had opted to walk in then, but on the occasions we were separated, I found myself catching her eye from across the room, her gorgeous smile and my heart lodged in my throat at the very sight of her.

And then one night she met Pop. When we'd stayed out too late and I had to get back, she offered to bring me home, stepping in to see Pop in his favorite rocking chair with his favorite sudoku. I found myself nervous, blushing – this scenario so foreign to me. But I also found myself wanting Pop to like her, really like her, like I do.

"Big fan," he'd said, standing to greet her, smoothing out his shirt.

She'd laughed at that, something soft and bashful, but filled to the brim with gratitude as she shook his hand. "Maybe one day I'll bring some extra cake over."

She walked by the walls filled with pictures, stopping to look at each one. She took a peek outside, her eyes lighting up at the sight of the lake, serene at that time of night. She spotted Pop's open *Sudoku Everyday!* book on the table, and when he asked her about it, she'd winced and told him, "I'm more of a crossword puzzle girl myself," as he unleashed the loudest bark of laughter I'd ever heard.

And when she gathered her things to leave, she'd turned to Pop and shook his hands once more, telling him, "It was so lovely to finally meet Gray's favorite person," smiling brightly as she said it.

I walked her out afterward, kissed her senseless against her car door, as she whispered, "I can see where you get it from."

"Get what?"

"Your humor, your kindness. Just...everything about you." She kissed me once more and I watched her climb into her car and drive off. When I went back inside, I heard Pop's laughter echoing through the house followed by a series of statements that unraveled me.

"Oh, you are in trouble, Gray," he'd said first. My answering smile made my cheeks go warm. His grin mimicked mine, as his eyes turned a little glassy, and he softly said, "Gran always used to give me shit about doing sudoku instead of crosswords." He laughed mostly to himself as I took another hit to my lovestruck heart. And then, for good measure, he ended with, "She's as wonderful as I imagined she would be."

Twenty-Three

Sabrina

There are scattered piles of paper all around me on the table. Lists for chocolate cakes, almond cakes, lemon cakes. Another list for Amelia's scones, muffins, and madeleines. Salted caramel and ganache and coconut mousse, too. I am organizing some final things around the shop, making notes on my clipboard, getting ready for tomorrow. It's Tuesday night, my usual day off, but I had some extra orders thrown in for the beginning of the week and I'd prefer to get a head start on everything.

I'm trying to finish up quickly, my brain already fried from all the paperwork today. I'm ready to go home, to talk to Gray, maybe see him tonight. We've spent weeks together, my own whirlwind romance, and he's still here. *I'm not going anywhere,* he'd said to me. The words that have played in my mind on a loop, worry seeping into the corners like the other shoe is about to drop.

If I was keeping one foot out of the circle before, I'm not sure where the circle stands now. My feelings are no longer in check. They haven't been for a while. Not since that souffle night. Or the night at the beach. Not since the wedding crashing and the rooftop dancing. If I'm being honest with myself, it's been a slow progression to this.

The whisper that started that night after the beach – the *love* – now bouncing around my heart, ricocheting against my bones. The bold, almost terrifying, feel of it whenever I'm near him.

These have been the best weeks of my life.

I even got to meet his grandfather on Sunday night. I smile now, reliving the moment. He was funny and outgoing, no nonsense. But he was kind and welcoming. Another Gray.

I lock up behind me and turn towards the parking lot, phone in hand about to text Gray that I'm done for the night.

"Hey," I hear a familiar voice say.

I stop and look up. "Hey."

Ben stands leaning against his car door, a sight I've seen so many times before.

"Let's take a ride," he motions to his car, this dance an all-too-familiar one between us. This isn't his dad's Cutlass he used to take us out in when we were seventeen.

This isn't even him at twenty-two, at my doorstep asking for another chance. This is...strange. *Why am I not telling him to fuck off?*

It's just us, and somehow that has always been much easier to handle.

The thought of Gray stops me briefly. It should absolutely be more than enough to dim the appeal of this odd proposition, but I find myself drawn to this. I find myself wanting to just get in one last time. The elusive closure I've been longing for.

A goodbye.

"Alright," I say. And I get in.

We drive past local shops, new and old. Past the high rises being built high above New River, some with beautiful intricate construction, others simple and efficient.

Our car rides were always mostly silent. Like we both enjoyed the comfort of the quiet among us, never needing to fill the space with constant noise and conversation. Sometimes we would talk, share secrets, laugh, but most of the time these car rides were a way to take a breath after a long day. A way for me to see the real Ben – or so I thought. The one nobody else got to see, the mask off. And I felt free to be me – as me as I was then with him around. I could let my hair down a little, too. I could aim to be a little more than *just enough,* not quite *too much.*

I watch him drive and I'm hit with a pang of *I miss this* – that nostalgic craving for simpler times, easier days. Those years when there were no responsibilities to tend to, nothing else to concern myself with. It was just us and quiet drives. The rest of the world didn't exist, and I could exist just like this, in this bubble with Ben.

Concern shows on his face now and I can tell something is weighing heavily on his mind.

I turn to him. "How's it going?"

He looks over, shrugs, gives me a small smile that doesn't quite reach his eyes. He looks ahead once more and in a quiet voice tells me, "I think Monica is going to call off the wedding."

Everything screeches to a halt.

"What? Why?"

He shakes his head slowly, unhappiness lingering in his eyes that I have to keep from trying to comfort. Seeing him like this, in such sadness, makes me realize that underneath it all he is a person with feelings. For so long, he was villainized in my head – a caricature of my anger and resentment, but he's human, too.

Maybe this doesn't have to be goodbye. Maybe we can figure out a way to be friends.

"She, uh..." he scratches his jaw. "She thinks I'm not over you."

My jaw drops to my lap. *What the fuck?* Okay, maybe not friends.

"Maybe she has a point," he shrugs again. "Maybe she could see how I've missed you. You know you were always the one for me, Bri."

What the fuck?!

No. No, I do not know that I was always the one for him. My heart is starting to beat faster, the panic taking center stage. He reaches over to grab my hand, this act also familiar in how many times we used to do it in our drives. But this time it doesn't feel like warmth and butterflies, it feels wrong. I immediately pull my hand away like I've been burned. All of this feels so confusing and wrong.

"Ben, forgive me here, but what the fuck are you talking about?"

He laughs a little at that. "I know it sounds out of left field, but you and I – we've always made sense. I've always loved you, you know that."

I know that?! My eyes widen, my breath comes in short spurts. "You realize you broke up with me, right? You realize the hell of a break-up that we went through? And you've always loved *me?*"

The rage is rising up to join the panic. I might throw myself out of this car if I don't calm down.

"I – "

"You what? Decided you were going to come back into town, plan your wedding here, ask me to make *your wedding cake*, and then tell me that you still love me? Are you out of your fucking mind?"

"I'm proud of you by the way. You've accomplished a lot here," he says then. It feels like a slap in the face. Like too little, too late. It feels like longing in the worst way. All these things I've wanted to hear from him for years and now he's thrown them at me in a span of ten minutes. A grenade of words exploding right in front of me, and I'm stuck dealing with the shrapnel.

"You don't get to do this to me now, Ben," I tell him, my mouth a hard line, quivering, the tears threatening to fall. "You don't. Where were these words six years ago? Eight years ago?"

"I was stupid, Bri. I messed up." His voice might be pleading, but I'm not even sure anymore. "I was so busy with my own things, worried about everybody else. I didn't even realize what I had until I lost it."

I roll my eyes so hard at that, an exasperated huff out of my nose. "You know what? It doesn't even matter." Six years ago, eight years ago, now. The words that I longed to hear then are just nothing but pandering now. Nothing but narcissistic desires because he can't have me.

He cannot have me.

He wasn't mine; he never was. He always had one foot out the door, looking for the next best thing, while I hungered for all of him, settling on the scraps I got.

One night, many years ago, we'd been out driving around town and we found a small park nestled in a residential neighborhood – a pathway leading to a small playground and some benches. We got out and sat on one of the benches, looking up at the stars that covered the night sky, eating our Taco Bell haul we'd picked up earlier. He'd looked over at me, smile on his face, and said, "I love you, you know that?" He said it as casually as telling somebody *"I love pancakes"* or *"I love this movie"* – a simple statement, some commentary almost void of emotion. But he'd said those words to me, the very first time he'd said them to me. It's a memory, a deep feeling, I carried around with me for so long. And for what?

Maybe he did love me, but he did so conditionally. And I loved him – whatever I thought love was at the time, anyway – but it was a love that would always end in heartbreak no matter how many times the story was written.

"You lost it, Ben." I look at him, eyes glistening, face probably red with anger. "It's too late for this. It is too late. I don't know what game you are trying to play, but this between us is done."

He nods but stays silent.

You don't get the girl this time. You get to watch her walk away.

"Can you take me back to the shop now?" I cross my arms, sit still in the passenger seat, looking out the window at this town. This town that was so full of life and love and hope and right now I want to burn it all down.

When he pulls into the parking spot, I unbuckle and get out. "Good luck," I manage to tell him. He's lucky he didn't get a *go fuck yourself.*

"Hey Bri," he calls out. "I'm sorry."

I feel the weight of those words like lead, but it's then that I realize, really realize, the truth. *No, you're not,* I think.

I reach into my bag for my own car keys when I hear footsteps shuffling towards me. I look up and see that it's Gray holding coffee, confusion on his face. He looks at me and then at Ben's car, the one I just got out of with Ben in the driver's seat. Back and forth once more.

"Hey. What are you doing here?" I ask, like I've just been caught doing something I shouldn't be doing.

I hear Ben's voice through the driver's window. "I knew something was going on between you two." The tone is resentful, bitter, uncomfortably familiar as he keeps his eyes on Gray.

"What's going on?" He addresses both of us.

"Nothing. I was just leaving. Good luck to you both," he says and drives off.

Gray turns to look at me. "I thought you were still working so I went to Amelia's and figured I would stop by. I sent you a text." His eyes narrow, "What was that?"

I don't know how much to say, but I opt to go for truth, something that has served me well with him so far. "I was closing up the shop and he was outside, asked if I wanted to go for a ride. It seemed like something was weighing heavily on his mind, so we went for a drive."

"Are you best friends all of a sudden?" He's trying to keep his tone casual.

"We have a history, Gray," I tell him, exasperated from tonight already.

"You're right. Sorry."

"He...uh, he told me Monica is thinking about calling off the wedding."

Gray's eyebrows shoot up. "Did he tell you why?"

I clear my throat. How the hell did I get mixed up in this predicament? "He's claiming Monica thinks he still has feelings for me."

Gray's answering laugh is bitter, and it catches me off guard. "Of course, he does."

"What?"

"And I'm sure he told you, too."

"I told him he was out of his fucking mind if that means anything," I say. "It was...so bizarre. So ridiculous. Saying all those things to me..." I trail off.

"Was it ridiculous? Or were you happy to hear it?"

"Excuse me?" I gape at him. Just yesterday Gray and I were together, happy, and now he stands in front of me debating my intentions. The past hour has been a total clusterfuck.

"Why even get into the car with him, Bri?"

Because I wanted closure. Because I wanted one more car ride. Because I thought maybe we could be friends. "I don't know," I say instead. And I feel terrible once I do.

"I want to be your front and center," he says.

"You *are*." I hold my ground, keep my eyes locked on his.

"Am I?"

"*Yes*," I tell him. "Where is all of this coming from?"

He runs his hand down his face and lets out a big pent-up breath. His hand finds his chest, rubbing at the center of it with his palm. "I want all of you Sabrina and you are holding back. I know you panicked that night at your place. You've got one foot out of this while I'm here, all in, waiting for you."

"There you go with assumptions again, Gray." I throw my hands up, frustrated that he thinks he can tell me how the hell I feel. That he can negate or create feelings for me. "I'm allowed to panic. It doesn't mean you don't have me. I'm right here!"

He shakes his head now, like he's not even listening to what I'm saying. "*I* want all of *you*. And if I can't have that, then I can't do this."

I am fumbling over anything that is trying to come out of my mouth. I grab onto the anger again. I grab onto whatever I can because I feel this slipping and I don't know if I'll survive it if it does.

"What do you want me to say? That I still have feelings for him? It's not the truth, Gray! What are *you* so scared of?"

"I want you to tell me that you're done with him!" he practically shouts, eyes wide at his own outburst. "But maybe you're right. Maybe I am scared that I will always be second best to him."

"Stop – "

"Because while you were waiting for Ben to come around, there was somebody right in front of you. Or was I not good enough?"

"Don't you – "

"You talked about how you never felt good enough and then you stand here and make me feel the exact same way."

I'm crushed at those words, crumbling slowly, the weight of tonight a burden I can almost no longer bear.

He's not letting me get a word in. So, still fumbling over these stupid words forming and trying to make their way out of my stupid mouth, I yell it out.

"Ben!" I freeze, realizing what I just said. A shot right to his heart and his face shows it.

The second I say it I wish I could take it back. I wish I could go back in time to five minutes ago, unscramble my stupid brain. I wish I could go back to thirty minutes ago and not even get in the fucking car with Ben. But hindsight is always 20/20, isn't it?

"This is coming out all wrong! Listen to me!" The tears are threatening again, balancing on the edge, ready to tip over and flood my cheeks.

He lets out a breath slowly, resigned. "Ben has no place here, but he is still here."

I flinch at those words. "Gray, please – "

"He doesn't deserve you," I hear him say, so quietly. "He never did."

"I know that."

"I don't think you do," he says, shaking his head. I stare back at him, unsure of what to say.

The silence between us is deafening, a void that could very well swallow us up. A long stretch of it that is taking me farther and farther away from him.

He sighs, something sad and quiet, and speaks. "I want to do this with you. I want to spend my time with you, and I want to watch you bake your beautiful cakes and then I want to bring you home and make love to you until we're so tired that we fall asleep watching *The Witching Hour* with seven glasses of water surrounding us. Because I love you, Sabrina."

The tears fall then, waterfalls down my cheeks. My heart beats furiously in my chest, louder and louder, like it's about to take off running and the only direction it wants to go is straight to him. It's the best thing anybody has ever said to me and it's the most heartbreaking, too, because it sounds a lot like goodbye.

"I love you," he repeats it, my heart swelling like it might burst.

I love you, too, I will myself to say. But the words are lodged in my throat, stuck behind a monsoon of tears and heartache, trapped behind fear.

He looks over to the parking lot then back at me, a mountain of sadness and hurt on his face.

Don't leave don't leave don't leave.

"I'm so sorry," he shakes his head, "But I need some space right now." He turns and walks away.

They always say they won't leave, they try to promise it, but for one reason or another they always do. I am so tired, so very tired. This, right here, is the last fight.

I collapse on the pavement and sit in the silence.

Twenty-Four

Sabrina

I muster up the energy to drive home and once I get there, I hear my phone ping again. It was going off the whole drive home. I looked over once, hoping it was Gray, but it was Liz. I read the latest message.

Liz: Where are you?

Bri: Elbow deep in self-sabotage. Where are you?

Liz: Coming over with ice cream.

I throw my things down on the floor, trudging over to the couch, sinking into the cushions. If only they could swallow me up. There's a knock on the door shortly after and I hear Liz open it to let herself in.

"That was quick," I call out.

"I was at Scoop." A fancy ice cream shop that opened a couple of blocks from my house. Jeff must be on shift. I know James was working late tonight. She helps herself to a glass of water, grabbing spoons in the kitchen before coming over to me.

"Thought you'd be with Gray tonight," she says with a smile, a little singsong.

"Me too," I reply shakily.

She notices my face then. "Hey, what's going on?" My eyes are red and puffy, a mess from crying.

"Where the hell do I even start?"

"How about at the beginning?" She sits down next to me, handing me a spoon.

I take a deep breath, will myself not to cry. "Ben was waiting outside of the bakeshop when I closed up," I tell her.

Her eyes go wide as she takes the lid off the pint. "Go on."

I tell her about the car ride and Monica wanting to call it off and Ben telling me he missed me after all these years. Liz just responds with variations of "holy *shit*" and "that *motherfucker.*"

I tell her about Gray being there when Ben dropped me off. I tell her about our fight. She listens, engrossed in the story, taking occasional sips of water.

"He was throwing all these things at me, and my brain was scrambled eggs, so when I went to get a word in, I called him Ben."

Liz spits her water out, the spray coating my face.

"Honestly, this seems about right for the night I've had." I wipe my face with my shirt.

"Crap! And then what happened?"

"He told me he loved me."

She chokes on the sip this time.

"Stop drinking water, Liz."

"Sorry, sorry!" She sets her glass down on the table.

"He told me Ben doesn't deserve me."

"That's the fucking truth."

"I know."

"Do you though?"

"Why does everybody keep saying that?"

She takes a breath, quiet for a minute.

"There was a feeling when Ben was telling me all those ridiculous things – one where I felt like maybe I finally won," I say. "I got the words I wanted. I got the love I thought I wanted."

Liz's eyes are kind, sympathetic, as she listens.

"I could walk away from him and break *his* heart this time," I tell her, almost ashamed to be feeling so vengeful and petty. "But it felt so wrong. It felt so, so wrong. Like, what game is he playing? Holding emotional bullshit over me like that?" I feel the anger build up in me again. I dig out a spoonful of ice cream – lemon mascarpone cheesecake – which is cold and bright and *dammit,* so good.

"Then in the aftermath, Gray told me he loved me. And that – oh my God, *that* felt like everything I had been waiting for my whole life." I start crying again, digging out more ice cream, trying to eat it while I'm a blubbering mess.

Liz cuddles up closer, arm around me.

"Am I the asshole here?" I ask.

"Should we ask reddit?"

"I'm serious, Liz. Why the hell did I get in the car?"

"I think you know the answer to that."

My answering sigh is heavy, deep, tired. "You know, it didn't matter what the question was, the answer was always yes. And it was always yes in the hopes that one day Ben would love me. That he would look at me and finally see how good enough I am for him, and he would *love* me."

Liz squeezes my hand. "Nobody will ever be good enough for him. That's what it is. And what a lonely, miserable life that must be."

I nod at that, finally seeing it. My fingers fidget with the hem of my shirt, twirling in the fabric. "Have I been chasing the ghost of something?"

"I think...the real question is were you so terrified of your feelings for Gray that you felt like it would be easier if you pushed him away?"

"I didn't mean to push him away."

"Of course not. It wasn't intentional or consciously done. Self-sabotage rarely is." She looks at me pointedly.

"I love him," I say, voice quiet and shaky like it almost doesn't have the strength to say such powerful words.

"I know."

"You do?"

"It was pretty obvious." Her small smile is kind, comforting as she eats the ice cream. "You are a brilliant light, and yet he made you shine even brighter."

We eat spoonfuls in silence, sitting in the discomfort of everything that has happened tonight. My mind is reeling, trying to make sense of it all.

"How did I get stuck in the middle of this nonsense, Liz? I am not special enough for this!" I huff out a laugh at my own joke, but I'm not sure that it even is one.

"Stop it. You are worthy of love, Bri."

I shake my head, wanting to fight the words she is saying to me, lip quivering.

"Okay, let's talk about worth, Sabrina." She puts her spoon down, sitting up straight, looking right at me. "You are worth more than what others think of you. You are worthy *despite* what others think of you. Though, really, the only person here *not* worthy of you and everything you have to offer is Ben. You, Sabrina Moss, built a business, built a *life*, with your hands and with your heart. You built this from sadness and grief and turned it into happiness and love. Don't you ever forget how strong you are. And you know what? Take away all of it. The shop, the cakes, the fancy magazine write up. You, in all your beautiful, imperfect human glory, are worthy of love. You are worthy of *everything*."

Her words seep into my veins, down into my sad, sad heart. Didn't Gray say something similar to me once? I'm lovable just the way I am.

"That has always been the battle, hasn't it?" I whisper, one lone tear running down my cheek.

Liz's answering nod is small. She puts her hand over mine again, squeezes just a little.

We finish the pint of ice cream in silence, channel surfing, sprawled out on the couch. Soon after she heads home, to my insistence, and I sit alone in my house, restless, angry, and heartbroken.

I fumble with my phone, the desire to just talk to him, to just listen to his voice on the other end of the line a force within me that I'm struggling to rein in. But I can't reach out to him right now. I have no right after I hurt him like that. After he asked me for space.

My breath is a heavy thing as I pace around my house. And because I am a glutton for punishment, I decide to make a souffle. Maybe to bring a piece of Gray back to me. Maybe in the hopes of it lifting my mood.

I work in a fog, going through the motions. My kitchen suddenly feels so big, too spacious, like it needs another body in it. My house is too quiet, missing personality, missing somebody else. I sit on the stool, staring at the wall for what seems like hours. Suddenly I remember the souffle, running to open the oven door.

I had forgotten to turn on the oven.

Twenty-Five

Gray

"I thought you were going to bring me some of that fancy coffee," I hear Pop say as I step into the house. He's at the dining room table, tinkering with an old watch.

"Sorry," is all I manage to respond.

"You alright? Looks like you've had a rough night."

"That's an understatement." I sit at the table across from him.

"What did I miss?"

"Sabrina and Ben out for a car ride."

He peers up at me over the rim of his glasses. "And?"

"What do you mean 'and'?"

"And then what?"

"I caught them in the act." Pop raises an eyebrow.

"Well, I caught her getting out of his car."

"Assumptions, Gray," he says in warning.

"We…had an argument about it." I scratch my forehead.

Pop listens quietly, still tinkering with his watch.

"I told her I wanted to be her front and center. That I didn't want to be second to him." I fold my hands together in front of me, white-knuckled, needing to grip something.

"Mm."

"And then she called me Ben."

"Ouch."

"Yeah. Ouch," I say, the bitterness still in my tone. "And then I left." *Again. I left her again.*

Pop is quiet for a long time, small tools taking turns in his hand as he twists this way and that, occasionally looking at me while I sulk like a sixteen-year-old.

"You remember the first time you came to live with me?" He sets the watch aside and looks at me, hands clasped in front of him, mirroring mine. "You were so upset. You didn't want to show it, but I saw it. You were angry. You felt so left behind. I couldn't blame you."

I sit still, listening.

"Do you remember what you told me that first night? You said, 'Pop, I'm just tired of being moved around. I want to feel like I belong somewhere.' And from that day, I made it my mission to make you feel like you absolutely belonged here."

"You did," I tell him quietly.

"That's good to know." He takes a breath. "I can't change what happened with your mother. I know she loved the open road and change and new scenery. And she ran any chance she could. I always told her she can't run from herself..." he shrugs, but I know it always weighed heavily on him – worrying about his daughter, hoping there was a way to maybe make her stay this time. "That doesn't mean that everybody else that comes into your life will push you to the side. There are good ones out there that will make you feel like you belong. You just have to trust them enough to stick with you. It's a process. Everybody comes with their own baggage, their own burdens. We all have our own responsibilities to tend to, but those that matter will always make space for you."

"Like you?" "

Sure, like me. But like Sabrina, too." He looks at me, makes sure I'm still listening. He knows I am.

"I don't know, Pop."

"You probably do. She's got a history with this Ben guy. It's a burden, at least it sure as hell sounds like it."

Tell me about it.

"Could she have been looking for your trust?"

I stare at him, heart beating out of my chest as I realize I probably fucked up. Her life has been nothing but people leaving. Of course, she wanted me to stay. She deserves somebody that will fucking stay. But I was focused on my own anger, my own disappointment. I don't think I was even listening to her.

"Aren't my feelings valid?" I ask quietly, looking down at the table.

"They absolutely are."

I run a hand down my face. "I might have been an asshole."

"Perhaps."

"But she didn't exactly make a great choice either."

"I can't answer for her actions. I can only say that I think this deserves a longer conversation."

"I told her I needed space."

"That's fair. So, take the space you need."

"And then what?"

He shrugs a little, picking up his watch. "And then you decide if you want to see her again."

I swallow, my throat filled with razorblades. A sharp pain sits in the center of my chest that won't let me breathe. "I miss her already."

"Then, I think you need to go after her."

"I told her I loved her," I say, almost sheepishly. The words came rolling out of me at full speed and there was no way I could stop them. They'd been stuck in my throat for what seemed like weeks, and I chose tonight of all nights to throw them at her.

He peers at me from the top of those glasses again, the smallest smile turning up at the corners. I sit with him while he finishes working on his watch, not able to turn off my mind.

Maybe, for starters, what I need is some sleep. I say goodnight to Pop, getting up to head to my room. His voice stops me then.

"Hey Gray," he speaks softly. "Your mother does love you. Just want you to know that. I know you felt tossed to the side. She chased so much in her life, but she always wanted you there with her. It wasn't what you needed, I know, but...we're all flawed. We show our love in different ways. Don't let that stop you from anything. Love deeply, Gray. Always."

I swallow around the lump in my throat.

"And, in case I never told you this, you healed me too. After Gran...well, you know."

"Christ, Pop," my voice shakes.

He reaches for my hand, eyes studying me, head nodding slowly. "I'm okay, Gray. I know you feel some sort of obligation to watch over me, but I'm alright. I can handle myself. You'll never be rid of me. This move..." he hesitates, then finishes. "It was about you."

I want to tell him he's wrong. I want to tell him that I'm here because he needs me. But maybe, I'm realizing, the only one that needed anything was me.

"I love you Gray, I always will. But you've got a life to live, too."

It's been a long time since I've cried and right now my eyes are fucking burning. "I love you, too, Pop."

"And maybe give your mother a call." He smiles at me then, reassuring and strong.

I walk to my room and close the door, falling face first onto my bed, stifling the tears that will come no matter what. I don't even bother to get undressed.

***

"Hey mom."

"This is a nice surprise," her scratchy voice over the phone harbors evidence of an early morning.

I woke up early, tossing and turning most of the night. I was too hot, too uncomfortable. My body ached in places I didn't even know it could ache.

"I was thinking...when would be a good time to come see you guys?"

Her silence has me almost worried I've lost the call, but then I hear her, quiet, hesitant, but her joy is pouring into me through this phone. "You can come whenever you'd like, Gray. We'll make the time."

I clear my throat. "How about next weekend?"

"That would be great." I can picture her smile now, and I'm surprised by how much I miss it, miss her.

"I miss you, mom." The words roll out like a freight train.

There's a hitch in her breath, a sniffle like she might be crying. "I miss you, too, honey."

I manage to find a cheap flight that will have me home by Sunday afternoon and take one long stabilizing breath in and out. A hug from Pop for bravery, a rub of my back from Nancy for encouragement, and my two feet guiding me not home, but to a place I have long since forgotten.

When I arrive at her house, she greets me outside standing on her porch, arms thrown open wide to welcome me. We have the same smile. She envelopes me into a hug, my muscles have kept their memory of them – strong hands that squeeze at my shoulder blades, thin arms that wrap around.

Dave comes up behind her then, greeting me with a handshake and a warm demeanor. I've always liked Dave and I'm happy to see them together like this, side-by-side, arms wrapped around, holding each other.

Their house is quaint – steps leading into a living room with a fireplace, a small kitchen off to the side, a deck that holds some plants. "I've been trying my hand at gardening," she tells me. "It's been very relaxing."

She is cautious with me, talking slowly, taking her time. It's been so long since we've been together like this, and I've never seen her house here.

"Are you hungry?" she asks then. "I could make something for us. Or we could go out to eat. There are some great places nearby."

I smile at that, digging up the memory of Sabrina from when I offered to make her breakfast.

"I'm not very hungry, yet. But we can stay in, I don't mind." Her refrigerator door is cluttered with postcards and magnets, souvenirs of states she's visited or lived in. And pictures of me – school pictures as a child, pictures of me and Pop when I was older, my college graduation, a more recent one from right before I moved back home. My life in pictures displayed in my mother's kitchen in a house I've never even seen.

"Do you want a beer?" she asks me later, the sun starting to set.

"Oh. Sure." Maybe it will calm my nerves.

We take a seat outside on the deck while Dave starts up the grill. She's close to me, speaking quietly, a conversation for just the two of us to hear.

"I'm sorry for how…sparse I've been the last couple of years," I tell her, twisting the bottle back and forth with my fingers at the neck.

"You don't need to apologize for that, Gray." Her eyes are kind, but sad. "I should be the one saying sorry. I should have said sorry to you a long time ago."

She had, the memory replaying in my mind. When it was decided that I would stay and live with Pop, she had quietly murmured, under her breath, how sorry she was.

"It took me a long time to realize it, to see how I hurt you as I chased the things for myself," she continues. "I never saw it that way. I thought you were okay. I did what I could, kept us afloat as best as I could, and I wanted you with me. You kept me strong. You kept me going. And then you decided to stay with Pop and everything I thought I knew fell apart."

"Mom..." I start, but she keeps going.

"I wanted you here so we could talk about this, so you could understand that I never meant to hurt you, Gray. I would never," her voice breaks, her eyes are pleading.

"I know that," I say quietly, my heart cracking just a little more.

Her hands fidget. She clasps them together, wrings them once, twice.

"Are you nervous?"

She looks down at them, laughing softly, nodding slowly. "I'm nervous to tell you this."

I raise my eyebrows, wait expectantly.

"Dave and I...we're getting married."

It's only the first day and this whole trip has already been a myriad of unexpected twists. My heart pounds in my chest, so I take a large gulp of my beer.

"It's time to stay in one place, to settle in." She hesitates a little, takes a sip of her wine. "I want to be comfortable somewhere for once. And I want that with Dave." She looks over to the grill where he stands, flipping steaks. "I'm sorry I couldn't give you the things you needed then. I'm sorry it took so long for me to look inward. For me to come around."

"I'm glad Dave could be that for you." The words feel odd in my mouth, too heavy for my tongue, but as difficult as it is to push them out, I mean them.

"This isn't just about Dave. This is about you. This is me asking for another chance."

I look at her for a beat. Her mouth is set in a firm line, her eyes show signs of worry now, but I think she's hopeful. There's a glow on her face, one I haven't seen in a very long time. One that makes me hopeful, too.

"I want us to have a relationship, Gray. A stronger one. And maybe that starts with me."

My head is swimming with information that I'm still trying to make sense of, but the impulsive answer I find myself giving her is the most honest one I've got in me.

"Okay," I whisper.

"Steaks are ready!" I hear Dave call out, bringing them over to the table on a platter.

She leans over then, a big warm smile gracing her face, eyes glassy, as she grabs and holds my arm. "I'm so glad you're here," she tells me, and I feel the weight lift, just a little, for the first time in weeks.

We spend dinner lost in conversation, the two of them talking about their life the past couple of years, talking about their plans for the future. I listen, intently, and watch how easy it is between the two of them. How she reaches over, links an arm with his, and he smiles at her like she hung the moon. "Sherri is the light of my life," he gushes, looking right at her.

It stirs up memories in me, ones I am trying to push to the side, at least for the time being, but when Dave leaves us alone again to talk after dinner, I find my mom looking over at me, a small smile pulling at her mouth.

"What made you decide Dave was the one?" I ask her, surprising even myself.

Her breath in is deep, her breath out is slow and thoughtful. "It wasn't any one thing, more like a combination of them that slowly built up over time. A lot of it was in how he made me feel...like I could do anything, and I could be anyone. Like I didn't need to keep running."

Like I didn't need to keep running.

"Who is she?" Her question pulls me from my thoughts, shakes me into the present.

My eyes find hers and I slowly begin, talking to her about my life like I've wanted to for years. I tell her about Sabrina - the anger that rose up first, the missing I feel deep down now, the heartache that has lingered for weeks, the worry that I fucked up, or maybe even that it's not me she really wants. I've been too much of a coward to even reach out to her.

"I don't know if I believe that," she smiles. "But I will say this," she presses a hand to her knee, leaning forward just a little, "and it's just how I feel so who knows if this can even be applied in a general sense. Lord knows I have no business giving anybody any kind of advice."

I snort at that, a soft chuckle that escapes my lips.

"The right person makes us feel comfortable down in our bones, the right person makes us hope for more," she continues, taking a sip of wine. "But the right person is still human, and we all make mistakes. Nobody is perfect, Gray."

I toy with the label on my beer bottle, taking in her words solemnly.

And when I fall asleep that night, surrounded by familiar feelings in an unfamiliar home, the weight dissipates a little bit more, sparkles of it floating up, disappearing into thin air.

We spend the weekend like that: in comfortable conversation, in small bits of laughter, in smiles. We take an afternoon to hike. She shows me around some of her favorite local spots - something she never had when it was just us. She proudly introduces me to her co-workers, giving me a small tour around the bar she now manages. When the weekend is over and I'm heading to the airport, I feel myself breathe easier. I feel myself wanting to come back again.

And I feel ready to go home.

This weekend was certainly an awakening, but it was learning, too. A realization that healing isn't linear, not like I once thought. There are ups and downs, detours and roundabouts. There is crashing down and starting all over again.

So, here I go. Starting all over again and ready this time.

***

I reach out to Ben the next day, finding out he's in town, and opt to meet with him during my lunch hour.

"I can't be your groomsman," I tell him. We're at a small café near Pop's house, sitting at a table outside, the heat adding another uncomfortable layer to this already unbearable conversation.

His shock is evident, but he recovers quickly. "Conflict of interest?" he manages to laugh.

"Something like that." My voice feels strained.

The silence between us is absolutely suffocating at best. "She's a special one," he says eventually, like I don't know. Like I haven't spent all this time finding out, figuring it out, falling deeply. I feel a desire to punch him in the mouth for it.

"She is," I manage to respond.

He nods at that, slowly understanding. "Gray?"

"Yeah?"

"I'm sorry I was a dick."

"What?" I'm not sure I've ever heard him apologize.

"That night you saw me with Bri. It wasn't...we were just out for a ride. It's always been complicated, you know?"

I don't know, I want to tell him, but maybe I should know. All the stories I heard, all the talk about Ben's love life. It always has been so complicated, hasn't it?

"How is she?"

"I don't know," I tell him quietly now.

"Oh."

"Yeah. That night was probably a mess for everybody involved."

"Shit." Now it seems like he's the one with nothing to say.

"You and Monica okay?" I ask and he flinches just a bit, realizing that I know.

"Yet to be seen," he responds, a little sad. It throws me off. I don't know that I've ever seen him sad about anything, let alone a woman.

"I'm sorry, man," I tell him, and I mean it.

"Whatever happens...we're still friends, right?" I'm not sure that I've ever seen this vulnerability with him. This whole conversation has been much stranger than I anticipated. And to top it off, I don't know that I have an answer for him.

"I'm not sure." What happens next? Where do we all go from here?

Did I hold on to Ben because he was my first true friend in college? Did I hold on because he was social and well-liked and supportive? Did I hold on because it started to feel like an obligation?

"Me neither, man," he responds. He stays quiet for a moment, but then he snaps out of it, keeps going like only Ben can. "Well, I'm going to go. I'm driving back home today."

"Have a safe drive home, Ben. Good luck." "You too." His hand reaches for my shoulder, hesitantly, but then he squeezes lightly and turns to go.

I watch him drive off and the weight almost disappears. There's one piece of it still on my chest, the heaviest, the most suffocating, the one that might do the most damage.

I'm probably going to need all the luck I can get.

Twenty-Six

Sabrina

THE SIP OF AMELIA'S coffee runs cold down my throat – a jolt of caffeine, ice, and sugar. I'm back at the bakeshop at the start of another slow week in the hot summer season where things are almost luxuriously quiet and calm. The type of quiet I would welcome if I wasn't deep into another broken heart and my mind wasn't unbearably loud. The type of quiet that serves to remind me that while I was trying to rewrite my own memories, I was stupidly making memories with him, too.

My phone pings then with a notification from a social media post. A new follower - a user suspiciously titled CynthiaB63 – who also liked my latest wedding cake picture. *Please, no.*

And when I see her profile picture smiling back at me, straight white teeth and light blonde hair, the finest lines around her eyes, I can't help but throw my phone at the wall. James jolts, Liz ducks.

Read the fucking room, universe!

James slowly grabs my phone, noticing it's still open to the picture. Their eyes go wide in understanding and say nothing else.

Bowls line the table, my scale set in the middle. I need to bake. I need to lose myself in cake for a little while. Cake always has the answers. Cake always calms my mind. I need to let it work its magic.

"James, play something good, please." My voice shakes.

He takes a minute to pick something, then turns it up, late 90s Shania Twain blasting through the speaker.

"Hype music," he says with a wink, and my gratitude for him knows no bounds.

Butter goes in first. It gets whipped briefly, then sugar is added. As it mixes it creates an almost sinful mix, lusciously smooth. I follow with vanilla bean seeds, making the mixture speckled and fragrant.

I love the sound of eggs cracking against a countertop. The flick of the wrist, the quick crack of the shell, breaking open and falling right into that heavenly mix. My hands almost falter at the memory of Gray cracking them against my countertop, the egg white that separated between his fingers.

Flour gets added in slowly, gently. The powder mingles in the air, leaving a thin film of dust on every surface. The thick batter slowly pours out of the mixing bowl, a mesmerizing lava-like flow that goes into cake pans and evens itself out.

Liz is dancing, James is singing. We keep it going. *Let's always keep it going.*

I don't need Gray. I sure as hell don't need Ben. I need these people, this life, this shop. I need this.

***

The following weeks – seventeen days to be exact – are brutal. A broken heart is the worst companion in the kitchen. I throw myself into work anyway – even more than usual. Between testing new recipes, photographing them, another local magazine write-up, and plans to finally open up the bakery, I don't have much time to be sad.

But I still am. Late at night when I drive home alone, when I want to call him to tell him a funny story and listen to his laugh on the other line. When I'm getting ready for bed and I unconsciously grab two water glasses instead of one. I feel like an asshole, like I deserve it. Like I made a big mistake and I'm in too deep to reach out to him.

It leads me to my mom one Sunday morning. I find her gardening outside in the summer sun, wide brim hat on her head and colorful gardening gloves on her hands. Knees in the dirt, elbows deep in flowers and herbs, her light gray bob pulled back into a ponytail.

"How did you get over dad?" I'm standing in the backyard, leaning over to peek at some zinnias in bloom.

She lifts her eyebrows at that. "Coming in with the hard questions today, huh?"

"Sorry," I barely shrug.

"Sit." She motions to her chairs on the outdoor deck. I do as she says, and she stands and comes over to sit in the chair next to mine, taking off her gloves one at a time. "What's going on?"

I laugh a little at that. "What isn't?"

Everything rushes out, whether I meant for it to or not. Gray and Ben. Magazine articles, success, and loneliness. The ongoing fight I've been in for my worth – losing every battle to nobody but myself.

Her breath rushes out then, chin in hand, looking at me like she wishes she could fix all my problems, make them go away. But she's always reminded me of my strength, too – a strength I like to think I've gotten from her. "Times like these make me worry that I've failed you," her hazel eyes that match mine shine with tears waiting to fall.

"I think he's the one that failed me, Mom," I tell her with a small smirk, but my eyes are glassy, too. "I tried to have a relationship with him, you know," I tell her softly, almost ashamed like I was trying to befriend the enemy. "And then he tried to keep it up with me. I just didn't know how to forgive him."

Her nod is small and sad, understanding. "I know that."

"How did you do it?"

She takes a minute to answer, thinking it over in her mind. "Well, Bri, let me tell you this. Forgiveness is not necessary for growth. That's a hard truth. But a desire to heal, a willingness to work on yourself – that is important. It took me a while to figure that out and some days were certainly harder than others, I think you know that." She takes another deep breath in, exhales slowly, quietly. "But your father and I – we didn't work. And sure, I wanted us to work, but maybe for the wrong reasons. And he clearly didn't. He made some shitty choices, of course he did, but now we're here. I can look back at our relationship for what it was and also understand that it was not right, it was never going to work. I don't know that I completely forgave him, but I had to let it go. I had to make peace with a lot. I've got you, and I'm happy. I'm not weighed down by something that no longer serves me."

"I'm proud of you, Mom."

She startles like I've surprised her.

"Cynthia liked a cake picture of mine," I blurt out then.

Her eyebrows shoot up again, but I don't miss the small smirk that pulls at her lips "Looks like somebody is extending an olive branch."

"I don't know if I can do it."

"You don't have to. You don't have to force a relationship or forgiveness, Sabrina."

"And...what if I want to try?"

"I think that's a decision you have to make," she says slowly, but her face is reassuring. "But let me say this – and let me say it clearly so you hear it – your father's choices were not a reflection of you. They were only ever a reflection of *him*."

I'm crying a little bit now, tears very slowly running down the sides of my cheeks.

"I'm sorry you've been keeping this inside and I'm sorry you've felt this way for so long, Sabrina. You didn't deserve it, sweetheart." Her tears fall then, too, as she slowly brushes mine away with her thumb.

We sit quietly in the blinding summer sun and almost unbearable heat, until we start talking again – about cakes and zinnias, Gray and Ben.

"Benjamin Sadler," she shakes her head. "He never knew what to do with you. You were too much brilliance for him, and he would have rather seen you contained, easy to manage. We don't need men that can't handle brilliance, Sabrina."

I'm inclined to roll my eyes. Everybody is starting to sound like a fucking broken record, but I know she's right.

"But this Gray character...seems like he could be a winner."

"He is. He was. I don't know. I made a mess of things."

"Messes can be cleaned up," she waves her hand.

"I'm trying," I say quietly. *I am trying to fix it, to fix me.*

She nods in agreement, speaks softly when she says, "I know. There's no need to fix yourself, though, okay?" Her uncanny ability to read my thoughts is jarring. "You are not broken. There could always be some upkeep, I guess," she laughs lightly, teasing. "But you are not broken."

"I love you, Mom." My lips quiver as I say it.

"I love you, too."

***

As the work continues, Liz and James make runs to Amelia's instead. I work with my back to the window so I don't look at the people walking by.

I know I messed up and so I aim to *clean it up*. Look inward, sit in the silence and the discomfort. Ask myself the hard questions and give myself the honest answers. Not sure if I'm succeeding, but I've given Gray the time and space he asked for. I think I needed it too. I think I needed to step back and look at this from a different angle, with a different lens. Navigate through messy waters, wade through the rough moments - the rough moments drawn out by thoughts of my past and my childhood, by Ben, by Gray.

And amid all of it, I do the most important task. I reach out to Camille at The Regency and let her know that I will not be taking on Ben and Monica as clients and to, respectfully, look for somebody else.

It's time to cut the cord. *Really* cut the cord.

I spent a lot of time angry with myself. For the number of years wasted, for the five minutes it took to throw it all away.

There Gray was fighting for me, always letting me know where I stood. A breath of fresh air when all the other romantic relationships in my life had been tumultuous and uneasy. And I pushed him away because the honesty, the certainty scared me. Because maybe I owed something to Ben. But I don't owe him anything. Not success or a toned body or a toned-down personality or to be single and waiting for him to come around. I don't owe him a fucking thing.

I do, however, owe it to myself. I owe it to myself to live the life I want to live free of anybody's bullshit. To surround myself with the people I want in my life, and those that want me in theirs.

I owe it to myself to break free of the dead weight, of the things that, like my mother said, do not serve me anymore.

Twenty-Seven

Sabrina

"Have you heard from Gray?" James asks, crunching on a piece of bacon.

We're at breakfast, James able to join us this time.

I shake my head. "He needs the space. The least I can do is respect that."

"How much space does he need?" Liz brazenly asks, taking a sip of her coffee.

"Don't know. Maybe he'll reach out to me when he's ready? Or maybe he won't." I shrug, trying not to let the sadness show.

"Don't say that," James says.

"It's possible, James. I hurt him. I know that."

"So apologize," he says.

"I don't know if he wants to hear from me right now."

"I think he would love to hear from you," Liz says firmly. "Apologize. And tell him how you feel, Bri."

"And what if he leaves again? What if...what if my apology and my love aren't enough?"

"I think if there's one thing that we are certain of here it's that you have always been enough for Gray," James tells me, wrapping his arms around me and holding me close.

"Your love is so much more than enough, Sabrina," Liz says, wrapping her arms around me from the other side until I am sandwiched by the both of them, a mountain of love surrounding me.

How did I ever get so lucky?

I consider their suggestions – reaching out, talking to him, apologizing. And maybe, if he doesn't accept it, then I can accept that. I can be okay knowing that I could love somebody else, that my heart could start over. And I can look back fondly on how he gave me back this city and helped me heal.

After breakfast, we walk over to the bakeshop. Liz and I are making three deliveries today; James is staying back to bake some cakes for later this week.

Once inside we move on autopilot: James to the clipboard to see the cakes that need to be baked, Liz to the fridge to start packing things up for the deliveries, me to the back office to check that everything is done as it should be. Autopilot like these last weeks where I've just had my blinders on, keeping focus on everything ahead of me, not wanting to look back. I think about our conversation at breakfast. The desire to talk to Gray, to see him, is starting to build up. It's getting almost too hard to ignore.

I push the feelings down – funny enough, much like I did at the start of us hanging out – and start boxing up the cake tiers and desserts with Liz. Our deliveries include one cake for The

Beachcomber, one cake for a backyard beach wedding, and one cake plus desserts to The Regency.

The backyard wedding goes quick – two tiers, rustic with bits of greenery. The Beachcomber takes us about half an hour – two bigger, taller tiers, brushes of deep red and gold. The Regency – a three-tier cake and a dessert table – takes us another hour. Once done, Liz and I head back toward the elevator.

Inside, she nudges her head in the direction of the buttons. "For old time's sake?" she asks.

I smile, a genuine smile. I feel like I haven't smiled in so long. "Definitely," I tell her, and she pushes the button for the top floor, taking us in the direction of the rooftop.

We run up the staircase, giggling as we do, then to the rooftop access door. I let Liz push the door open – no alarm – and we walk into the evening air. Humid, windy, the sun sinking into the horizon, coloring the sky a striking hue of blue. We walk through the air conditioning systems and up my favorite staircase until we're at the very top overlooking this beautiful city sparkling like diamonds in the glow of the sunset.

It's not until I take a deep breath that I notice a shadow moving near us.

"Shit!" I hiss to Liz. "Somebody else is up here!"

The shadow emerges then, and I almost faint right there.

Gray. Tall and strong and perfect. Deep blue eyes like the ocean that are a little hesitant as he comes forward, the stubble along his jawline, that fucking hair.

"Thanks, Liz," he says then, handing her a caramel cold brew he had in his hand. "Good to see you, by the way."

Liz winks at him, taking the coffee and sipping from the straw. She smiles at me and walks down the steps and back into the hotel.

"Wha..?"

"I bribed her to bring you up here."

"That traitor." I look back at Liz, then over at Gray again.

He bends down suddenly and picks up a Nutella Delight that he had resting on the ground, passing it over to me.

I gasp. "Is this real life?"

He smiles at that. "I've missed you."

"Me too," I whisper back, standing a distance away from him, too far for my liking but unsure how to proceed. I'm too stunned to even take a sip of coffee.

"I messed up."

I shake my head. "No. No, I did."

He takes one step closer, testing the waters, making sure it's okay. I stay where I am. "I'm so sorry for how I acted, Sabrina."

"You were upset, Gray. It was valid." I take a deep breath, the coffee cup in my hands suddenly obtrusive and awkward so I set it down at my feet. "I hurt you, and I never meant to do that."

He nods at that, something small.

"I'm so sorry for getting in that car with Ben," I tell him. "For the things I said."

"But leaving you was not the answer."

"You needed the space. I think I needed the space, too. To really figure some things out, you know?"

He takes one more step closer. "Did you figure some things out?"

"I'm working on it."

"That sounds hopeful."

"It is," I smile, tentatively.

He is very slowly closing the gap between us. I stay still, feeling frozen in place.

"I should have trusted you more," Gray says.

"I should have given you more of me."

"You gave me everything."

"I didn't. You were right. I was so scared. And I was still tied up in other things." I shake my head at that, trying not to let the anger resurface, trying to lead with acceptance. "That night, I was looking for closure and what I got was a mess."

He looks down at the ground briefly, out across the city, then back to me.

"I'm not making their wedding cake," I say. "If there even is a wedding."

"I'm not going to be his groomsman," he says.

"Oh."

"I probably should have done that from the beginning. You were always more important than him."

I soften at that, my heart beating furiously in my chest. "I should have told you how I felt from the beginning. How I *feel*."

He takes one more step closer. Now we're inches apart. "And how do you feel, Bri?"

I look at him, taking a step toward him, the gap almost nonexistent. "I love you, Gray," I whisper it at first, testing the words on my tongue, letting them float in the space between us.

He stiffens, a quick intake of breath like he's holding it.

"I always worried I wouldn't know how to love anybody else. But the truth is, I've only ever loved you. It's only ever been you," I tell him. I look at him in front of me – his kind eyes, his good, good heart – and I gather all my courage, take it to the very edge, and jump.

"I love you, Gray. So much." The words leave my lips and the pure joy of saying them out loud to him has me exhaling in relief, smiling from ear to ear. "And I want this with you, too. All of it. Chocolate souffles and *The Witching Hour* and Amelia's and this rooftop with Marv who is probably going to come up here any second and arrest us. I want all of it, every day. And I think I have since the very first day I met you when you smiled at me and all I remember thinking was *you belong here*. You belong here with me."

He grins at that, eyes glistening, hands a little shaky. "Yeah?"

"Yeah," I nod. "I love you. I've never wanted to say that so much to somebody else and I never want to stop," I laugh a little at that, my eyes watery.

He leans in then, grabbing my face in his perfect hands and he kisses me. Kisses me like he's coming home, like he needs me to breathe, like I am the only person in this whole entire world.

"I love you, too, Sabrina," he whispers against my lips. The words hit just as hard this time around, pack just as much of a punch. It leaves me winded and weightless, dizzy and hopeful. "I meant what I said that night. I want to be with you, do everything with you, all in. You deserve people that stay, and I'm yours. I want to eat that delicious ice cream in bed with you."

My grin overtakes my face. "There's nobody else I'd share the world's best truffle mac and cheese with."

He chuckles. "There's nobody else I'd fall off a bike for."'

I laugh. "There's nobody else but you." My face is serious now, the smile fading into a thin line as I repeat those words to him again, "There is nobody else but you."

Gray's eyes meet mine, understanding in them as he listens.

Just then the music starts below, thumping bass, poppy rhythm, the sound weaving through the air up toward the rooftop. I hear it then. "Cake by the Ocean".

"Can this be our song?" Gray asks.

I laugh at that, loud and joyous now, unable to be contained. I start to sway, moving to the beat. He follows and soon we're dancing on the rooftop, this time closer.

It's still terrifying handing this man my heart and allowing him to do what he wants with it. Whether that is to keep it close and safe or to stomp on it with a combat boot, I'm ready to trust. We're ready to trust. He's shown me how, healing the broken parts of me, and loving them anyway.

I'm ready to fall right into water. With him by my side, holding me up, keeping me close. Always.

"Hey guys? Are you done yet? Marv said hurry up," Liz calls out from the stairwell.

We walk out, hand in hand. Down the elevators, through the double doors, and out into the world – our favorite city before us, ours for the taking.

— · —

EPILOGUE - SABRINA

Eight Months Later

"The president of your fan club insisted on being your first customer," I hear Gray say as he walks in with Pop, holding the door open for him.

"Ed!" I call out, walking over to give him a hug.

"Wow. This place looks great," he responds, and I take a minute to look around, to see it like he must be seeing it.

After months of planning, I finally opened Sabrina's Sweets to the public, to share even more baked goods with the rest of this wonderful city. And this I did for me. In looking at this bakeshop, this vibrating, vibrant space, I see how much it has always been for me.

I set up a countertop with a glass divider and filled it with cake stands and platters, desserts on display. It's simple, and still with the backdrop of the bakeshop I've made so many cakes in over the years. James wrote a menu on chalkboard, and we were able to add small bistro tables and chairs just outside.

We're just doing a soft opening right now. The menu is small, testing the waters. Cookies, cupcakes, brownies, tarts, and a small number of premade cakes to go. I hope to offer more seasonal specials as time goes on while continuing to book weddings. I also got Susana from Amelia's and Marcos to work part time with me. Some days have been a little hectic, the chaos that comes with learning something new, but it's been fun, too. Days filled with laughter and joy in this space that has always held my heart. Happiness remains embedded in it, down into the core of it, and I couldn't be prouder.

"You did good, Sabrina," I hear Liz say next to me, her hair back to hot pink, in a French braid down her back.

"We did good, Elizabeth," I reply, looking to her and James, who stands behind the counter, organizing some of the display.

"This is incredible Bri," Gray gushes. "You did it."

He comes over to kiss me in greeting, soft and loving, causing the butterflies in my belly to erupt. It never gets old. His arm wraps around my shoulder as he whispers, "You never cease to amaze me."

"Suck up," I smile, the blush creeping into my cheeks, and kiss him once more.

Pop has walked over to the counter, eyeing the cakes, perusing like he's making the most important decision in the world. He strikes up a conversation with James, and Gray walks over to say hey and join in.

The past months have certainly been the definition of a whirlwind. Gray did join my group, almost seamlessly. We joined boisterous social outings with Liz and Jeff, James and Marc, soaking up the friendship, the love, the delight of New

River. But we spent quiet nights at home, too. A lot of Funyuns, ice cream, and *The Witching Hour* on my couch.

"Look at them," Liz mutters beside me, a smile pulling at her mouth, and I do, grinning at their animated conversation. The door jingles then and Marc walks in. We erupt in greeting, James the loudest of all, coming around from behind the counter.

About a month ago, we all went out to dinner – a local spot with the best burgers and a long list of beers on tap. James and Marc joined us last, James running up to the table, flashing his hand in the air, waving it frantically.

"Are you okay?" Jeff had asked.

"I'm engaged!" he'd shrieked.

Marc was right behind him, and we jumped up with congratulations, reaching over to give hugs and kisses. Liz winked over at me, and I smiled in response. We both knew.

Marc had reached out to us one day, said he wanted to plan a romantic proposal featuring a lemon tart, the dessert they shared on their first date. The proposal itself included that lemon tart, some champagne at the beach, and one glorious sunset – the kind that sets the sky on fire.

We listened as James gushed about the perfect details – our resident romantic getting his happily-ever-after – and I felt the most immense, unyielding joy for them both, for the beginning of a new chapter for them. And as I listened, I felt Gray's hand on my thigh, a quick squeeze that felt like a kindling of a flame and a whole lot of hope.

All of him – his presence and warmth next to me here in this shop and in my life – it continues to feel like hope and love, comfort and support.

I go up to him now, grabbing his hand, intertwining our fingers, and squeezing. His smile lights me up from the inside and I wonder how I ever went a day without it.

"I love you," he whispers in my ear.

"Okay, lovebirds," I hear James say, packing up a 6-inch cake for Pop to go.

"Ooh, good choice, Ed," I tell him. He's picked out an almond cake doused in an amaretto syrup and slathered with a salted caramel buttercream. If Pop were a cake, well, he'd probably be that one. Nutty, sweet, secretly the best cake out of all of them.

"Please tell me you're not going to eat that whole thing yourself," Gray says.

"Mind your business, Gray," Pop says, then stage whispers to me, "Pain in the ass," winking and smirking as he does. It makes me laugh. "I will share with Nancy and the Old Fisherman and maybe you."

We stand together and chat. Gray's hand sits in mine, a gentle reminder that he's here, that he has been, and that he's not going anywhere. Perhaps, I'm slowly learning, I'm worthy and deserving of all of it.

And as for Ben, he never did get married. I think they tried to work things out but ended up calling it quits a couple of months later. I heard most of this from Liz and James, who recounted all the drama from social media to me. The dissolving of it, the friends that stood by Ben, and those who took some steps back.

I had Liz and James manage all the social media in the past months, giving me a much-needed reprieve. But they kept me in the loop, letting me know that Cynthia kept liking pictures, commenting on things here and there. My father started following the account, too. Now that the bakeshop is open, I wonder if I'll see them waltz through those doors. The thought is so nerve-wracking, but I like to think I could do it. And if they wanted to open up a conversation? Well, we'll see.

"I'm going to take Pop home now and finish up some work, but I'll see you later, okay?" Gray says now, kissing me goodbye. I give Pop a big hug, thanking them both for stopping by.

Gray's work continues. He's managed to get some great new clients, including me who did need a new website upgrade. His work is still freelance and flexible, allowing us all the time we could want.

As they walk out, Jeff comes in, followed shortly by Amelia and then Luca; then my mom and Tina; Christine and her new boyfriend. The revolving door of community, of friendships I've made throughout the years, leaves me emotional. It's a tangible thing, seeing this outpouring of support from everybody I've had the pleasure of meeting in the last several years. They are here for me and my heart swells and swells at the very sight of it. It's almost too much to handle, and when I close up at the end of the day, I feel so overwhelmed with gratitude that I have to take a moment to just sit with it in the glow of the parking lot.

"Proud of you, Bri," James tells me, breaking the silence.

"I'm so thankful for the both of you," I tell him and Liz. We come together in a group hug, one that is strong and joyous.

And when I finally drive home, I roll the window down, breeze flowing through my fingers, and I head home to somebody waiting for me.

"You're never getting rid of me," Gray says later, sitting on my couch, talking around a mouthful of Boysenberry Cobbler ice cream I'm feeding him from the pint.

I chuckle. He spends most nights of the week here, but there are still times he stays with Pop. Checking in on him, making sure he has what he needs. It's important to him and I know he needs that. Which is why the next words out of his mouth surprise me.

"I'm just going to stay here all the time and eat all your ice cream and Funyuns."

"Do you...want to stay here all the time?" He stills, looking over at me, the lightest tinge of pink on his cheeks.

"I don't need you getting sick of me," he says lightly.

"I would never."

He laughs softly. "You say that now."

"Okay, maybe just minimally sick of you. And in that case, I can go upstairs and lock the door and avoid you."

"You make a point," he tilts his head. But he's skipping around it. And now that he's opened the door to this, I need to know.

"Gray," I say softly. "Do you want to be here all the time?"

"I'd love to be here all the time, Bri. You know that." He looks down at his hands, the ones slowly massaging, kneading the arch of my foot.

"What if...you moved in with me?"

"What?"

I shrug, the words just falling out so easily. The conversation comfortable and easy as it has always been. "I want you here all the time, too."

"Yeah?"

"Of course, I do, Gray." I set the pint of ice cream down on the coffee table now, maneuvering over to him to sit on his lap, arms around his neck.

"I would love nothing more than to wake up with you every morning and go to bed with you every night. And Ed isn't too far away. You could work there, you could work here. You could do whatever. I just want you here with me," I whisper the last part.

Maybe this should make me nervous, or scared, or confused. But it doesn't. Because all I see is moving forward, all I feel is secure and safe and loved. Such a sure feeling that I've never felt with anyone ever. I know where I stand with him, where we are. He never lets me forget it; he never makes me doubt it.

And so, I allow myself to do the same. To let him know how much I love him and how much I want him with me, always.

"I love you," I whisper against his lips. "Always will. You belong here, Gray."

He kisses me in response, something sweet that slowly turns into longing, into desire and a deep love.

"Okay," he says softly once he pulls away.

I meet his eyes, smile like I can feel my heart trying to jump for joy out of my body, and whisper back, "Okay?"

"Okay." He nods once and smiles, one big joyous grin that overtakes his whole face.

He returns to kissing me and it never fails to feel like anything less than magic, like he is my home and anywhere he is is where I'm meant to be.

"We should celebrate with some chocolate souffle," he says.

"Is that code word for sex?"

He lets out a loud bark of laughter. "No, but I guess it can be."

I laugh with him, too, my favorite thing to do.

"I love you, Sabrina," he whispers, forehead resting on mine. His hands move to grip my own, his heart beating underneath my palms, beautifully, thrumming under my fingertips, grounding us both here. He breathes in deep, slowly, and smiles, "I belong here. With you."

Acknowledgements

This book has been a labor of love from the very beginning and, while writing it was a stressful event, the support from those around me has been heartwarming and fulfilling. Very big, enthusiastic, genuine THANK YOUS go out to:

Nicole, the first person to read this, who gave me feedback and support (even when you didn't know what to do because I'm super weird about it) and not-so-subtly reminded me that CLAVICLE IS NOT A SEXY WORD. Here's a new book for your bookshelf.

Sara, the second person to read this. For your kindness, your ear, your constant advice, your feedback, your support. Thank you for being you.

Adjani, for your insight, your tips, and your never-ending enthusiasm (even when I didn't have it in me) in the form of several exclamation points. For listening to me stress about everything. Thank you!!!

My mom, who took me to all the bookstores and libraries when I was a kid. Who let me follow my (several) passions and who continues to support me every day.

Friends and family who have shown enthusiastic support by texting, commenting, and following on social media - please know that it means so much. Honorary mentions to Stefani, who always makes me laugh, and Brian, who, in the early years, had to listen to me whine about too many dumb boys.

A special shoutout to Joe D and The Triangles. I like to think you would have gotten a kick out of this one.

Lucy, who was so kind and patient and informative, and brought to life my characters in a wonderful cover.

And Brad, for everything. Unwavering support, laughter, hugs, advice that I don't want but you give me anyway, listening to my nonsense, and all the love. Sorry this isn't Steinbeck. (It's better.)

And to you, reader, for picking up this book! I hope you love it, and if you do, please feel free to leave a review or tell a friend!

About the Author

Natalia has been reading and writing for as long as she can remember. Born in Argentina, now residing in Florida, she spent over a decade in the culinary field, but now spends her days wrangling kids and writing love stories. Her hope is to continue to write stories about lovably messy people falling in love.

Find her on Instagram @nw.writes

9 798988 751212